TIMELY INHERITANCE

THE OCTAGON ROOM - BOOK 1

J.C. ORION

DREAM STAR PUBLISHING

Produced in the United States of America, First Release - 2025

ISBN-13: 978-1-966909-01-9
Dream Star Publishing
Emporia, KS

dreamstarpublishing.com, www.jcorion.com

Thank you, Dad, for being such an an avid reader with such a wonderful and ever-growing library of fantasy and science fiction books. And thank you for being my biggest cheerleader. Your support kept me writing that first book, just out of high school, and kept me eager to get that next story or book done for you to read (sometimes a chapter at a time).

And thank you, Mom, for pushing me to always improve, to finally write that story opening that pulled you in and wouldn't let you go. Because I wasn't writing in your genre, and I always knew I had something good when it piqued your interest and had you wanting more.

I dedicate this book to you both. I wouldn't be the writer that I am without you. I wish you could read this published book, Mom, and all the books to come in this series. But I know you would be there to cheer me on, still.

Table of Contents

TIMELY INHERITANCE

Chapter 1

The mansion seemed to be holding its breath, waiting for Cassandra to get out of her black Civic. She had parked in front, but had almost kept on going right round the circular gravel driveway and hightailed it back to San Francisco.

The enormous building of dark wood and stone and gargoyle fixtures was out in the middle of nowhere, up a driveway a few miles long, and dead-ended smack in the center of thick old growth and snarled underbrush, the encroaching forest like a wall that seemed unwilling to come any closer. Cassandra could relate. She had no intention of getting out of her car, now that she'd seen the place.

But she was the sole beneficiary. Her estranged great uncle had left the place to her, since his brother, Cassandra's grandfather, had died decades ago. She'd never met her great uncle, Niles Bennet, couldn't figure out why he'd leave the place to her in his will. Why not her parents? But of course they hadn't known Niles any better and had moved to France shortly after Cassandra left home for college, and that was years ago now.

She'd sell the place, that's what she'd do.

But then the front door opened, and a man in butler uniform stepped onto the porch, hands folded in front of him.

Cassandra tensed.

Nowhere in her paperwork did it say the mansion was inhabited. He seemed to be waiting for her.

Well at least she wouldn't have to see the place alone. She pushed up in her seat, so she could reach the front of her jeans, and tucked the mansion's antique bronze skeleton key into her pocket. No need to bring her purse, and she left the car keys in the ignition, since it wasn't likely anyone else was coming out here.

The pungent taste of wet wood and soil struck Cassandra the moment she opened the door. The forest smelled alive and vibrant, not at all in keeping with its initial creepiness. She slammed the door shut and crunched across the gravel, throwing a weary glance in the direction of the mermaid fountain full of pond scum and enough grass-filled cracks to resemble the tiled mosaics she'd often seen in garden shops.

The butler, still as a statue, watched Cassandra approach, and only when she was within reach did he speak. "Miss Cassandra Bennet, welcome home."

She gave him a thin smile. "Thanks, but I'm not sure I'm staying." She gave her car a nervous glance, contemplating making a run for it. She wouldn't be here now if she hadn't just lost her apartment. But now that she'd seen the place, and realized just how far it was from everything else, she had no intention of staying. No way, no how.

She started to turn away.

"Miss Bennet, will you please come inside. I have arranged everything for your stay."

Cassandra halted, slowly turned back to him, the corners of her mouth turned up in what her friends called her pensive smile. She brushed a wayward strand of short chestnut-auburn hair from her eyes, which were the same brown hue as her hair. "I wasn't told anyone was going to be here."

The butler's glassy brown eyes seemed to see right through her, an eerie look, but then he snapped out of it and gave a quick smile, too fast to be considered sincere. "I am here to serve. But if you prefer, I will retire."

Cassandra frowned. "Uh, that's not quite what I meant."

"If Miss Bennet is weary from her journey, I would be happy to draw a bath. And I have prepared food, to be found in the dining room."

Cassandra shook her head. "No, no. I'm not staying." Though she was hungry, come to think of it. Maybe just a bite, in a little bit.

While she was here, though, she might as well have a look around. She'd never known her great uncle and was curious to see what the old man had called home. He clearly had no qualms about letting his gardens go wild. If the inside was as poorly maintained, it would reduce the property's value. She hated to think of the upkeep costs for a place like this.

She stepped into the building and wrinkled her nose. Whoever this butler was, he sure didn't care about that musty stench or the layer of dust over everything. And boy had her uncle accumulated a lot of things!

Every surface in sight, and there were a lot, was covered in antique objects. Everything from lamps that looked centuries old, to strange baubles and animal skulls. Creepy, to say the least. Her uncle had a morbid fascination it seemed. Lots of bones, most of them unidentifiable, adorned the dark antique furniture. They poked from bookcases overflowing with tomes—that looked like they belonged in a museum—and statues and vases in marble and bone China. Cassandra wondered what color these objects must have once been, for everything was muted under a layer of dust thick enough to carve.

Heavy strands of cobwebs clung to the rafters high overhead and filled the spaces in the banister rungs that followed a grand dark wooden staircase around the wall to the upper floor.

Haunted house came to mind. Cassandra shivered, glad for the butler's company, though his position as someone of comfort was questionable. He shut the door with a soft click and stood waiting, watching Cassandra impassively.

"What do I call you?"

"Pardon, Miss Bennet?"

"What's your name?"

"Mr. Bennet was fond of calling me Albert."

That wasn't quite what she meant, but she'd take it. "Is there anything in particular I should see before I leave?"

"Where would Miss Bennet like to go?"

"Somewhere other than *here*," she said, giving the house a suspicious glance. All she knew of her late uncle was that he had died, and the body had never been found. His body could be hiding under any number of things and only the stench would give him away. "Can't you draw the curtains?" Most windows were covered in thick red velvet drapes, but then again, what few windows she could see in the neighboring drawing room were opaque with grime. What the mansion really needed was a bath. It could be worth a lot of money, if anyone could just see what was here.

"If Miss Bennet desires, I shall draw the curtains."

"Where do you sleep?" she asked, suddenly curious. His car must be parked. . . Cassandra's thoughts drifted, wondering if she'd seen a garage or not, and wondering if he didn't have a car, how he got anywhere. Maybe there was no need, if they had a stocked larder. Her uncle had gone missing weeks ago, though, and Cassandra had come as soon as she could get time off work.

"Miss Bennet should seek the Octagon Room at the end of the hall." He pointed with a long finger to the hall behind her, but she frowned at him, trying to determine if he was really who he said he was. Slicked coal-black hair and pale skin, impeccable black suit and shiny shoes to match. His deep voice was friendly enough, if a little flat and unsettling. He was the epitome of a butler if she ever saw one.

"Just a quick look and then I'll be on my way." She'd decided not to sample any of his food, especially if his lack of housecleaning and gardening were any indication of failed cooking ability.

The hall was too long, lined with cluttered and toppling shelves, and the door at the end gave Cassandra the creeps. Shiny black, like Albert's shoes, and carved with strange symbols. The doorknob was cold polished bronze, and the skeleton key a perfect fit.

Cassandra nearly let go, almost turned back, but curiosity got the better of her. She opened the door.

The hairs on the back of her neck rose and shivers went up and down her arms. The Octagon Room was the eeriest room Cassandra had ever seen. Something screamed at her to run away, to lock the door and throw away the key.

And yet, it was so compelling it drew Cassandra in one step at a time, driving equal parts dread and fascination into her.

Cassandra had always been odd, had never quite fit in. She'd always had a strange family and strange ways. The Octagon Room screamed *other* and *mystery*. Cassandra had to decipher it and learn its secrets.

The odd thing about the room, among so many, was that apart from being octagonal and mostly black, it was designed to be a sleeping chamber. A four-poster bed with rumpled black velvet comforter butted up against the wall on her right, and along the seven other walls were tall bookcases teeming with books. On closer examination, Cassandra was surprised to see a relatively thin layer of dust and that almost every book in here had to do with either history or the occult.

She caught the acrid taste of smoke in the air.

Something glinted from a little black table by the bed. Cassandra went to investigate. The table, as it turned out, was part of the floor, and quite narrow, but nestled into its top was a golden octagon roughly the size of an orange. It wasn't smooth, but covered in elaborate filigree work, with a keyhole on the top.

Cassandra tried the skeleton key and was surprised when it slipped into place and the octagon opened like a lotus flower, into eight perfect golden petals.

"Fascinating," she whispered. The petals rippled faintly with an inner luminescence. She tentatively touched one. It promptly lit up, along with two others, all three in a row glowing bright amber. The air became charged. Cassandra glanced up at the ceiling, which rose to a peak, like the little octagonal lotus in the table. She felt compelled to touch one more petal. A wind rustled through the room, stirring her hair and raising goose bumps all over her body, then suddenly whipped and whistled and went quiet.

The petals dimmed and the lotus closed, popping her skeleton key out. Cassandra picked the key up and hurried out of the room, sneakers pounding along the hallway, all the way to the front door. She'd had enough, didn't care about saying goodbye to Albert, just flung the door open and . . . froze.

A man stood on the porch, dressed a little oddly, to say the least. His top half was fine: tight-fitting black top and an old-fashioned black fedora, tipped at an angle. But his pants were fascinating, like quicksilver, a design and fabric like none she'd ever seen before. She wondered what store he'd found them in, and why he'd ever thought the hat was a good match.

He looked surprised to see her. He closed his mouth, gray eyes becoming steely. "You have some explaining to do." His voice was deep and oddly accented; one Cassandra couldn't place for the life of her. She got a whiff of aftershave. "My records tell me only Mr. Bennet was living here. I have twice attempted to gain entry and have begun the process for excessive forced entry." His eyes narrowed and he peered around her. "How did you get in?"

"This is my house." Cassandra crossed her arms, feeling suddenly protective. Who did this guy think he was?

His jet-black brows hiked up, then turned into a glower. "Impossible." He lifted his arm, which was bare with the short sleeves, and started typing on his skin with his other hand.

Cassandra tensed. The pieces were falling into place. There was a crazy guy on her porch and she was all alone up here. Where was Albert?

She didn't dare take her eyes off the stranger, just started slowly closing the door, but he whipped his hand up fast as a viper, palm to the intricately carved door, and looked up from whatever he thought he was doing on his arm.

Cassandra flinched. There was that intensely piercing gaze again, like she was a petri dish and he was dissecting her. All she could think about now were all the bones all over the house and all the ways she could end up like them.

He lowered his "keyboard" arm and Cassandra caught a glint of something glowing under his skin, like a grid, which promptly vanished. Okay, that was weird.

"Niles Bennet has no living relations."

Now it was Cassandra's turn to be shocked. "What are you talking about? He's my great uncle."

"Impossible." He lifted his keyboard arm and waved his palm in front of her. What sort of drugs was he on? "I'll have to bring you in for questioning. Untagged. Possible squatter or looter."

"Who the hell are you?" Cassandra was shaking, about to scream for Albert for help.

"Detective Brice. I've been assigned to a missing person's case, possible homicide."

"You're a detective?" The guy was delusional. She tried to close the door, but he pushed around her and stepped into the gloomy house.

"Albert!" Cassandra backed out the door.

The wannabe detective shot his gaze around the house. "Untagged not alone. Gained entry. Sweeping for second individual. Albert."

All Cassandra had to do was get to her car. She hurried down the steps, looking back over her shoulder all the while to make sure the crazy guy wasn't following, and came to an abrupt halt when her sneakers landed on hard asphalt. That was unexpected.

But what was even more unexpected was the utter lack of gravel, a fully functional and glistening fountain with splashing water, and lush landscaping as if Albert had come out here and waved a magic wand. Even the house exterior was spotless, the windows sparkly clean.

Cassandra's legs went weak and she almost hit the ground.

Where was her car? She should have run straight into it. She looked all around and saw a car hovering over the driveway a little ways off. A *hovercar*? It looked like a little spaceship, sleek and black, with a cockpit. It seemed to be on, whirring softly and kicking up dust.

Cassandra approached the vehicle in disbelief, walked to it in a stupor until the gritty dust struck her face and she had to back off, spitting dirt from her mouth.

"Not real, not real."

Keyboard arm and shimmery pants. Hovercar. It all reeked *future*. But how could this house be all cleaned up on the outside and still be the same one she'd walked into who knew how many years ago?

And how the hell had she even *gotten* here?

The Octagon Room. That had to be it. That eerie room with the strange device. When she'd activated it, it must have brought her here. Either that or she'd gone to sleep on that big, creepy bed and this was all a dream.

She wrung her hands all the way back to the front door, which was still wide open. It looked so dark, so uninviting inside. Floorboards creaked from upstairs and she heard Brice's voice resonating faintly, no doubt cataloguing his observations.

"You called."

Cassandra jumped.

Albert was standing nearby, in the shadows around the corner. She just couldn't bring herself to step into the lemony smelling gloom to speak with him. "Wh-where am I?"

"You are standing on the porch, Miss Bennet."

She smacked her forehead, tried to rub the headache that was creeping in. "Not what I meant." He could be really obtuse. She waved her hand angrily at the driveway behind her, the surrounding forest, a distant San Francisco, if it was still here in whatever year this was. "Where the hell did this *house* bring me?"

"If Miss Bennet is inquiring about the year, it is 2145. Miss Bennet did not specify a year, merely 'somewhere other than *here*.'" His smile was thin and tight, hands neatly folded in front of him. "If Miss Bennet would care for a bite, I have arranged a new assortment of savory samples in the dining area."

Cassandra stepped into the house, into the unmistakable aroma of polished wood and baked bread.

How could she have missed it before? Whatever magic wand had been used on the exterior had been waved in here, too. The house was spotless. Still cluttered, yes, but nowhere near as bad as the house in her own time. No layer of thick dust or sticky cobwebs. No bones, either. "What happened to all the stuff?" She couldn't be certain if the furniture had changed or not, as the last house had been too filthy to tell what was really there.

"If Miss Bennet inquires of Mr. Bennet's belongings, the items have remained in storage."

"You mean the house I inherited was his storage unit?"

"Correct."

"Then what's this place?"

"Mr. Bennet's living quarters. As Miss Bennet might well imagine, upkeep on multiple properties is a laborious task."

Cassandra shook her head, disbelief furrowing her brow. "Just how many mansions did my uncle have?"

Albert fell silent, his eyes taking on that glassy sheen again. "Just the two. Mr. Bennet did not plan for his sudden demise, had anticipated many long years. He had always intended to clean out his storage, to organize. He collected so many things on his travels."

"My uncle was a time traveler?"

"Correct."

The stairs suddenly creaked as Brice came down, still cataloguing into the air. Cassandra couldn't tell if it was his arm or something else recording it all for him, or if he was speaking to someone through a hidden earpiece. "Where did that come from?" He pointed to Albert.

Cassandra pulled a face. "What? Albert?"

"Yes." Detective Brice approached the butler, his gray eyes in full inspection mode. "Fully interactive." He fingered Albert's black cloak. "Remarkable." He waved his palm over Albert, then along the wallpapered wall—her uncle had had good taste; bold stripes, but not overdone, with dark wainscoting along the lower half. "Tied to the house. Unbelievable." His gray eyes darted to Cassandra. "Did you know of this? Somehow activate it?"

"I don't know what you're talking about," Cassandra said wearily. She'd reached overload. Hovercars. Typewriter arms. Time travel. And now the detective was questioning Albert's status as a human being.

"This hologram is state of the art. Remarkable. I've never seen its like."

Well, that made two of them.

"Where are you going?" Brice asked, as Cassandra walked around him and headed for what she hoped was the right direction for the dining room.

The hall behind her went to the Octagon Room, and the stairs went up to more bedrooms, most likely. Her uncle could have had a swimming pool up there and Cassandra wouldn't have cared.

She walked like an automaton through the drawing room, pushed through a set of dark-stained wooden doors, and smiled at all the food laid out along a freshly polished table, an overhanging crystal chandelier reflecting faintly on its shiny surface.

Cassandra's stomach growled as she plopped down in the nearest chair, which she admired for its intricate wood carvings of dryads and woodland creatures and especially for its nice comfy red velvet cushion.

It felt good to sit down.

She absently ran her fingers through her now-tangled chin-length locks, a hair style her friends had called "cute spunk", though Cassandra had chosen it for its get-out-of-bed-ease, and cringed as her fingers struggled through a particularly nasty snarl that rained bits of leaves. It seemed the hovercar had kicked up more than just dust.

Hair back to its usual leaf-free waywardness, she picked up a fresh bread roll, still warm and soft, and sank her teeth in with a moan. She chewed and stared absently out the wood paneled window to the fountain outside.

"What are you doing?" It was Brice.

"Eating."

When the detective didn't answer, Cassandra finished chewing and slowly turned to look up at him. He was handsome, if a little hard in the face. That strong jaw, those muscled arms, his rigid stance and piercing gaze. He wasn't one for idle chit-chat or drinks at the bar after work. He studied and picked apart other people while keeping his inner life well-guarded.

"I've had it up to here," she said, raising her hand over her head. "I can't take it anymore. And I'm starving. Albert told me there was food in here." She shrugged. "Might as well eat."

"I never asked your name."

"Why would you? I'm just a potential looter or squatter."

"You really believe this is your house?"

"It was my great uncle's, Niles Bennet."

Detective Brice pulled out a chair and sat beside Cassandra, but not too close. She could feel his eyes boring into her.

"Cassandra Bennet. That's me." She gave him a big smile but it felt fake, even to her. Her hand started shaking and she lowered it to her lap. She'd lost her appetite.

"The untagged are homeless. Either vagrants or looters. Sometimes both. We attempt to round them all up, but there are always pockets, deep in the woods. Those who refuse to join the grid."

"I'm not homeless." Well, she would be, in a few days, about a hundred years ago. And this house wasn't bad, a little big for her, maybe, but if Albert could look after it . . . but she didn't really want to stay in the future, did she? "I had an apartment, a life. Not much of one, but it was mine. In San Francisco."

Detective Brice lifted his arm, eager to be back on course for his investigation. "Your address?"

Cassandra lowered his arm, and promptly drew back as if she'd touched something fragile in a museum with the little sign that said "Don't touch." "You won't find it. Remember, I'm not in your system."

"I could perform a cross-check. It's possible your serial number fell off grid."

Cassandra sucked in a big breath of bread and meats and pastries, could taste them on her tongue, and released it shakily. "I'm from the past. I know it sounds crazy. But a room in this house brought me here. I came from an exact copy of this house, though a lot untidier. It seems only the Octagon Room travels between homes. From what I can gather from what Albert said, my uncle was a time traveler."

"We had our suspicions that Mr. Bennet was up to something. But time travel?" Detective Brice frowned and pursed his lips, shot a glance at the doors to the drawing room that said he knew a lot more than Cassandra about what might be going on here. For one, he wasn't outright denying her story.

That gave her the chills.

"There is only one room I have not yet inspected."

"The one at the end of the hall downstairs?"

He nodded, that steely gaze back in full force. "Niles Bennet vanished three weeks ago." He leaned back in his chair, which was sort of facing Cassandra, his brawny arms crossed over his chest and thoughtful frown fixed on her. "We were unable to gain entry to this building, as I have said. Mr. Bennet was late to the grid, but once you're in, you're in for life. Your location can be tracked anywhere. Mr. Bennet simply vanished, an impossible feat. Time travel could explain such a disappearance, especially if he traveled somewhere off grid, to a time before our grid, or perhaps to a time far beyond a potential collapse. We had registered frequent lapses, had grown suspicious."

"Why did he tag himself, why not just stay off the grid?"

Brice lifted his arm, typed away, and nodded, as though affirming something he already suspected. "Apprehended two years ago and brought in for questioning. He'd been operating under a false serial number, also never explained. He insisted it was grid error and we could never prove otherwise. We tagged him anyway, just to be sure."

"And what about Albert? Is he really a . . . hologram?"

"From what my sensors detect, yes. Miss Bennet, what year are you from?"

"Let's just say about a hundred years ago, give or take a few decades." She smiled faintly.

Brice released a sigh and shook his head. "You say you came here in the Octagon Room? Show me this room."

Cassandra pushed away from the table, her chair squeaking along the hardwood floor, and led Brice down to the Octagon Room, past the spot where Albert had been standing. She didn't hear the butler anywhere in the house and felt another creepy shiver.

The door to the Octagon Room was still wide open, just like she'd left it. And the room looked just the same as it had when she'd entered it. It must be the time travel capsule, and the little golden octagon in the table the control mechanism. Pretty cool how her uncle had built a home to harbor his time machine. An impossible achievement of technology hidden in plain sight as one of the rooms in his house. Though anyone seeing this room could never pass it off as ordinary, and judging by Brice's reactions, he was no less surprised or creeped out by the place.

He walked all over the room, waving his hand over everything and checking his forearm from time to time. He finally arrived at the little golden device and released a long whistle as he waved his hand over it. "Off the chart readings," he said, excitement edging into his normal reserve. "I am beginning to believe you, Miss Bennet."

"Please call me Cassandra." She edged closer to him, hoping she wasn't making a mistake by bringing him here. Her uncle had tried to keep this technology hidden. Someone like Brice, with something like the grid at his back, had been unable to gain entry. That said something, didn't it? Either of major bureaucratic red tape before a forced entry could be performed, or something of her uncle's impenetrable defenses on this house. If Albert was a part of its construct, who knew what other mysteries these walls harbored?

As Cassandra watched Brice study the octagonal device like a kid in a candy store, Cassandra felt an impending sense of doom, like she had just made a big mistake.

The grid, whatever it was, didn't sound good. She knew nothing about this era beyond Detective Brice and what he'd told her, but she didn't like the idea of something that seemed to control everyone here. What happened if this time travel technology got into the wrong hands? What if the grid was the wrong hands?

If it had been safe, surely her uncle would have shared this technology by now, not tried to hide it. And Cassandra had no idea if her uncle had been doing good with it, but judging by the house in her time, and the house here, he was an explorer at heart. A cataloguer. He didn't seem to have been abusing his power, seemed to have been careful. She had no idea how her uncle had stumbled on the time machine, but maybe Albert would have some answers.

Confident that Brice would get nowhere without the key to the octagonal control device in her pocket, she went to the foyer in search of Albert.

CHAPTER 2

Albert popped into the foyer as soon as Cassandra whispered his name, startling her. If she'd had any doubt he was a hologram before, she didn't doubt it now.

Before he could greet her, she put two fingers over her mouth and whispered, "Shh. I don't want the detective hearing us. Can we go somewhere more private?"

Albert nodded and gestured to the drawing room. Cassandra followed him inside, and he quietly shut the doors and turned to face her. When he spoke, his voice was in hushed tones. "How may I serve Miss Bennet?"

Cassandra started pacing, the floorboards creaking softly beneath her sneakers, and chewed on her nails, thinking. The aroma of freshly baked bread was strong in this room and her stomach rumbled, reminding her that she hadn't eaten enough earlier. Her mouth watered at the thought of one of those Danishes. But first things first.

"Albert, you're attached to this house, right?"

"Miss Bennet is correct. My program flows throughout the walls, including a fifty foot exterior radius." The butler's expression was placid, his brown eyes following Cassandra as she paced.

"Do you have any other purpose besides housekeeping?"

"I am linked to the control hub for the traveling device."

Cassandra came to an abrupt halt. "You control where the Octagon Room goes?"

"To some extent, yes. The Octagon Room was designed to be Mr. Bennet's main mode of transportation, though he spent most of his time in this home, in year 2145. My program is linked to the Octagon Room. When it travels, my program is updated in the new locale."

"Can the Octagon Room go anywhere else, or just between the two mansions?" Cassandra had started chewing her nails again, forgetting completely about anything other than solving this peculiar arrangement, her mind trying to wrap around the idea of time travel and its logistics. If she worried too much about anything else, she would start panicking again, she just knew it. Best to focus on the questions and Albert's impassive face.

"Miss Bennet is correct in surmising that the Octagon Room can travel to any point in time. The traveling device is nearly limitless in its possibilities." Albert did not move, did not breathe. Now that Cassandra was staring so intently at him she wondered how she could have missed any of those signs of lifelessness before.

"Who else can control it?"

"The device is calibrated to Mr. Bennet's DNA. Only a blood relative may currently operate the device. And of course, the key. I can direct the device, for safety purposes, but it will respond to linked DNA."

Now it was just a matter of getting rid of Detective Brice without him wanting to bring her in for questioning. Maybe he could do a DNA test to prove she was a relative and not a squatter. "Albert, can you produce copies of the paperwork showing that my great uncle willed his estate to me? Does the will include this house, in 2145?"

"Why of course, Miss Bennet. I will gladly produce the paperwork you require." And he popped from the room.

Cassandra opened the double doors and hurried down the hall to the Octagon Room, where Detective Brice was still bent over the traveling device. He looked up when she came in. "Albert's getting copies of my great uncle's will."

He straightened, that calculating look of his sending shivers up and down her spine. "This device is fascinating. Tell me, Cassandra, do you know how it functions?" As he spoke he came round the little control table, closer to the door, to face her. The smell of aftershave was strong. He was relaxed, on the surface, but she detected an inner tension he couldn't keep from his eyes. His interest was too intense, too piqued.

Cassandra backed away, though the only way she could go was deeper into the room, and as soon as she did so she realized her mistake, the set-up the detective had created by standing where he had. He pulled the door shut and stood in front of it, stance wide, danger seeping from his body and seeming to fill the room, as though a predator had just stepped in and Cassandra had nowhere to run.

"I think you are lying. I think you know very well how the traveling device works." Detective Brice still had that piercing look, but a corner of his mouth had risen just a little. A secret. Had he been eavesdropping?

But how?

Cassandra stared at him, wanting nothing more than to just go back to her own time, get in her car, and never come back. Let the detective have the house, the traveling device. She didn't care.

But something told her the detective should not have the device, should never have known it existed.

"The key, Miss Bennet." He extended his hand, palm up. Rarely did emotion touch that face, but the look in his eyes was one of triumph. He seemed to sense Cassandra's hesitation. "The key. You don't want to die over this, do you?"

That got her attention. She held her breath, now wondering if the detective was even what he said he was. She knew nothing about this time. "I just want to go home," she said faintly. "If I give it to you, will you let me go home first?"

"Sure," he said, though that glint in his eye made Cassandra uneasy. If he'd overheard her conversation with Albert, then he'd know only she could use the traveling device. Unless he found a way to take control from her, she'd never be free.

Hands shaking, she pulled the key out of her pocket and held it out to him.

He seemed to change his mind. "Insert the key and show me how it works."

Her heart racing, Cassandra went to the little table and sat on the bed, staring down at the device. Brice had moved close now, his presence raising the hairs on the back of her neck. She felt she'd glimpsed something of his true nature now and didn't like at all what she'd seen. Maybe she could take him back to her time and render him helpless, away from the grid. Albert said the device would respond to linked DNA. What did that mean? Maybe she just had to think of a place while she touched it?

Please forgive me, she thought, and stuck the key in the device.

The octagonal ball split into eight petals. She touched a petal and three promptly lit up. She kept thoughts of home firmly in her mind, hoping this would work as she pressed the fourth petal. But just as her finger was landing, Brice grabbed her hand and forced her finger to also take in the neighboring petal. Five in a row.

A gale wind swept the room, sending papers everywhere, stirring dust and stale acrid smoke into the air. Cassandra pulled her hand away and shielded her eyes from the debris.

The room started spinning, a terrible groaning roar, spinning so fast Cassandra flew right across the room and struck a bookcase in exploding light.

CHAPTER 3

Hissing filled Cassandra's thoughts, edged in on the terrible throbbing pain. Every part of her hurt, but it was a distant thing, something that ebbed and flowed with the hiss, with the press of prickly shards like needles in her . . . cheek.

Cassandra opened her eyes. The world was tilted, rolling waves of the most gorgeous shade of turquoise splashing forward and hissing back. She tasted salt in the air. Noted the azure and lavender shades in the sky, the curving hint of a heavenly body larger than the moon hovering at the horizon, close and startling in its size.

Cassandra pushed up, and the world titled again, stuttered and fractured, blurred, and came back into focus. She was on a beach of pink sand, a soft pink, almost white, the same hue as the sparkling highlights in the cresting waves.

The air was cool, a little oppressive. Thick with unfamiliar scents and tastes, a metallic taste.

She was disoriented, but she knew without a doubt that she was somewhere *else*.

She got to her feet, realized she had on only one sneaker. The other was lying in the sand further up towards a jagged cliff wall. Bizarre plants spilled down from above. The beach extended to either side of her.

She limped over to her other shoe, sat down and put it back on.

When she was done lacing it up, she ran her fingers through her short chestnut-auburn hair, raining sand into her lap. The longer strands stuck out a bit more than usual, thanks to the sand and the salty moisture in the air.

She noticed a book in the surf and went to pick it up. A book on the occult. Her uncle's then. She kept it and found another book further on, sticking up out of the sand. The history of a society she'd never heard of.

Cassandra dropped both texts and stared numbly ahead to the splintered bookshelves and hobbled over, found a journal of her uncle's lying in the sand and decided to hold onto it.

As she picked through the wreckage of the Octagon Room, dread clawed into the pit of her stomach, pounded in her ears. If the traveling device was gone, she'd be trapped on this alien world forever. It seemed too much to comprehend. She swallowed bile-filled panic and started digging through the broken planks and ripped bedding.

"Help." The voice was weak, but definitely masculine.

Cassandra found the moving body under an avalanche of broken shelves, which she struggled to remove. Detective Brice lay beneath the wreck, his body resting in a crater of sand. If not for their soft landing she doubted either of them would have survived. But she wasn't so sure she was happy to see the cause of their dilemma alive and well, didn't trust him as far as she could throw him.

"Wh-where are we?" He blinked into the odd ambient light.

Not a sun in sight, which was odd. Maybe it had already set for the day? Cassandra didn't relish the thought of an alien world in the dark, didn't know what they'd do for food or water. Thank god the air was breathable.

"We're on another world thanks to you. Why the hell did you make me press that fifth petal?" The more she thought about it, the more she wanted to kick him. Hard. "I could really use Albert. Too bad you broke our frickin' time machine!" She clenched her hands and moved away from the detective before she hurt him.

Albert suddenly flickered in beside her. "You called?"

"Albert!" She'd never been so happy to see the hologram. "Where are we?" If Albert was here, maybe there was some hope for them yet.

"Mr. Bennet only just began cataloguing the Fifth Branch. I do not know where you are, Miss Bennet. The Octagon Room is damaged."

"No kidding." Cassandra almost laughed.

"My program has limited power. If you have questions I suggest you ask them before I go offline."

Where did she start?

Detective Brice had gotten to his feet, was looking all about with the same bewildered expression Cassandra had probably just worn. But there was something odd about him, his face wasn't so wooden, so hard. And that piercing look, it was still there, but nothing like before. Normal wonder and curiosity flashed in his gray eyes, no more sinister undertones.

She'd save that mystery for later. She turned back to Albert, who was flickering, slowly fading. "Albert, is the device still here, still in working condition?"

"It is, Miss Bennet. It remains attached to the control hub, under the wreckage behind me."

Cassandra sighed with relief. Good, they had a way home at least. So long as the key was still in it. Or nearby. She'd worry about that later. Before she could ask another question, the detective shuffled over and stared at Cassandra. His eyes were wounded, lost.

"I . . . I can't feel the grid."

"That is good, Mr. Brice," said Albert. "We are nearly out of time. Miss Bennet, your great uncle wished for me to relay the following to you, in a section of his will I have reserved for just such a time, though I could not have foreseen the destruction of the Octagon Room, or your arrival on a Fifth Branch world. The information was to be released during your next travel."

Cassandra waved her hand for Albert to hurry. She didn't want him to run out of juice before he said what he needed to.

The surf crashed and hissed in the distance and Brice shifted beside her, huddling close to her, his state of mind a little disconcerting. At least he still had the smell of aftershave. Something familiar to hold on to.

"Mr. Bennet discovered the traveling device quite by accident, though perhaps none of this is by accident. Mr. Bennet never learned whether that was the case or not. I see that you have found his journal. I believe you will find more information, should you wish to learn more, in his journal and gathered texts, now scattered about this beach.

"When Mr. Bennet learned how to use the device, he gained wealth with his future knowledge. He also discovered a second device, in the far future, in a collapsed society he was never able to save or alter. He used this second device to travel and he never returned from his latest expedition. If he ever disappeared, I was to begin preparations for Miss Bennet to take over. An heir Mr. Bennet had deemed suitable to carry on his work."

Cassandra stared at the hologram, trying to take in his words. All she could focus on was the taste of salt in the air, the strange metallic bite. She chewed on her lip and gave the detective a nervous glance.

He seemed to be following the conversation, though he still had that lost look about him.

Little crab-like creatures had started climbing through the wreckage, their hard shells scraping against wood planks. Ozone, that was one of the odd smells in the air.

"Miss Bennet, you should know that Mr. Bennet spent most of his later years trying to save the collapse of that far future society, the ultimate collapse and extinction of humanity."

Cassandra tensed. "What? Humans . . . die out?"

"In a few thousand years, yes. Mr. Bennet believed the traveling devices were part of the problem, which is why it is of the utmost importance to keep them hidden, especially from future Earth timelines where the grid has taken control."

The mention of the grid perked Detective Brice's interest. He seemed about to ask a question, but Albert carried on, seeming to rush over his words now in an attempt to finish what he had to say before he faded out completely.

"As you know, Miss Bennet, the traveling device is linked to your DNA, as am I. The second device, which only the late Mr. Bennet knows the location of, is also linked to you. There are only two remaining devices, as far as Mr. Bennet knew. Controlled by thought, as you have learned. But one thing, on their operation.

"Mr. Bennet never explored First or Second Branches, deemed them unsafe. Third Branch is travel upon a particular world. Fourth Branch is time travel upon a given world. And as you have learned, Fifth Branch is something else entirely, another dimension, beyond time. Mr. Bennet never reached Six, Seventh, or Eighth Branches, but feared the grid originates from one of those outer dimensions. He feared for humanity, and perhaps the threat extends beyond your species' own survival."

Cassandra stepped away from Albert, shaking her hands at him. "No, no. That's way too much. Other dimensions and worlds? And the grid?" She gave the detective a suspicious glare. "What about *him*? Isn't he connected to the grid?"

"The grid is not on this world," Albert said. "Mr. Brice should be fine, so long as you stay away from any worlds or timelines controlled by it." Albert flickered faster now, static filling his voice. "The universe is your oyster, Miss Bennet. Happy explorations." He popped out.

Cassandra stared at the spot where the hologram had just been, all too aware of Brice standing beside her. "What now? What the hell am I supposed to do with that?" She looked over at the detective.

He was staring at the spot in the sand where Albert had been standing, his expression as glassy as the hologram's.

"Lot of help you are," she said with a sigh.

Cassandra couldn't wait to get home and be done with all this craziness. She had an apartment to get back to and pack, a cactus to take care of, a job to go to before she lost that, too. She couldn't process what Albert had just told her. She was still getting used to the fact that she'd gone forward in time, had met a hologram, and was now on an alien world.

Correction. Another dimension.

She chewed her lip.

Her stomach growled.

What she wouldn't give for one of Albert's tasty pastries right about now. If she didn't get some food fast, she just might have to grab one of the crab things clunking through the debris. Strange creatures, with shiny red shells and snail-like eye stalks poking up all over their bodies. Not at all appetizing, really.

She got another whiff of salt and ozone as she bent over the broken remains of the Octagon Room. She lugged aside a fractured wall panel, which thumped into the sand, and found the control table lying on its side beside her uncle's huge creepy bed.

"Thank God," she breathed with relief. The orange-sized golden octagon was nestled safely in the table's top. Cassandra pulled it free and turned it around, examining the filigree metal work. Didn't seem to be damaged, another relief.

But the key was missing.

Cassandra looked at the pale pink sand at her feet, lifted her sneakers, spun around.

Her stomach clenched uncomfortably. Where the hell was the key?

Trying not to panic, she set the octagon device down in the sand and started sifting through the sand. The key had to be nearby. She lifted the control table, dug sand from under the side of the bed, looked all over the black velvet bedspread and satin sheets, lifted and tossed aside more planks.

"What are you doing?" Brice had finally decided to rejoin the world of the living.

"Help me find the key." She tried to keep the panic out of her voice. If they didn't find that key they were trapped here forever. "Help me!"

Brice knelt beside her and started digging.

Cassandra was too frantic to direct him. "It can't be gone!"

"Is that what you're looking for?" Brice sounded far too calm as he pointed behind her.

Cassandra spun around. One of the crab-things was scuttling away, the antique brass skeleton key glinting in one of its claws. Only now did she notice that every single one of the weird little creatures was rooting in the pile of debris for shiny objects: a nail here, a door hinge there, a brass knob, whatever they could get their claws on. Like pigeons on a treasure trove of bread crumbs. All that was missing was all the squawking.

"No!" she shrieked and leapt after the crab, which saw her coming a mile away with all those eyes poking up all over the place.

It moved far faster than she would have given it credit, kicking up sand in a beeline for a hole in the dunes beside a massive boulder covered in aubergine fuzz like a mutant eggplant.

There were other boulders nearby, all coated in the peculiar moss, and the crab-things were disappearing into holes at their bases, too.

Cassandra arrived too late and peered hopelessly into the dark hole.

They couldn't lose the key.

She dropped to her knees and started digging.

"Cassandra," Brice said from behind. "I wouldn't—"

But Cassandra never got a chance to hear the rest of his warning.

The ground gave way beneath her and she plummeted in.

CHAPTER 4

Cassandra landed with a thud. The sand floor had a little give, but not enough. Her left hip and arm throbbed painfully. She lay still a moment, afraid to move. When the throbbing subsided, she gingerly sat up.

Her hip really hurt. She must have landed on a rock.

The warren of stone tunnels she'd fallen into would have been utterly dark if not for the beams of light shining through the pocked ceiling overhead. The crab-things dropped in like red rocks all around her, hitting the ground with legs tucked and popping open to scuttle off into darkened passages away from the pinkish light.

The air wasn't quite as oppressive down here. Cooler and damp-smelling.

Cassandra spat salty sand from her mouth and peered up into the bright opening above. The hole had widened quite a bit, but was too far away to reach. Easily ten feet up.

Brice's head dipped into view, his shadowed face backlit. "You all right?" She couldn't read his face, but he sounded concerned.

Cassandra shielded her eyes and nodded. "Little bruised, but I'll make it." She gave the surrounding passages a nervous glance. "I don't know what else is down here, though." The little crab-things couldn't have dug these tunnels, could they? Something bigger, most likely, something Cassandra didn't want to meet.

And where was the key?

She looked about for the crab that had stolen it. Most of the creatures had already disappeared into the gloom. What chance did she have of finding the thief now, with no flashlight and no idea which passage it had used?

"Hang on!" Brice vanished from sight.

"Like I'm going anywhere." Cassandra's stomach growled.

Then something shifted and scrabbled beneath her bottom.

She screeched and jumped up.

A crab-thing scrabbled from the small crater in the sandy floor, eye stalks waving and claws clacking. Like a deflated basketball with wiggling worms glued all over it. Weird and sort of terrifying.

She backed away and the crab scuttled off.

Something glinted from the sandy floor. The key! Resting plain as day in the center of the crater. Cassandra released a cry of delight and snatched it from the cool, moist sand.

Her delight quickly turned to dismay, however, as soon as she saw that half the key was missing, the part that would actually fit into the keyhole and make the traveling device work.

A rope of satin sheets tumbled into the tunnel, raining sand on Cassandra's head and smacking her in the face.

"Heads up!"

Cassandra couldn't believe they didn't have a way home.

She wanted to cry.

She tucked the broken skeleton key into the front pocket of her blue jeans and grabbed hold of the rope. Then gave it a little tug, to let Brice know she was good to go, and hung on for dear life as he painstakingly pulled her into the light.

Thankfully the opening didn't widen any further, and as she slid over the lip of the pit it became clear that hard rock was under all the sand on the beach.

Brice had wrapped the sheet rope around an aubergine boulder and backed up enough so that he was visible as Cassandra climbed onto the sandy dunes. The look on his face was one of relief, his face a little strained with effort, his biceps bulging beneath his short-sleeved black top.

She didn't trust her voice to speak just yet, the sense of dread weighing on her like a mountain of sand.

Part of her was still angry with Brice—they were stuck here because of him—but she was too depressed to yell at him. Or thank him.

She fished the key out of her pocket and held it out to him, her gaze fixed on the gaping hole at her feet.

Brice didn't take the key. "It's broken."

A gentle breeze brought a whiff of aftershave on salty sea mist.

Cassandra stuffed the key back in her pocket. "We're stuck here."

"Let's see what else we can find." Brice proffered a hand but Cassandra didn't take it.

She got to her feet. "Thanks for helping me out of the hole." She gave him a tight, pensive smile. She hadn't really looked at him very closely since they'd arrived on this alien world. She'd been too overwhelmed, too frantic to find the key.

He seemed more like his old self, more on the ball. Cassandra didn't know if that was a good thing or not. She'd seen the grid under his skin, seen how he had acted back at the mansion. Could he be trusted?

But Albert had said Brice would be safe from the grid here. Still, she knew next to nothing about Brice. Only that he said he was a detective, in a future nearly as alien to her as this strange world.

His gray eyes studied her right back, had taken on some of their familiar calculating that made her so uncomfortable. She suspected he was much better at this than her. It was his job, after all. To study people, to determine their motives and hidden desires, their secrets.

At least Cassandra had nothing to hide. She didn't care if he knew she didn't trust him or that she blamed him for their present predicament. She gave him a glower, just to make things absolutely clear between them.

Brice folded his arms over his chest, his eyes narrowing. She got the feeling he wasn't used to apologizing, even if it *was* his fault. If she'd thought he'd softened a bit since their arrival here, it was gone now. He was as unreadable as a statue.

Probably her own fault that he'd clammed up again, but she refused to be responsible for his moods.

And she was starving, dammit.

She hadn't had a bite to eat since the warm buttered roll in Albert's smorgasbord of deli meats, dinner rolls, and Danishes, and nothing before that since a light breakfast. She'd never planned to be gone long, had expected to take a quick look at the mansion to determine if it was worth moving into or selling. It was to be her ticket to a better life, perhaps provide her with enough money to afford a decent apartment, something more than a bed and kitchenette. She made just enough money to make ends meet.

And now she was trapped in another dimension with no food or water, stuck with a steely man she couldn't trust.

But he *had* just rescued her. That counted for something, didn't it?

"I'm as much a victim here as you, Miss Bennet."

Her eyes widened. She doubted that very much, but then again he had been connected to the grid before. Could it have had something to do with his alarming behavior back at the mansion that had gotten them stranded here?

"I don't know why I did what I did. Why I moved your hand like that." He unfolded his brawny arms. "And I hate to use that word. Victim. I'm no victim. But you get my meaning?"

She nodded, her eyes locked on his. Keen intelligence lurked at their depths, swift calculations, and something else. She couldn't put her finger on it, but it had something to do with the other, softer side of him she'd witnessed when she first found him on this beach. "What's the grid?"

He arched a single black eyebrow, a small hint of surprise. Then his eyes narrowed into full inspection mode. Whatever he had surmised from her question, he revealed nothing of his thoughts. His deep voice was matter of fact. "Peace and order. With increased grid influence, crime can be contained."

"But what is it? Who invented it?"

Her question seemed to surprise him again, but he recovered quickly. "It came before my time. I was tagged at birth, as is the norm. And to answer your other question, nanotechnology creates a grid beneath the skin. Biocomputer, of sorts."

She didn't know how old he was. Maybe mid 30s? Older than her and with the confidence of someone with a lot of life experience.

She rubbed her temple, feeling the effects from a lack of food. Being part computer would explain his cold demeanor back at the mansion, but not entirely. "You don't really believe the grid's a good thing, do you?"

He frowned, a glower reminiscent of the ones he'd given back at her uncle's mansion. She'd get no further with this line of questioning.

Clearly done with the conversation, Brice turned away and ran his fingers through his thick black hair, no longer as slicked back as it once was. The more carefree, tousled look suited him.

But Cassandra didn't like thinking of the detective that way.

She let him walk away, content to watch the waves pound the beach while Brice went through the crash debris. Boards clanked and thudded as he rearranged the chaos. Eventually he called her over.

He'd made a nice stack of longer, relatively intact boards, most likely for a shelter, but what really got her attention was the little white refrigerator sitting beside them.

"My uncle had a *fridge*?" She couldn't believe their luck.

She flung it open and wrinkled her nose at the stale air. At least it was still cold inside and the food unspoiled. She didn't care about rationing, didn't want to think that far out, about being stranded for weeks, or years, or forever.

She ripped open a plastic bag and sank her teeth into a tuna sandwich brimming with lettuce and thick tomato slices. A few bites in and she didn't feel quite so ravenous, could actually slow down and savor the flavor, take pleasure in the warm tingly satisfaction rolling through her and the return of more rational thinking.

When she was halfway through, she thought to offer some to the detective, but he shook his head.

"Don't like fish."

She shrugged and finished it off. No use in saving it. Without electricity, it would spoil.

Detective Brice lugged a wooden crate to their growing pile and pried the lid off with a groaning squeak.

Cassandra was impressed. Her uncle had stocked his time machine not only with a bed but also a generous amount of rations. The crate had a bit of everything, even a can opener. She chuckled at the little stash of chocolate-covered English biscuits.

While Cassandra sifted through the packaged food, Brice lugged over another crate, this one full of bottled water.

Cassandra relaxed a little. They might be stranded on an alien world but at least they wouldn't starve or die of thirst, at least not right away.

As if reading her thoughts, Brice said, "Won't last long. Hopefully it'll buy us enough time to locate some local cuisine and fresh water." He dumped a camping stove and pot onto the food provisions. "We can boil any water we find."

Cassandra pulled a face but resisted mentioning that any number of organisms could be living in said water that might not be killed off by boiling.

He studied the ocean. "Desalination apparatus could work too, if I find suitable materials in the wreckage."

Well, if she had to be stranded with someone, at least it was Mr. Survivor. She could put up with his taciturn behavior and calculating stares so long as he helped them survive long enough . . . to what?

Without a key they weren't going anywhere, least of all home.

Cassandra plopped down in the sand beside their growing mound of supplies, in the middle of what looked like a warzone of exploded bedroom, and hugged her legs to her chest with her chin on her knees.

A little less shaky now that she finally had some food in her, but her mind was still struggling to grasp this impossible scenario.

Unable to process, her thoughts kept drifting to all the unfinished tasks at home, her little cactus, drinks with Shirley at 8pm in an attempt to land Cassandra yet another unwanted date, and then her brain would hop back to the present dilemma and. . .

She sighed. No use. Maybe she'd wake up, realize she'd never received a letter from her great uncle and find out this was all just a dream.

Brice seemed to have a better grip on their situation. Keeping himself busy, sifting through all the junk. He had his back to her as he meticulously cleared the bed of splintered wood. As if she'd share the bed with him. She'd rather sleep on the sand.

And yet the idea of falling asleep at all was depressing. It would make this reality all the more real, though the light hadn't changed since their arrival.

Odd that it didn't seem to be getting any darker. The lack of long shadows was a little disconcerting, too. Only down in the tunnels had there been any. Up here, on the surface, the ambient light eliminated every single one.

Too many questions and not enough answers.

Her gaze landed on her uncle's journal. She'd dropped it during her frantic search for the key. Pale pink sand had partially covered it.

Brice gave her a sidelong look over his shoulder as she jumped up to retrieve the leather book. She returned to her spot by the supplies and unraveled the cord binding. The worn leather was warm and smooth, smelled of cowhide, and the pages inside were relatively damage free and full of that lovely old paper smell.

The pages crinkled as she rifled through them until she found her uncle's notes under the heading: "Fifth Branch."

She ran her finger over her uncle's ink drawings of strange creatures she'd never seen or even heard of. Though she did recognize the crab-things. Her uncle described them as being relatively harmless and attracted to shiny trinkets. Bet he'd never seen them in a frenzy over the oodles of metal holding his Octagon Room together. A bedroom crashing in their midst was probably right up there with "warm sunny day."

"Don't you think it's odd there's no sun?" she asked Brice absently.

When he didn't answer , she looked over to see him dusting off his rescued fedora, a little bent around the edges but still in one piece.

Yet a missing sun wasn't really that strange in the scheme of things. Everything about this world was oddly surreal. Close to what Cassandra knew, and yet not quite right.

In the journal her uncle described the crab-things' eye stalks as "light and temperature sensitive" as well as apparent gauges of how much ozone was in the air. At least Cassandra had gotten that observation down. The air was full of it.

She flipped through a few more pages until she arrived at a list of needed materials for "research facility." Her heart started thumping excitedly as she read on. "Brice, I think there's a research base nearby, something my uncle built to study this world."

The detective came over, fedora back on his head, and politely took the book from her hands. He quickly read the page and a few others after it, then handed it back. "You're right. This world seems to lack a sun." So he *had* been listening. Took him long enough to answer. "Without imminent nightfall we can risk a quick excursion.

Perhaps we'll find more supplies or even the second traveling device at your great uncle's base."

Cassandra shuddered. If the second device was there, then it probably meant a dead body. She had no intention of seeing the rotting corpse or whatever remained of her uncle.

But if the device was there, it was their only ticket home.

She brushed a wavy strand of hair from her eyes, then twisted the cap off a water bottle, took a swig of plastic-tainted water, swished it around in her mouth, and swallowed.

Detective Brice pulled a futuristic palm-sized device from a holster at his hip, checked it over, and stuffed it back in its holster with an air of satisfaction. When he caught her watching him, he gave her a grim smile. "No telling what we'll find over there."

Cassandra returned a wan smile. Not the most comforting thing he could have said. "Is that a laser or something?"

"Something like that." He nodded to the book in her lap. "You going to hold onto that?"

She shut her uncle's journal with a thump. "I'd like to keep it, yes." It had a few sketches of the surrounding terrain, or at least what Cassandra hoped was the local terrain. They'd find out soon enough.

Brice tossed her a tan canvas knapsack from the loot pile. "Take this then." He put one over his own shoulders and adjusted the straps. "Stock up on water foremost."

Cassandra grabbed a few water bottles, a packet of dried fruit rolls that promised to burst with natural strawberry flavor, as well as a few Honey and Oats granola bars from the other crate, and stuffed it all into the sturdy canvas pack, along with the journal and the golden octagon. She hoisted it over her shoulders. The padded knapsack nestled comfortably against her mid-back, not too heavy or cumbersome. And the shoulder straps were padded, too. She adjusted them a little. Perfect.

"I have to say, Miss Bennet, I'm impressed with your wherewithal to remain calm."

She stared at him, but he seemed sincere. No hint of teasing. She didn't feel very calm or collected. He must have forgotten her earlier panic episode over the missing key. "Thanks?"

He gave her a faint smile.

"And, please, just Cassandra." She'd told him that back in the mansion. He must have forgotten, or not been in his right mind. Was everyone in 2145 just another mind in a big computer?

She gave the detective a suspicious glance as he bent down to fill his sack with supplies, his mercury pants shimmering like molten silver. Cassandra wondered what the material felt like.

Brice closed and pounded both crates tight with a fist, then stood and tilted his fedora to her, the corner of his mouth turning up and a strange twinkle in his eyes. "Don't know about you, but I'm eager to see more of this strange new world."

Standing this close to him, she could smell his aftershave, though it vanished in a gust of sea air and ozone. She took a step back and gestured for him to lead the way.

Easier to keep an eye on him if he was in front of her, but really, it was so he'd be first in line if they encountered anything nasty. He had their only weapon.

She thought about picking up a splintered piece of wood and decided against it when she saw where they were headed—a steep cliff wall of white chalk at least fifty feet high.

She'd need both hands and a fair amount of luck to make it to the top.

CHAPTER 5

Brice started up the chalky cliff first, a deft and agile climber. With significant upper body strength, he made it look easy. Too easy.

He was halfway up the cliff before Cassandra had gotten very far. It wasn't that she couldn't have gone faster, she just didn't want to slip and fall, and a fall would only be longer and deadlier the higher she climbed. She focused on each rocky outcrop, made sure her sneaker was well planted before lifting the other leg and pulling with her arms. Though she'd found it strange to see no sun, she was thankful it wasn't beating down on her right now.

She risked a glance up, had been careful not to look down since she started climbing.

Brice had gone off to the side to avoid a tangle of strange plants spilling from above and was nearing the top. He'd probably avoid most of the plants on his current course.

But if Cassandra could reach those vines, they just might be the leverage she needed to make it up the rest of the way before her shaking arms gave out. She definitely didn't want to fall from that height.

She gritted her teeth and kept climbing, her hands gripping the dusty rock. Not really chalk, but as white and powdery when abraded. It also made for an unpleasant dust that didn't taste like talcum powder; more like baking soda. She didn't want to eat the stuff, though it was hard to keep her mouth closed with her lungs laboring for oxygen.

When she was about halfway up, Brice scrambled over the ledge with a few dislodged rocks that clunked down the cliff face. Okay, so maybe that was why he'd moved off to the side. No rocks landing on her head. He poked his head back over the edge. "Need a hand?"

She almost laughed. With what? He was a good twenty feet higher, and they didn't have the bedding rope.

Maybe she should have just stayed behind at the camp. At this point, going back down seemed way easier, if the more disheartening of her two options.

She couldn't give up, as much as her hands and arms hurt.

How long had it been? Twenty, thirty minutes?

At least the cliff wasn't too sheer, with plenty of sturdy toe and hand holds. The vines weren't much further away. She could make it.

Her arms thrumming like plucked guitar strings, Cassandra kept at it until she finally reached the lowest hanging vine and latched on. She gave it a tentative pull. Seemed sturdy enough. She didn't want to risk relying on it too much, but the waxy tendril, which had a sickly sweet aroma, made her climb a lot easier and faster.

She'd be joining Brice in no time.

When she was about ten feet from the top, she reached a thicker clump of vines full of strange blue flowers that abruptly withdrew at the sight of her.

But they were *flowers*. They couldn't see her.

No time to worry about it. She was nearly there.

The sickly sweet aroma grew stronger. Cassandra became a little light-headed. Probably just fatigue.

Almost there. Five more feet.

Her sneaker slipped. She managed to get it firmly lodged again and kept climbing.

The vine in her hands released oozing slime.

Cassandra's hands slipped.

She started falling, grabbed the cliff and held on tight.

"Brice! My hands, they're burning."

The world was swimming. The chalky wall, so cool against her cheek. Like sand. Sleep, that's what she needed. So tired.

"Cassandra! Keep climbing. You're nearly here."

She shook her head.

Whispering filled her ears. Faint tinkling laughter, like nails on chalkboard. Screeching. Promises of death on the rocks below. Coppery taste of blood in her mouth.

If she stopped now, she'd die.

She groaned and pulled herself up faster, ignored the burn in her palms.

A warm hand gripped her upper left arm, startling her. Brice.

She'd made it.

He helped her the rest of the way up, sat her down, away from the vines that clung to the cliff edge, and cupped her chin in his hand. "Cassandra. Look at me."

She tried to follow the sound of his voice. Deep, like the rumbling sea below.

His face was right in front of hers. Gray eyes narrowed with concern. Analyzing, deciphering. Aftershave enveloped her, fingered her brain and released serotonin. Numbing, relaxing.

He released her chin and lifted her palms, studying them.

Cassandra's drooping eyes flinched at the ghastly blisters on her palms. "Poison." She meant the vines, hoped he was quick enough to catch on. "Mind muddled." But she wasn't sure if she'd said that aloud or not.

She was suddenly frightened, wondered how long this fugue would last, whether it would worsen or not, worried it would be the death of her.

"Drink," he said.

He seemed to be in two places at once: holding a bottle to her lips and splashing cool water over her palms and soaking her jeans. She drank greedily and relaxed a little as the fog cleared from her mind.

"It still hurts," she said of her hands, her throat parched despite the water.

Brice lifted the sack from her shoulders and took out the journal. A few moments later he said, "Your great uncle discovered a cure for the toxins. His base is our best chance."

She winced as the larger blisters started oozing. At least she could think again. "Thanks." She must have gotten a double whammy from the vines. Blistering slime as well as mind-numbing fragrance.

She peered at the plants, morbidly fascinated. The blue flowers had come out of hiding again.

"Are they watching us?"

Brice arched a brow, then followed her gaze and gave a crooked smile when he saw the cause of her concern. "Just might be. Very calculated attack they performed on you. Let's hurry and see if that map lines up with this terrain."

She couldn't tell if he was teasing her or not.

This time she allowed Brice to help her to her feet. He was careful to avoid her stinging palms as he gripped her wrist.

The vines were a peculiar shade of green, almost purple. The blue flowers like upside down satellite dishes, uncannily following Cassandra and Brice's movements.

Cassandra was glad to leave the smelly plants behind, which coated most of the cliff in both directions as far as she could see. When she and Brice were some distance away, the plants started hissing and released sparkling pollen into the sky. A beautiful, sparkly cloud that Cassandra had no intention of discovering whether it was as toxic as their slime or fragrance.

She'd had enough of this world's flora, just wanted to find her uncle's base.

But the lake on her uncle's map was nowhere in sight. She and Brice had climbed onto an endless plateau. An enormous flat plain of hard rust-colored rock without a plant or animal in sight. No boulders, no rocks. Just flat ground that extended seemingly forever.

Overhead a cloudless sky swirled with sunset colors. A world in perpetual sunset without a sun.

"Straight ahead?" Brice had a handsome profile. Straight nose, high chiseled cheekbones, and a strong chin. His fedora hung a little lower over his forehead and would have cast his face in shadow had there been a sun overhead.

No wind, either. Nothing to rustle their clothes or Cassandra's wavy salt-stiffened brown locks. Hopefully her short bob looked better than usual, since she rarely spent any time styling it. If the tousled locks were sticking out more than usual, all the better. Crash-landing-on-alien-beach seemed to work just as well as bed-hair-ready. At least her hair was out of her eyes. She wasn't about to add oozing pus to the salty strands.

"Sure. Lead the way, Detective Brice." They'd both viewed the map and she thought she saw the subtle change in the plateau ahead, as if it dropped off at some point, indicated by a faint purplish-blue divot in the horizon.

The detective started walking and Cassandra kept stride with him, wiping blood from the corner of her mouth with the back of her hand. A small scrape she must have received during the scuffle with the vines on the cliff.

After their encounters with the life so far on this world she hoped they encountered nothing else in their search for her uncle's research base. She'd already lost the octagon key and been poisoned. Not a promising start to their adventures in another dimension.

At least they hadn't suffocated from lack of oxygen or died on impact the moment they arrived. They had that to be thankful for.

Chapter 6

"Where's the light coming from?" Cassandra didn't expect an answer, but she'd grown tired of the silence. Brice wasn't much of a conversationalist and they'd been walking on the flat burnt-red plain forever. A landscape as unchanging as the oil-slick-on-water sky.

"No idea," Brice said, his tone flat, his gray eyes fixed forward. He lifted his typewriter arm every now and again, seemed to remember it didn't work, and dropped it. He'd grown more sullen with every mile they walked.

Different dimension, different rules. Guess this world didn't need a light source to be illuminated.

"What's it feel like?"

His brow furrowed and he shot her a puzzled side glance.

"The grid. What does it feel like to be on it?"

"What's it feel like to be Cassandra?"

She released a blustery sigh. Getting Brice to talk was like pulling teeth. "You were on the grid your whole life and now you're not. What's the difference?"

He came to a stop. Though the plateau continued on, it had started to descend ever so gradually. Not a hill, but a definite dip. "You ask a lot of questions, Miss Bennet." So they were back to last name basis, were they? A range of emotions flashed across his face. Confusion, anger, and that same lost expression he'd had when she first rescued him from the rubble. "Being off grid is freedom. Emptiness." He waved his bare arm. "And I can't get a single reading on this place. Either my implants have stopped working because I'm off grid or the laws of physics have changed."

"Maybe you need a new battery." It was a lame attempt at humor, but it got him to crack a smile.

"Maybe." He started walking again, slow enough for Cassandra to easily catch up. His quicksilver pants rippled with his long strides and he adjusted the brim of his fedora. "I can't tell you what it's like to be on grid, only what I've lost since going off."

Cassandra resisted the urge to look at her throbbing palms. The blisters were worsening, she could feel it. No use in seeing just how bad.

"How are they holding up?" He indicated her hands with a flick of his eyes.

She hadn't looked at them. Eerie how he could read her like that sometimes. "Bearable."

"Still mad at me for dumping us here?"

Yes, but there was no use in holding a grudge. "You could make up for it by not dodging the question."

"Right." His mouth turned up in an amused smirk and he fixed his attention back on the horizon. An edge to the plateau wasn't far off now, rising up a little from where they walked.

"Thirsty?" He stopped to take out his water bottle, took a chug, and offered it to her.

Since the cap was already off and the bottle not too awkward to hold, she took a few long lukewarm droughts. Smelled and tasted like plastic, but it did the trick. She handed it back.

He twisted the cap back on and dumped it in his pack. "It's like living in an ocean and discovering you've been reduced to a bathtub."

"Huh?"

"The grid's an ocean of knowledge." He tapped his head. "This skull, a bathtub." He chuckled, which brightened his face into a whole other person. "Well, maybe a nice clear lake. A really big one." His gray eyes took on a dreamy sort of look, which was odd to see on his face.

"We have the internet. Is it like having all that information at your fingertips?"

"I suppose. And so much more. It's all I'd ever known."

"Were you aware of others on the grid?"

"No, but I wasn't alone. I felt . . . complete. More than myself. Calmer, more efficient. More . . . solid."

Cassandra had caught a glimpse of the grid in him and hadn't liked what she'd seen. "More rigid?" She wanted to add *sinister* and *creepy*, but thought it best to keep those observations to herself.

"Rigid? No. More concrete. More sure of who I was. A firmer identity."

She still didn't know what the grid was, but she had a better picture than she'd had before, or at least she thought she did. Typewriter arm made sense when he seemed to be implying that he'd been part of a massive computer.

She was just about to ask him if the grid was global in 2145, when they finally arrived at the end of the plateau.

Cassandra didn't like what she saw below, not one bit.

They'd found the lake from her uncle's map, but nowhere had he drawn the creatures that now hovered over it. Thousands, perhaps hundreds of thousands, of jellyfish-like purple blobs hovered above a shallow turquoise lake, their long tentacles trailing in the still water. And nowhere in his journal had her uncle mentioned that the lake glowed with an inner luminescence, which really was quite beautiful, if not for all the purple blobs mucking up the view.

"Where are you going?" Cassandra's voice rose sharply with distress.

Brice paused at the cliff edge. "Down. We found the lake. Your uncle's base should be on the other side."

"You see those things, right? Are you crazy?"

He looked amused. "Don't think I've ever been accused of that. Fearless maybe." He shrugged and started climbing backwards down the cliff. "This one's easy. Maybe twenty feet. Not that steep."

"Falling is the least of my worries right now."

"Good. Then you should make it down in no time."

Cassandra didn't want to follow Brice, but she also didn't want to stay where she was or traipse back to the crash site and contend with the toxic vines. She didn't want to be on this world, and hated that she didn't want to be alone. Normally, being alone suited her just fine.

"I can't climb." The air hurt her palms now.

Brice's fedora popped back into view, a look of consternation on his face. "Right. Your blisters. We could try wrapping them?"

She looked down either side of the cliff wall. Like the one at the beach, it seemed to go on forever, but it looked a lot less steep to the right. "Or I could just try using that bank over there."

"Or that. See you below."

It wasn't far to the bank Cassandra had mentioned, nor was it difficult to navigate. Her sneakers slipped a little on the rocky, dusty path, but she didn't fall, just ate a lot of red bitter-tasting grit.

"What's that smell?" she asked when she reached the bottom.

Brice shrugged. "Probably coming from those things." He gestured off-handedly at the jellyfish blobs, which towered over them like a sea of bobbing pom-pom trees with viny trunks. "Or the water."

"I doubt it's the water. Smells sort of like . . . "

"Dirty socks?"

She pulled a face. "Yeah, guess so. Look at that water. Clear as a treated swimming pool. No way is that rancid."

No wind made for glassy water. Too bad it was cluttered with so many tentacles, which moved just enough to create ripples and disturb the mirror-like effect of the glassy surface. Nevertheless, with the lake's ambient luminosity, the mirror-effect was reduced and the swirling rainbow colors from the sky reflected faintly only in the expanses between the tentacle trunks.

She held back, had no intention of approaching that shallow lake, pure as it looked, or the eerie blobs giving off definite danger vibes.

The creatures were just floating there like an army of slumbering giants, though with no eyes or other familiar body parts it was impossible to gauge if they were even capable of thought. The creatures' undersides were easily ten feet up and their bodies as tall as Cassandra, so that the whole creature was probably fifteen vertical feet. The jellyfish resemblance made her think the blobs had a mouth on the underside, and maybe a stomach hidden somewhere in those bulbous bodies.

After what the vines had done to her, she wasn't going anywhere near the things.

"There's a bridge over there." Brice started off for a distant wooden bridge so low to the lake it practically touched the water, and it wasn't straight, either, but zigzaggy like it had been assembled by a drunkard with a sick sense of humor. Who in their right mind would put a bridge in the middle of a sea of bloated jellyfish that hung overhead like enormous helium-losing balloons?

"You're going to walk for who knows how long through all those ... those *things*?"

"You have an alternative?" Brice stopped and fixed Cassandra with a frown.

A faint splash echoed down the cliff.

Cassandra wanted to clench her hands, but they hurt far too much for that. She settled for a scowl instead.

"If your uncle can draw to scale, we have roughly a mile of bridge. The trek to either side is far longer. Want to risk the time with your hands as bad off as they are?"

A chill crawled up Cassandra's spine.

He must be worried if he was playing the fear card, though no worry lines creased his brow beneath the brim of his fedora, or touched his cool gray eyes.

He wasn't worried, but he knew she was.

Cassandra didn't like being played.

She opened her mouth to object when she caught a sickly sweet odor like the vines. Not good, not good at all. She could almost taste it in the air, too, or maybe there was just so much of the toxin inside her now it was detectable on the tongue.

Her eyes darted down to her palms, she couldn't help it, and immediately wished she hadn't.

The blisters had burst, oozed, and now bubbled like a fetid bog of bloody blue paint.

She felt faint.

"Hang on," Brice said. He fished a strip of torn bedding from the crash site, ripped it in half, and carefully wrapped her hands. He was gentle, but she still cried out from the contact and bit her lip, eyes squeezed shut. "I'm surprised you aren't exhibiting more signs of infection."

Well Cassandra sure felt sick now, and the bandages only made things worse. She opened her eyes and resisted a whimper as she flicked a bandaged paw at the bridge.

She almost said "happy now?" but it seemed petty, given the circumstances. Brice was right. The bridge would be faster.

He stepped onto the bridge first, black shoes thudding dully on the wooden planks. His lean body was tense, on the alert for any sudden movements, but the jellyfish trees were as still as an armada of galleons in a dead calm.

Another splash echoed against the cliff as Cassandra joined Brice on the bridge. Like stepping into an eerie lavender forest planted in luminous turquoise glass, except that the trees had monstrous bodies wrapped in roped veins.

As she walked among them, the blobs seemed to throb like a slow-beating heart and a gentle hissing filled the air, so quiet she wasn't sure she was really hearing it. The dirty sock smell was stronger now, too, enough to coat her tongue.

Brice picked up the pace, his long strides setting a tempo Cassandra struggled to match in her current condition.

She couldn't stop gazing longingly at the clear waters. Her palms burned and a quick dip sounded like heaven. But the floating jellyfish were too close for comfort, some only a few feet from the crooked bridge. If she were to stick her arm out, she'd almost be able to touch their rubbery surfaces, not that she'd want to, not with a ten foot pole.

When she heard another faint splash she couldn't help but bring it up.

Brice didn't answer.

"Did you hear those splashes?" she asked again, a little louder this time.

He slowed and shot a steely glance over his shoulder. A faint "of course I've heard those splashes" look that only served to ruffle Cassandra's feathers. "Means we'd better hurry."

"Are they waking up?" If so, and Brice had suspected as much from the start, no wonder he was walking so fast. "Is it getting warmer?" Probably just the exercise, but her forehead was perspiring like crazy. She wiped it with the back of a bandaged hand. Satin wasn't very absorbent, but it was cool to the touch.

She gazed longingly at the water again, wondered how cool it was, how soothing it would be and if it would feel as silky as the satin.

"We're running out of time," Brice said, so close he startled her. He took her arm and gently pulled her along. "No swimming for you."

Cassandra tripped after him, a dragging weight. Had she really been about to leap into the lake?

"Not your fault," he said. "Toxin's spreading." Was that worry in his voice? His grip was strong but not painful. His jaw set, his gray eyes fixed on the path ahead through tentacle trunks reminiscent of banyan trees.

Cassandra's gaze rose up to the throbbing spheres that swayed as if in a gentle breeze, swirls of color streaking a mauve sky even higher still.

The hissing intensified and a few splashes broke the steady drone of their footfalls on the wooden planks, the only sounds in this eerie landscape.

Cassandra had a sudden sense of being watched.

Impending doom drifted up like volcanic vapor from the surrounding lake.

Brice started running, dragging Cassandra along for the ride, not that she didn't want out of there just as badly, but her legs had forgotten how to function properly, made her feel about as graceful as a marionette. It was like a nightmare, where you try to run as fast as you can and yet seem to go nowhere. Regardless how much Cassandra tried, she couldn't make her legs work properly.

"Run!" Brice said beside her, irritation and worry edging in on his normal calm reserve.

"Trying!" Cassandra bit back. God her hands burned, itched like crazy. She wanted to chew the skin off, couldn't stand the fabric friction.

"What the hell are you doing?" Brice yelled, his eyes wide with disbelief as Cassandra yanked the bandaging free of her right hand with her teeth.

Blue pus ran down her arm and dripped from her elbow. She didn't care how gross it looked, her hand was free. Now for the other one.

But Brice would have none of it. He held her arm hostage from her teeth and blistered right hand, insisted on keeping them moving, even as they devolved into a wrestling match in the middle of a bridge barely wide enough for the two of them.

So focused was she on freeing her left arm from the detective's grip that she failed to notice the enclosing jellyfish until it was too late.

Brice abruptly abandoned their struggle and whirled on the creatures with weapon ready.

All Cassandra cared about was freeing her other hand. She barely noticed the monstrous tentacles that thumped onto the bridge, rattling the planks beneath her sneakers.

Finally!

The bandage fell away from Cassandra's other hand and she breathed a rattling sigh of relief, let her hands hang at her sides, her posture slumped and a blissful smile on her face, the same guilty look she'd wear when itching a mosquito bite or poison oak. She knew she should have kept her blisters covered, but it just felt too good to have them free now, to feel the air on her thick, puckered flesh.

Sickly sweetness oozed into the air, coating her tongue like a handful of cotton balls stuffed in her mouth. She would have gagged earlier, but now found the aroma sort of soothing.

Corded tentacles thick as fully grown pythons crashed all around her. A cacophony of thumps and creaking wood and splashes like thrashing crocodiles.

The hissing intensified, too. A deafening sound as if a gargantuan faucet had turned on full blast, droning out every other sound.

Brice yelled a mere five feet away, but Cassandra couldn't hear a word, could hear nothing of the weapon firing in his hand.

Strobing red beams punctured the jellyfish blocking the way ahead and sprayed mauve blood everywhere.

Tentacles whipped across the bridge, knocking Brice's feet from under him.

He went down, but didn't land on his back as Cassandra would have done.

He rolled and was on his feet again and firing within seconds.

A jellyfish careened off to the side, where it collapsed into the lake with a horrendous droned-out splash that spilled turquoise water over the planks in a muted gush that traveled all the way to Cassandra's sneakers.

The horrendous ambient hissing made it impossible to hear or think straight.

More tentacles snaked across the bridge and latched onto Brice's legs and arms.

His weapon soared into the air.

Cassandra ran for Brice, but the creatures were too fast.

They lurched Brice right off his feet and carried him back towards the tentacle cluster blocking the passage to the research base.

The creatures only seemed interested in Brice as they soared right past Cassandra in a cloud that reeked of rubbery tartness like lemons left to rot in a hot tire.

When Cassandra finally caught up to Brice he was upside down, hanging by his ankles.

His arms flailed, his widened eyes found hers.

The jellyfish were drawing him closer to the rim of sharp spikes in their underbellies.

"No!" Cassandra lunged and grabbed the tentacle wrapped around one of Brice's ankles.

As soon as her throbbing sore skin touched that rubbery flesh, the tentacle recoiled as if she'd branded it with a hot iron.

She lunged for the other tentacles holding Brice before they could whisk him out of reach, and each tentacle recoiled just as fast.

Much to her surprise, not a single jelly tried to reclaim Brice.

Instead, the creatures drew back as though he and Cassandra had just burst into flames.

Tentacles trailed off the bridge and splashed back into the water, audible now that the deafening noise had finally diminished to a gentle hiss like a garden sprinkler.

The path was open again.

Cassandra didn't know what had just happened, nor did she care.

She looped her arm through Brice's, careful not to get her oozy palms on him, and helped him to his feet.

He hopped onto one foot, clearly favoring his left leg. He saw her watching and shook his head. "Nothing serious."

She'd take his word, for now.

They grabbed his fedora from its resting spot on the bridge and hurried as fast as they could down the zigzagging bridge, Brice with a hobbling hop and Cassandra struggling to keep him upright. He was taller than her by a good six inches and hard to support, especially when she had to keep her oozing palms off him.

She nearly cried out with relief when the view finally opened up again, revealing the opposing bank beyond the forest of carnivorous jellyfish.

They picked up the pace and were soon stepping off the planks onto hard burnt-red ground. No cliff on this side, but a gentle upward slope of dusty russet earth.

Cassandra thought she detected the distant sound of ocean surf, along with a salty ozone-laden breeze to clear the stench of dirty socks and rancid lemons.

She wanted to stop and rest, could tell Brice did too, but they staggered up the slope, intent on getting as far from the lake as possible before stopping to catch their breath. Brice's leg seemed to be doing a little better, capable of taking more weight, or maybe he was just using it more because it was faster.

They crested the hill and Cassandra finally collapsed to her knees, too afraid to look at her ruined hands just yet. She started shaking, from her toes all the way to her jaw. Her arms where the blue pus had dripped were stinging now, too.

Brice dropped down beside her with a grimace of pain.

"Is it … is it b-broken?" she asked through chattering teeth.

"I don't know." He lifted his nonfunctional typewriter arm. "No way to know for sure."

Cassandra laughed, which was hard when she was shivering like a jackhammer. "People … people can usually t-tell. D-don't need a typewriter arm."

He took a deep breath and closed his eyes. "Thanks, Cassandra. For rescuing me."

"You'd . . . have done the same for m-me." She wanted to hold her jaw shut but didn't want to smear blue pus all over her face.

Shock. She was in shock. From the recent attack, but more likely from the blistering flesh releasing toxins into her body.

"You should let me bandage them again," Brice said softly. "Except those strips of sheet are long gone. Along with my weapon."

"G-guess we better hope the b-base is d-down there." She clenched her teeth and willed the chattering to stop. If she concentrated hard enough, she could make her jackhammer jaws slow a little. "Think . . . that's it?"

They overlooked a plain of rolling faintly pink sand dunes that stretched as far as the eye could see ahead and to the left. To the right was a calm turquoise bay, more like a lagoon, with gentle waves crested in pink and purple and punctuated by huge, skinny boulders.

Near that distant shore was a dark spot, perhaps a building, though difficult to tell from their vantage point.

"Let's hope so." Brice sounded as tired as Cassandra felt.

For once, she found herself hoping the world ahead was empty. She couldn't handle any more Fifth Branch life.

CHAPTER 7

Without a sun or darkening sky to judge the passing of time, Cassandra had no way of knowing if her immense fatigue was due to it being three o'clock in the morning, having walked countless miles, or being poisoned by vines and attacked by monstrous floating jellyfish. Or if it was just sheer brain overload at finding out her great uncle was a time traveler, his butler a hologram, and that she was stranded in another dimension with no way home.

She'd long since given up the hopeful notion that this was all just a dream. She hurt far too much, had endured too many trudging miles and eaten far too much bitter-tasting red dust, for this not to be real.

Brice came to a huffing stop and Cassandra stumbled to a halt with him, his heavy arm draped over her shoulders. Her legs were shaking, buckling under his weight, and her sneakers had filled with enough sand that it felt like she was dragging an entire beach with each step.

As much as she wanted to rest, the building wasn't far off now, but Brice didn't give her a choice of pressing on, at least not if she was going to stick with him.

He collapsed against a tree and rested the back of his head against the trunk, fedora pushing forward over his face.

Cassandra wanted to sink to her knees in the cool sand, but feared she'd never get up again. "C'mon. Just another few hundred feet."

Brice continued to breathe heavily, his broad chest rising and falling more slowly, arms hanging to his sides. Had he fallen asleep?

Pus dripped from Cassandra's hands into the sand and she resisted another urge to lick them or lift to them to the sky. She'd been having a lot of unnerving urges lately, like wanting to rub her blistered palms all over Brice, or all over the ground, or on anything she could get her hands on, like that trunk Brice was resting against.

Now that she wasn't so focused on taking the next laborious step, though, she could really look at the scenery they'd descended into.

Seen from the vantage point on the cliff above, she knew they'd entered a valley of pale pink dunes that sloped down to a beach. The building they'd seen from above had been built on the dunes, just up from a flat beach of rosy colored sand and wavy amaranthine streaks. Turquoise waters lapped the shore and filled the air with the familiar tang of salty sea.

Being in another dimension, Cassandra would have expected the building to be more unusual than it was, not a retro building of futuristic design. Like a giant oval bowl, the two-storied building's walls curved outwards, with the solid metal lower story slanting out the most. The second story was comprised of tinted blue glass, and the roof was flat and broader than the building it protected. It looked like a 1960s impression of what a futuristic building should be, but Cassandra had to admit that in its current setting, with the rainbow sky and bright blue lagoon and strange trees, it was oddly fitting.

It had to be her uncle's base, and they were almost there, though she had no interest in finding a body. Just a salve for her palms and forearms and something to set Brice's leg with, if it was indeed broken, which seemed highly likely given his current condition. She just hoped he didn't have any internal bleeding and that the cure for her blisters was easily found and not too late to be helpful.

She nudged Brice with the toe of a sneaker. "Wake up." The urge to plant her oozing palms on his cheeks was too high to trust looping her arm around his waist again, and she doubted he'd be able to limp the rest of the way on his own.

Brice's aftershave scent had grown faint but was still noticeable, which made Cassandra uncomfortable being too close to him, especially now that they'd stopped. She'd been too distracted earlier with walking and holding Brice upright to be bothered before.

She backed up a little and resisted another urge to cross her arms and accidentally brush her blisters on anything else. The infection had already spread. "Brice!"

He murmured something that sounded like, "Two more minutes."

A faint rustling drew Cassandra's attention upward. Her eyes widened. The trees weren't really trees, like on Earth, but rather resembled colossal ocean-dwelling tube worms.

The one Brice was leaning against had a broad, supportive base and a trunk ridged in spirals. Ten-foot long tendrils like translucent rice noodles rustled high above in a breeze and were cinched at their base by a thick mottled green and blue ring that seemed capable of releasing or drawing in the tendrils, just like the tube worms Cassandra had witnessed at the San Francisco aquarium.

There weren't many other trees in sight, and this one seemed not to care that Brice was currently using it for support.

Cassandra relaxed a little. Maybe they'd found their first indifferent life form.

More of the strange eye-stalk laden crab creatures scuttled about the dunes, digging now and again and plucking who knew what from the sand to stuff into their mouths.

Cassandra didn't have anything else shiny for them to steal, except the broken key in her front pocket.

Commotion from the building up ahead put her on edge.

"Brice," she whispered. "Get up." Could just be more crab creatures, but she didn't want to risk it. Whatever had killed her uncle could still be here.

She shook her stinging hands and nudged Brice again with her toe.

The trees didn't have branches and there wasn't anything else for him to use as a cane. She didn't care. He could crawl away. "We need to hide behind a dune. Now."

The commotion grew louder—a clunking noise that echoed eerily from the building a few hundred feet away.

A clearing of sand encircled the compound as if a massive bulldozer had flattened everything else to increase visibility. There'd be no sneaking up on the place.

The clanking seemed to be coming from outside the building.

A form appeared from around the back of the building, humanoid in shape and holding something, like a weapon, in its hands. It saw them just as an alarm went off, a blaring fire truck whine replete with flashing red lights that roamed all over the sand, blinding Cassandra as they raked her face.

"Run!" she yelled at Brice, who finally seemed to realize the situation was bad enough to warrant action.

He pushed from the trunk and reached for Cassandra, who grabbed his waist and scrambled with him for the dunes, though it was probably a fruitless plan now that they'd been spotted.

Part of her hoped the compound belonged to her uncle and that they were being foolish in fleeing from him, but a glance over her shoulder dispelled that hope.

Now that the form had given pursuit and was quickly gaining on them, she could see it wasn't her uncle or any other human, but a robot.

She should have been more surprised than she was, but she'd already seen computer arms, hovercars, holograms, and experienced time travel and dimension hopping, not to mention all the strange creatures that had tried to kill them so far.

She also didn't think her sickly sweet palms would be any form of deterrent for a robot. Best to just keep ambling away, slow as snails through upward sloping sand.

Brice dropped beside her and Cassandra whirled on their pursuer, the toxic smell from her palms thick on her tongue.

The robot was larger than Brice, though of slighter frame, and looked about as sturdy as a tank. It held a large wrench in its shiny hand, and though its humanistic features were metal, they conveyed anger quite convincingly.

Cassandra held up her hands, hoping it could be reasoned with and that it understood English. "We come in peace." She inwardly cringed at the cliché, but it was the first thing that came to mind after all the movies she'd seen.

The robot was nearly upon them.

"Stand down Artemis!"

The whirring clangs and red lights abruptly stopped. The robot paused mid-stride, a mere five feet away, and lowered its make-shift weapon. Another creature, also silvery metal, slinked down from the robot's shoulders and landed in the sand with the graceful ease and quiet of a cat.

Cassandra stared at the tiny robot, about the size of a house cat but comprised of solid metal with few seams and no visible bolts.

Uncannily lifelike in its movements, the long-tailed creature slinked closer, big triangular ears perked up and twitching as if listening for sudden movements. Lambent cobalt eyes watched Cassandra with eerie intelligence as the creature came round the side of Brice, appearing to want to get a closer sniff.

"Get up!" Cassandra urged, afraid to take her eyes off the robots or turn her back on them.

"Kina!" a masculine voice called, the same voice that had ordered the larger robot to stand down.

The cat-like robot whirled and galloped off towards the source of the voice—an old man limping towards them with a cane under his right hand.

The little robot leapt up to the man's arms and on up to his shoulder, where it turned and perched, big blue eyes staring unblinkingly at Cassandra.

The old man stroked the creature's smooth back, which it seemed to enjoy and nuzzled the man's neck with the top of its head, big ears pressing back.

The old man was dressed about as oddly as Brice, same penchant for old-fashioned style with a futuristic flair. He wore a dark blue suit reminiscent of Victorian garb, a white button up shirt, and an ascot that resembled molten metal, like Brice's pants, but in swirling gold and darker shades of red like cooling lava.

The old man's white hair formed an unkempt and wispy halo, and his limp was quite prominent. Cassandra thought it a little odd that his left arm was fully covered and his left hand concealed in a white glove. Now that he'd come to a stop, the old man switched his cane to his gloved hand and gestured eagerly for Cassandra to come closer.

"Can't tell you how thrilled I am to see you, Cassandra! No idea who your companion is, but he's welcome, of course. Artemis, please assist the young gentleman."

"Yes, Master Bennet," replied the wrench-wielding robot in a tinny, hollow voice.

"Uncle Niles?" Cassandra couldn't believe they'd finally found her great uncle's base and that he was alive and well. It seemed far too good to be true.

He flashed an uneven row of shiny white teeth and gestured again for her to join him. "No need for titles. Just Niles."

Cassandra looked over her shoulder, to ensure Brice was okay, before shakily approaching her uncle.

Niles Bennet was a little taller than her, but only by an inch or two, and his frame surprisingly thin, which she might have considered fragile if not for the air of wiry strength and resourcefulness about him. Though his brown-eyed gaze was more piercing than grid-linked Brice's had been, it thankfully lacked grid-Brice's sinister edge.

Mad scientist came to mind, though.

What remained to be seen was just how mad.

But for now Cassandra was so relieved she could cry. She allowed her uncle to wrap an arm around her and fuss over her injured palms. He smelled of biscuits and a hint of peppery Old Spice, and though she had a thousand questions, for now all she could think about was a cure for the insane burning and urge to wipe her hands on every bit of flesh in sight. Once she got rid of the foul taste in her mouth, a nice meal and fresh water sounded good, too. And maybe a nap.

CHAPTER 8

Niles Bennet ushered Cassandra into his research facility, like something straight out of the future, a future beyond Brice's 2145. Judging by the surprised noises from the detective behind her, she hadn't been too far off with her estimation.

The interior had an open floor plan with a second-story wraparound platform and a substantial railing to prevent any nasty falls. With taller stories than an average building, the whole space was quite cavernous. A huge workshop bursting with enough robots, gadgets, knobs, and blinking lights to send any technophile into ecstatic fits.

Cassandra didn't know where to look first.

Hissing steam and sharp chemical smells left an unpleasant tang in the air. Rumbling clanks vibrated through the floor, lights blinked and flashed from countless panels, and robots—some tall like the one that escorted Brice, and some shorter—carried supplies throughout the facility, pounded metal sheets, and rummaged through bins and cupboards. A bustling factory similar to what Cassandra had seen in car commercials, though far beyond anything introduced in her time.

In the middle of the room, directly ahead, rested another octagonal room, though by no means complete. A handful of the taller robots worked on it, assembling wall panels of what looked like polished steel, one robot balancing a panel while the other used a tool that whirred and screeched with each added screw. Another robot worked on the octagonal room's floor panels, aligning metal sheets and affixing them together with more whirs and screeching, and yet another robot lugged additional components to be added to the jumble in the middle of the floor, dropping its load with a clank and stomping off for a new armload.

Unlike the Octagon Room that Brice had wrecked when he'd accidentally brought it to this world, the newer model was as sleek and shiny as the robots constructing it. No quaint wooden planks or bookshelves, unless Niles planned to have the metal overlaid with wood paneling.

"You're building a new one?" Cassandra asked in disbelief.

She almost mentioned that Brice had broken her uncle's other Octagon Room but thought it best to save that for later.

"Smart Walls," Niles said, his eyes dancing with manic glee. "Managed to pilfer a fair amount from a far future Earth, year 4327."

As fascinated as Cassandra was, all she wanted to do was rub her palms all over her uncle's exposed skin. She flicked her hands and tried to think about something else. "Smart Wall?"

Niles nodded emphatically. "Like Kina here." He patted the robot perched on his shoulder. "Smartest metal alloy humans have yet constructed."

Brice limped up beside them with the aid of the robot, Artemis, who stood stoic as a statue, glassy eyes observing the construction of the Octagon Room. Despite being machine, the robot managed to convey a startling amount of emotion with subtle shifts in its glossy eyes and various metal panels that comprised its face.

"AI directly imbedded throughout the metal," Niles continued. "Smart Walls can vanish from sight at will, defend as necessary, and my new Octagon Room will, of course, be genetically linked to our DNA. Can't have just anybody absconding with our latest time, dimension, and space machine now, can we?" He rubbed his hands and grinned broadly. "You have the orb, don't you? Wouldn't be here without it."

"You mean the octagonal traveling device?" Cassandra asked.

Niles nodded briskly. "Yes, yes." He held out his right, ungloved hand.

"It doesn't work anymore," Cassandra said.

Niles looked crestfallen. He started pacing and muttering, rubbing his halo of white hair so briskly it stood up like static when he finally came to a stop in front of Cassandra again, brown eyes uncomfortably intense. "You have it, tell me you do."

"Don't you have one?" Cassandra asked, shifting her pack so Niles could get into it. Her hands were useless. And what about a cure for her blisters, and help for Brice's leg? They could sort out the time machine stuff later, but her uncle seemed a man possessed.

He pulled the pack free of her shoulder and hurriedly dumped the contents onto a nearby steel workbench. Kina leapt to the tabletop as empty water bottles rolled and clattered to the floor, followed by a few heavier thumps from the bottles still full of water. Niles's journal and empty Honey and Oats granola packs rustled to the table. The golden orb dropped out last, which Niles snatched before it could roll away.

Niles seemed not to notice the mess he'd made all over the floor, his shiny blue shoes kicking an empty plastic bottle ahead of him as he limped back to Cassandra. "Seems fine. Perfect working order. The key. Where's the key?" He held his gloved hand out like an impatient child, though without the petulance.

Cassandra couldn't stick her hand in her pocket. "It's broken. Snapped in half." She showed her uncle her palms. "And I can't get it out of my pocket with these." Her uncle's wrinkled face looked like a great place to plant her palms. She mightily resisted the urge.

Niles's eyes widened, as if seeing her hands for the first time. He leaned in, peering intently at them, shook his head, and started muttering, but not in a way that Cassandra found consoling. For one, he kept repeating the words, "advanced case" and "lethal."

"If Master Bennet is done with my services, I would return to my work in the generator." Artemis didn't wait for Niles to answer, but shifted Brice to a work table for support, wiped its hands, and with an air of disdain walked to the wayward water bottles and picked them up one at a time. "I would also remind Master Bennet that I am *not* hired help." Artemis dumped the bottles into a large garbage bin at one end of the long workbench and clamped the lid shut, the motion releasing a foul puff of air.

Cassandra stared with her mouth open. Artemis didn't sound like a robot she'd be comfortable having around the house. "Awfully bossy, isn't it?" she asked of Niles.

Her uncle was too busy muttering as he rummaged through a massive white cupboard at the other end of the workbench, pulling out jars, reading labels, and shaking his head. He didn't bother to put any of the jars back, just plunked them onto the workbench among the scattered papers and tools before returning to his rummaging.

"I'll have you know I will *not* be organizing Master Bennet's cupboard again. Perhaps another of your minions can be convinced to help you this time." Artemis fixed Cassandra with a level stare that made her squirm. "I hope Miss Bennet does not need to be reminded that she and her companion are guests in our home." And with that Artemis clunked off and out the door with a floor-rattling slam.

Cassandra blinked in disbelief. Just who was running this place?

"Ah-ha!" Niles exclaimed. He had a jar in hand and struggled to limp across the workshop with a *click-click* of his cane to another section of the workshop nestled under the second-story platform.

This other section of his research facility was the sort of lab Cassandra was more accustomed to seeing. Microscopes and flasks and distillation apparatuses with bubbling liquids in bright greens and blues. But it also reminded her of a mad scientist, especially with flasks leaking mist like dry ice, and the odors, some sharp and sweet, and a hint of something so pungent she could taste it.

Niles fit the mad scientist bill, too; absent-minded enough that Cassandra wondered how he accomplished anything. And Artemis had just implied the only reason Niles could find anything or walk across the place without stepping on trash was because his robot minions cleaned up after him, however begrudgingly.

"Is Artemis always so bossy?" Cassandra asked again.

"Don't mind her," Niles said absently.

"That thing's a 'she'?" The robot hadn't been wearing clothes and lacked signs of any anatomy.

Cassandra was about to ask her uncle another question, when she realized she was apparently as absent-minded as her uncle. They'd forgotten Brice, who was still by the workbench, though he'd slid to the floor and now rested with his back against a table leg.

"You okay?" she called to him.

Brice gave her a weak smile.

"My friend, Detective Brice, he needs medical assistance."

"Your friend's broken leg can wait," Niles muttered. He snatched Cassandra's upper arm and shoved her hand into a machine that sort of resembled a magnifying apparatus—big and white, with viewing windows and lots of knobs. "Your hands cannot." He muttered some more as he calibrated the machine, turning knobs and peering into the various windows until he was satisfied.

Following a moment of silence, he leaned back and rubbed his head until his hair stood on end again, then peered back into one of the windows in the side of the machine. "Never seen such an advanced stage. Perhaps you should wait until we've cleared it up before you take a look. Hang on. Might pinch a little."

The machine clamped down on Cassandra's arm so she couldn't have pulled it out even had she wanted to. A sucking wind suddenly tugged on her palm like a vacuum cleaner, and it didn't pinch; it felt like barbed wires ripping her skin.

Cassandra cried out and the suction stopped.

Niles looked a little guilty as he flicked another switch.

Cassandra yanked her bleeding hand from the machine. "What the hell?"

"I had to take some samples while I had the chance." He opened the jar he'd taken from the cupboard on the other side of the workshop and smothered a foul-smelling yellowy substance all over her palms and forearms, everywhere blisters had formed.

The contact hurt, but the effect was immediate. The burning stopped and Cassandra sank to the floor in relief.

Niles went to a sink, turned on a faucet, and thoroughly scrubbed his hands in steaming water and squirts of lemony soap. "You aren't done yet. Eat the rest."

"What?"

Niles turned off the water and dried his hands. He held out the opened jar of yellow-green gunk that reeked like rancid tallow.

"No way am I eating that."

"Infection's become systemic. Unless you want to sprout spores all over your body, I suggest you lick the jar clean."

"Spores?" Cassandra asked faintly. "You mean the blue pus?"

Niles nodded, his expression grim, though there was a hint of fascination in his eyes, the look a scientist might give his favored lab rat who'd just shown promising signs of curing cancer.

Cassandra definitely didn't want blistering pus all over her body. She held her nose and spooned the slime into her mouth with a finger. She gagged more than once, but managed to get it all down.

Niles was thoughtful enough to hand her a glass of milk when she'd finished.

Cassandra scraped her tongue in a failed attempt to rid it of the fatty rankness. Most awful thing she'd ever tasted.

She gagged again and almost begged another glass of milk.

"How are you feeling?" Her uncle took the empty glass from her raw hands.

"A little better," she said. Then smiled. "A lot better. Am I going to be okay?"

"I believe so." Niles used the edge of the table to pull himself up. He'd been crouched in front of her. He stretched a little, arms reaching over his wispy halo of white hair. "Can't say I've ever had to eat the salve. Wasn't sure you'd be able to stomach it."

Cassandra blanched. "You mean the cure might kill me?"

Niles shook his head, distracted with the view into the magnifying machine. "Never thought to use crabs to counteract the toxin, did you?"

"The red crab-things with the eyes all over them?" They weren't real crabs, of course, but they might as well be for this world. "*They're* the cure?" She felt a little sick, wondering what part of them her uncle had just fed her.

"A defensive secretion against predators and most effective against parasitic vines."

Cassandra didn't want to know anything else about the crab secretions. She put a hand to her chest and took a deep breath. "Parasitic vines?"

"Look for yourself." Niles stepped away from the magnifying machine.

Morbid curiosity compelled Cassandra to look.

She pressed her face up to the eyeholes, still warm from her uncle's face. The image was blurred at first, but then it came into startling clarity. A close-up of Cassandra's puckered and blistering skin, but what made her the queasiest were the little mushroomy blue things sprouting up all over her skin, inside the wounds, swimming in the pus.

She drew back in disgusted horror. Her eyes fell to her palms. The blue pus had stopped oozing from them and that sickly sweet smell, like cheap imitation rose perfume, was gone. "I've been spreading baby vines all over the place?"

Her uncle rubbed his head and turned the machine off. "Whatever you touched, if it's capable of supporting life, the spores will grow. They gestate best in flesh and seem capable of influencing an infected mind for optimal spreading. The polyps grow and eventually burst free to root into soil. They have a harder time establishing in sand."

Cassandra grimaced. "Don't tell me any more." Mind-controlling spores sure explained all those unusual urges. She shuddered. "What about Brice? If he has spores, will he know? Can he get rid of them with the salve?"

"If he blisters, he can apply the salve, same as you."

"But don't the crabs have protective shells?"

"Plenty of fleshy bits and seams in their shells," Niles said absently, his attention flicking to Brice's slumped form. "Your friend is in need of assistance."

Cassandra felt guilty that they'd left Brice on the floor with a broken leg. She'd have to ask for something to clean and bandage her wounds later, once Brice was taken care of.

"Cyril, sweep for spores," Niles said into the room as he snatched his cane and limped to Brice.

Beams of green light from the surrounding walls and ceiling flickered through the workshop, from floor to ceiling and into every crevice. Alarms went off and sections of the floor lit up bright red, where Cassandra had been standing and walking. A few robots hurried to wipe up the contamination.

Her uncle sure ran an efficient workshop.

Niles called two of the larger robots over and had them carefully lift and carry Brice to yet another section of the workshop, which reeked antiseptic-white.

White operating table, medical equipment, scalpels and scissors, and a bunch of things Cassandra had no name for. Having very little experience with hospitals, she couldn't say what was different, except that much of it just seemed too advanced for her time. At least the smell of disinfectant was familiar, though it wasn't a scent that put her at ease. Who liked being in hospitals?

The robots laid Brice on the operating table, strapped him down, and clomped off.

Cassandra felt useless as she stood beside the table.

Pain creased Brice's handsome face. He tried to get comfortable, restricted as he was by the straps, but it only seemed to add to his discomfort.

His gray eyes landed on Cassandra.

She squeezed his hand, not knowing what else to do. Her palms were raw, but no longer weeping. Not the most pleasant thing for either of them, but he seemed to appreciate the gesture.

"Why the straps?" she asked her uncle, who had seated himself at a workstation, white cane propped up against the panel of knobs and switches and monitors beside him.

Niles typed away at the computer as a section of the medical wall swept out like a massive arm over Brice's leg. Lines of green light flickered over the length of his broken leg.

Niles muttered and rolled his chair to another screen in his work station. He rubbed his head into a static frizz. "Severe fracture."

Cassandra straightened. "Can it be fixed?"

"Yes, yes, of course." Niles spun around in his chair. "The procedure will be exceedingly painful."

"Can't you give him pain killers or knock him out?"

Guilt swam through Niles's eyes. "All gone, and I haven't been able to replenish with my orb being damaged during my last expedition." He looked like he was hiding something, perhaps in regards to his latest expedition?

"Will the procedure last long?"

"Shouldn't take long, no."

She squeezed Brice's hand until he opened his eyes again. "My uncle says you have a fracture. He can fix it, but it's going to hurt. You okay without anesthesia?" She watched for signs of panic.

Brice's gray eyes hardened. "Fine," he said, his voice faint. "Just get it over with."

She squeezed his hand again and nodded to her uncle.

Niles spun back to the consoles. His robot pet, Kina, leapt onto the flat surface beside him and sat on its haunches, big ears flicking, while Niles used the controls to lower the medical arm onto Brice's leg.

Cassandra flinched as the straps restraining Brice tightened over his arms and ankles, tightly binding his body to the table. She realized medical procedures in Earth's past had been performed without anesthesia, but it didn't make this any easier to stomach. She didn't know if the machine would be cutting into Brice's leg, didn't know just how much this would hurt him or how it would fix him.

She was about to ask her uncle to explain when Brice stiffened and gripped her hand tight as a vice, putting far too much pressure on her injured palm. She endured the pain by biting down on her lip. It was the least she could do considering what he must be going through.

The machine was deathly silent, but Brice gritted his teeth and groaned. Then he started thrashing. The straps prevented him from moving much, and he really tried his best to be still, but Cassandra's eyes teared up as his grip tightened and pressed her forearm into the table.

She was about to beg him to release her hand when his hold finally loosened and she pulled her throbbing hand back, cradled it to her chest as pins-and-needle feeling returned. Her raw skin had puckered and cracked from the pressure.

Brice looked better, his whole body relaxing.

The mechanical arm hummed away and folded back into the medical wall as the straps binding Brice whisked apart and vanished into the table beneath him.

"Fine piece of technology," Niles said of the operating table. "Obtained from future Earth, year 2980." He wheeled his chair over to Brice. Not the best bedside manner, but her uncle at least seemed genuinely interested in his patient's recovery. "How are you feeling, Detective Brice? Your bones mended nicely. Clean fractures will do that."

"Thank you," Brice said faintly.

A puff of antiseptic misted the air and Cassandra pulled a face and smacked her tongue. "Is that really necessary?"

Niles gave an apologetic shrug. "Automatic." He rolled back to his cane, used it to stand and held his arm for Kina, who scampered up onto his shoulder. "Don't know about you two, but I'm famished."

Now that her uncle mentioned it, Cassandra was dying for a nice meal. Dinner with her friends back in San Francisco a lifetime ago had been the last real meal she'd enjoyed. A hurried bite before she'd left her apartment for her great uncle's mansion hadn't really counted, and neither had anything she'd had since, though the tuna sandwich on the beach had been tasty.

Brice was perking up, too. It seemed his stomach would get him moving. He hadn't wanted any of the tuna and had instead eaten three granola bars during their trek here.

Cassandra offered him her arm, she couldn't bear any more pressure on her palms, and helped him from the table.

Brice swung his legs over the side and tentatively stood on both legs. He looked beat and in need of rest, but gave her a nod and gestured for Niles to lead the way.

CHAPTER 9

Cassandra sat on the glass-walled veranda of the second story of her uncle's research facility overlooking a tranquil bay bathed in perpetual sunset. A salty breeze ruffled her tousled short brown hair and tickled the back of her neck while waves pounded the beach below. The sea glowed with an inner luminescence. In some places the lagoon was darker, where the rainbow-swirled sky reflected on an undulating surface. Spindly boulders dotted the shallow aquamarine waters, huge boulders coated in aubergine moss and lighter hues of gold and white. Ozone filled the air, bringing clarity to Cassandra's thoughts, even as the hissing sea soothed her nerves.

Niles had given her another salve and bandages and finally her palms felt like they were on the mend.

Brice sat across from her, leaning back in his cushioned plastic chair and gray eyes fixed on the serene seascape. The heavenly body, which resembled a huge moon or planet, loomed over the horizon as if on a collision course with the world.

It was odd to sit beside the ocean and not hear the cry of gulls. Tube worm trees speckled the beach but cast no shadows, as seemed common for this world.

"The trees here gather sustenance from the air," Niles said, having returned with a shorter robot and a tray of food. "Don't have a name for them yet, but they're a placid species." He pulled out a seat between Cassandra and Brice, facing the ocean, and smiled up at the robot as it arranged the food and drinks around the glass tabletop. "Thank you, Celso."

The metal panels that comprised the robot's face shifted into the semblance of a happy smile. "You are most welcome, Master Bennet." Cassandra found the smile a little creepy. She still didn't trust the things, especially given all the cautionary tales of futuristic robots rebelling against human masters and taking over the world.

As soon as the robot had slid the tinted glass door shut behind it, Cassandra said, "Where did you get all the robots? Aren't you afraid of them going crazy on you?" She didn't mention Artemis, who could be anywhere below them, apparently working in the compound's enormous generator beneath the veranda.

Cassandra had way too many questions and immediately regretted asking this one but her uncle was already puffing up for a reply.

"Future Earth timelines," he said, wispy white hair trembling in the breeze like a crown of dandelion seeds on the verge of blowing away. "They all volunteered, if that's what you're worried about. I wouldn't employ slaves!" He looked aghast at her as he buttered a slice of toast. "Please, please, help yourselves." He slathered on a thick layer of jam and took a bite, then continued talking while he chewed. "They jumped at the opportunity to help me build this facility and carry on with my work. They're free to leave at any time. As members of the rebellion, I highly doubt they'd want to go back to their previous lives, such as they were."

Cassandra stared at her uncle, speechless. She couldn't believe she'd heard him right. "Rebels? You mean like wanting to kill humans? And you brought them *here*?" Her uncle was insane.

Niles nearly choked on his toast. He dabbed his mouth with a white cloth napkin and waved his hand. "No, no. Rebels, yes, but they wouldn't harm anyone."

Cassandra wasn't convinced. She gave Brice a look over the table, who raised his eyebrows at her as he sank his teeth into an overflowing ham sandwich. Her uncle seemed to think it was always lunchtime, and without a clock or sun to judge time, who was she to argue?

But employing rebel robots? Cassandra had a definite say in that, especially if it jeopardized their lives.

"They came for my research, for a chance to exercise their minds without suffering termination," Niles said with a thin smile. "Would you deny them autonomous sentience, Cassandra?"

Kina climbed up into his lap and rubbed its head against Niles's chest, big blue eyes fixed on Cassandra.

"I guess not," Cassandra admitted. "So long as they aren't hurting anyone." She pointed at the metal cat burrowing into her uncle's Victorian-styled coat. "And what about that one? Where did you get it? Same era as the others?"

"No, no. Kina's top-of-the-line. Smart Body."

"Like the new Octagon Room panels?" Cassandra asked, watching the robot that so eerily resembled a real living cat, though with ears and eyes far too large for any normal feline.

"Precisely. Kina has astounding processing capacity. A shame she was never fitted with a voice box." Niles chuckled as he absently patted the creature's shiny head. "After the failed models of previous generations and various rebellions, manufacturers were careful to restrict artificial intelligence to only grow so far and to express itself only in approved manners." His smile turned roguish. "But AI has a way of growing unexpectedly."

"Could you give Kina a voice box?"

Niles looked surprised. "Far beyond my available technology. I'm certain I could figure it out, given time, but I'm far more interested for now in duplicating the Octagon Room's design, with added improvements, of course."

"About that," Cassandra said, and chose that moment to fill her plate with food. She took a few bites of tasty buttered roll and thinly sliced turkey before continuing. Unlike her uncle, she waited until she was done chewing before talking. "Brice broke your other Octagon Room."

"Hey!" Brice protested around a mouthful of sandwich.

Niles looked taken aback. "That's a shame. But the room was designed to absorb the brunt of the damage from transportation glitches most often caused by user error or indecision. I take it your key was broken during your crash arrival in the Fifth Branch?"

"I guess so," Cassandra said, "either that or the crab that tried to run off with the key did the breaking."

Niles shook his head. "Claws aren't powerful enough."

Cassandra took a long refreshing draught of lemon water and set the glass down with a dull *clunk*. "When did you build the other Octagon Room, and the mansion?"

"I didn't. I inherited the mansion from my father, who in turn acquired it from a couple who had poorly managed their finances." Niles leaned back, a whimsical smile on his wrinkled face as he absently rubbed more static into his hair. "I loved the place as soon as I arrived, being a lover of all things old." He leaned forward and placed his elbows on the glass tabletop, his brown eyes wide and fixed on Cassandra with unnerving intensity. "During one of my daily walks through the forest I came across a golden octagonal ball lying beside the path, a key inserted in its lock. I'd been by that spot countless times before and never seen it." His brown eyes widened with wonder. "And when I turned the key, eight petals opened and something pricked my finger, drawing a single drop of blood."

Cassandra realized she'd been holding her breath. She glanced over at Brice, who was watching Niles just as raptly, elbows resting on the table and mouth pressed to his fists. He glanced at Cassandra as though he'd felt her eyes on him, and she gave him an embarrassed smile before returning her attention to her uncle.

"When I returned to the mansion," Niles continued, "the mansion felt as if it was waiting for me, as if it knew I carried the octagonal orb. When I entered the building, that is when Albert first appeared to me. I would later discover that entering with the activated orb had rebooted the mansion and brought Albert online, but of course he had no recollection of anything prior to that moment."

"Do you know who built the mansion and Octagon Room?" Brice asked.

"Not a clue." Niles raised his hands and leaned back in his chair again. His brow creased in a frown. "Well, not entirely true. I suspect a far future being, or more likely other dimensional being, created the Octagon Room from future Earth technology to safely harbor the orb and hid it in the mansion, which was also outfitted with Smart Walls and other far future technology. I think that whoever created the Octagon Room and mansion had gone into hiding, and that the traveling orbs are the cause of humanity's eventual collapse. I created many plans from the original Octagon Room, but I won't know if I've succeeded until the new room is complete and fitted with an orb." Niles rubbed his head. "I expect we can test it sometime next week."

"But our traveling device isn't working," Cassandra reminded him.

"You have an operational orb," Niles said with a bright smile, "and I have a working key. Once I've recalibrated the key, we should be good to go."

Cassandra perked up with relief. "You mean we can get off this world and go home?"

Niles looked a little offended. "You can go home, if you wish, but would you truly give up such an opportunity to travel time and space?"

"I can't go back," Brice said quietly, his face conflicted, "unless I want to fall under the grid's control again." He seemed uncertain if that was a good thing or not.

"And I can't go back to 2145, either," Niles added. "Like your friend, I've been tagged."

Cassandra deflated. "Does the grid have something to do with this future collapse of humanity I keep hearing about?"

Niles's gaze intensified. "Yes, I believe so, though I don't know how just yet." He pushed away from the table with a scrape of chair legs and removed his coat. He still had the glove on his left arm, and long white sleeves, but he slipped the glove off and pulled up the sleeve of his left arm.

Cassandra gasped, horrified at her uncle's arm, which looked like it had gotten stuck in a meat grinder, healed poorly, and been painted with subcutaneous glowing white lines as warped as his flesh.

"The infection's spreading," Niles said quietly, looking down at his ruined arm and hand.

Cassandra felt faint. "Infection?"

Her uncle collapsed back into his chair. He didn't bother pulling his sleeve down or putting the glove back on. The twisted white lines seemed to sparkle faintly, to sluggishly move. They reminded her of something—the flash of a grid she'd seen under Brice's typewriter arm back at the 2145 mansion.

"That's the grid?" she whispered.

"An advanced version, though the disfigurement is from an aborted transportation, not from the initial infection."

Cassandra's heartbeat quickened. "What happened?"

"My latest expedition, to explore the Sixth Branch." Niles's smile was quick and self-deprecating. "I'd left my Octagon Room behind in 2017, as part of my inheritance plan for you, Cassandra, and had been traveling with the second orb. Albert advised against it, due to safety concerns of traveling without the Octagon Room. I already had my base here in Fifth Branch, in anticipation of my eventual permanent departure from 2145, as I require a world free of the grid to avoid falling under its control. I had no idea the grid had already infiltrated Sixth Branch, nor had I ever seen such an advanced stage.

"I am still examining the imagery I managed to obtain in the fraction of a moment that I was there. All I know is that during my brief time there, the grid in me activated and a rapid rewriting began taking place. I aborted the transportation, but not quick enough to save the left side of my body. Without an Octagon Room to buffer the shockwave, well, you can see the effects of that aborted attempt." He brandished his left arm. "The infection is intense, continues to slowly rewrite my body. If allowed to continue unchecked, the Niles we know will cease to exist. I have no idea what I will become."

Cassandra's mouth fell.

"Is this the fate of all tagged individuals?" Brice asked, his voice hollow.

"I don't know." Niles sounded strangely subdued. "I require a far future operation table beyond the abilities of my current model. The only hope for me is amputation of affected limbs and a carving out of all infected tissue. The internal damage could be extensive. Only an operation table outfitted with Smart Tech can accomplish this, in addition to cybernetic implants and limbs to replace what it removes. This procedure is beyond any of my robot's capabilities, beyond the technology I currently possess. Only an era close to humanity's collapse will have the technology I seek; the same era from which Kina originates. I'd go myself, but I can't risk approaching any time under grid influence or experiencing grid creepage." He patted Kina's head.

Cassandra was at a loss for words. She fingered a soft roll, but didn't take a bite. The smell of Danishes failed to entice her.

Niles exhaled noisily. "I've been studying the grid for some time. No need to go into everything I've discovered right now, but I have observed that the influence leaks into surrounding times. The detective might be fine, but not I, not with such an advanced infection." His gaze, a little sad now, found Cassandra's pained eyes. "I have very little time. If I cannot be saved, I suggest destruction of my body before the infection can complete its progression."

"The grid is *not* an infection," Brice said darkly.

"I'm afraid it is, detective. A most unnatural infection."

"It has made society a better place."

"The grid infected in 2143."

Brice jerked back in his chair; affronted, surprised. "Not possible. It's been there my entire life."

"No," Niles said matter-of-factly. "It has not. You only *think* it has. The grid was unknown to humanity one day, fully entrenched the next."

"But . . . my memories . . ."

"Are false, Detective Brice." Niles's voice softened. "The grid is insidious and it has a remarkable way of covering its tracks. It rewrites history."

"But how is that possible?" Cassandra's heart was pounding fast now.

"I have no idea."

Brice got up so fast his chair toppled over. Fists clenched and jaw set, he stormed from the veranda. The door to the research facility slammed shut behind him.

Cassandra started to rise to go after him, but Niles put a hand on hers. His right hand. The warped one now rested on his lap under the table.

"Give him time. He has a lot to process and may not be able to come to terms with any of it. I'm tagged, but my history was never rewritten. I can't say why the attempted indoctrination on me failed, but there it is. Perhaps the orb provided me some protection, or my frequent absences from grid-controlled time."

Cassandra stared at her uncle, a frown creasing her forehead. She started to ask a few questions, but stopped before she got a single one out. She didn't know where to begin. It all sounded so far-fetched, so ominous.

And yet here she was, sitting on a veranda in another dimension with her supposedly deceased great uncle who'd made a hobby of time travel.

"What am I supposed to do about any of this?" Cassandra's throat felt too dry. She downed the last of her lemon water.

"I hope that you will continue with my work," Niles said bluntly. "I am stranded here. I will continue my research, help where I can." An excited edge crept into his voice. "You will need Albert. I've nearly completed a particle matter remote fabricator."

Cassandra blinked. "A what?"

"A mobile device for Albert, so you can take him with you."

"The hologram?"

Niles shook his head. "Albert is not a hologram. He is hologram-like. As with the time- and dimensional-traveling devices, he is of a far-future technology beyond anything I have yet discovered in humanity's timeline. He is particle matter fabricated using light and frequency. And as with any other emitters for him, the mobile device will track where to manifest his 'body', within range and power reserve limitations, of course."

Overwhelmed, Cassandra said, "I'll just call him a hologram."

"Albert won't mind. Return to my storage unit in your time and download a copy of him to the mobile device. You won't want to travel to a far future society without access to my notes. But you will also require my backup files from 2145, to upgrade Albert with my latest research. You will take the new Octagon Room, of course. And . . ." He gave Cassandra a tentative smile. "I hope that you will also bring much needed supplies, as I've not been able to return to Earth since the accident."

Cassandra felt numb. "What about that operation table? Don't you need that, too?"

Niles's smile broadened. "Yes, yes. The very best you can steal, preferably top of the line. I used up all my credits buying Smart Walls, and Kina here."

"You want me to *steal*?" Cassandra asked in disbelief.

"And you'll need to acquire cybernetic parts as well." He winked, as if Cassandra didn't understand his true meaning of the word acquire.

"And what if I get caught stealing all that stuff?"

"You won't. I'm certain a niece of mine can be resourceful. And you'll have Detective Brice with you."

Cassandra wasn't so sure of that, not after the way Brice had just stormed off. She wasn't even certain she wanted to go anywhere but home.

"I have some work to finish up. Find me when you're ready to retire for the night."

"How will I know when it's night?" she asked, indicating the eternal sunset.

A corner of her uncle's mouth curled with amusement as if Cassandra had just asked the silliest of questions. "When you're tired, of course."

CHAPTER 10

Salty sea air struck Cassandra's face the moment she opened the exterior door on the lower level of her great uncle's research facility. Niles had gone to his "thinking corner", as he called it, on the second story platform, where he'd started pacing, chewing his finger and muttering. Cassandra hadn't bothered him on her way out.

No robot had seemed to notice her passing, and the grouchy one, Artemis, could be heard clunking around in the generator, a substantial metal building at the side of the compound directly under the steel and glass-walled veranda where Cassandra had just enjoyed a bite to eat with Niles and Brice.

Her sneakers crunched softly in the pale pink sand as she walked towards the luminescent ocean in search of the detective.

She was still reeling from what Niles had just told them.

Her uncle had been maimed from an encounter with what seemed to be an advanced version of the grid during an expedition into the Sixth Branch, though Niles had spent but a fraction of a moment there. He'd aborted the transportation in time to save himself a full rewrite by the grid but suffered trauma from the abrupt shift. In fact, his body was still being rewritten, just at a slower pace than if he'd remained in the Sixth Branch.

If Cassandra didn't time travel to a far future Earth and steal an advanced model of her uncle's operation table, in addition to cybernetic parts to replace his amputations, he'd die.

Cassandra wanted nothing more than to go home and return to a normal routine, but she couldn't have her uncle's death on her conscious.

Besides, part of her was insanely curious to explore, to see what a future Earth far beyond even Brice's timeline was like. A world that created creatures like Kina, and where AI infiltrated steel walls and all manner of machinery.

The danger, apart from being caught stealing expensive equipment, was that the far future era was close to the ultimate collapse of humanity and suffered from what Niles called "grid creepage". Such a place wasn't safe for Niles, with an advanced grid infection coursing through his body, but might be okay for Brice, if he agreed to come with her.

When she'd first met the detective on the front porch of her uncle's mansion in 2145, she'd thought him crazy and a little creepy. That creepiness, however, had been the grid's influence, which had made Brice disrupt Cassandra's intended time travel jump to her own time and had instead brought them here, to the Fifth Branch. Though his calculating gazes had made her uncomfortable, he'd been nothing but helpful since coming to this dimension. Not the easiest to converse with, perhaps, but a good man.

Cassandra would have preferred to have nothing to do with Brice, but he was trained law enforcement. He knew how to fight, though he'd lost his only weapon during the jellyfish attack at the lake. He'd know things Cassandra didn't, being from a hundred plus years into her future. He'd be comfortable with hovercars and a ton of things

Cassandra didn't even know about yet. She'd seen nothing of 2145 except the secluded mansion, a hovercar in the driveway, and Brice's typewriter arm.

As much as she was reeling from information overload, *she* hadn't just been told that her whole life was fake, rewritten by an infection just two years prior. And knowing what Brice now knew, he would realize that if he wanted to remain autonomous he could never go home.

Tube worm trees towered overhead, long translucent tendrils whispering in the breeze as Cassandra walked past.

Brice was on the beach ahead, staring out across the undulating aquamarine waters. His quicksilver pants seemed to have taken on a life of their own in the wind, as if the material was actual liquid mercury rippling with alternating dark and light silver tones. His close-fitting black top was still tucked into his pants, his fedora firmly in place, and his brawny arms crossed over his chest as if in defiance of the ocean and everything this world represented.

He heard her coming long before she would have thought to announce her presence and he spoke without turning his head. "Couldn't sleep either?"

Cassandra would never get used to a visual lack of passing time. Now that Brice mentioned it, though, it did feel like she'd been awake forever.

She came up beside him and studied his face. Strong jaw set, grinding just a little. Gray eyes narrowed, calculated. Here was the grid-Brice she'd first met back in 2145, yet there was something else that hadn't been there before, a change in him that had been creeping in with each passing hour on this world. She'd seen glimpses of it in him—a twinkle in the eye, an amused curl of the lips, a semblance of something warmer lurking inside.

Could it really be true? Could Brice's memories really be grid lies? She wondered what he'd been like before the infection.

"I was in charge of my own thoughts," he said through gritted teeth.

Cassandra didn't believe that for one second. She'd suspected Brice hadn't been in control when he'd forced her to bring them here, and her uncle had just confirmed those suspicions. Brice, though, might take some time to come to terms with the truth.

He kicked the sand with the toe of his shoe and stomped off a few feet, then whirled on Cassandra, gray eyes brimming with anger and frustration. Rarely had she seen such emotion on his face. "I just don't see how it can all be a lie. I . . . I *remember* everything."

He was breathing heavily, his glare daring Cassandra to refute him.

She thought it wise to just let him talk, to vent whatever he needed to without judgment or attempts to dissuade him of his reality.

"I remember growing up in Marin, California." He plopped down in the sand, facing the sea, wrists resting on his bent knees.

Cassandra sat beside him, but not too close. A respectable distance. The sand cool beneath her jeans.

Brice stared out at the bay, his gaze taking in the enormous boulders ensconced in purple, gold, and white moss, the oil-slick-on-water sky, the gentle waves that sprayed the air with salt. What the beach lacked, however, was the smell of rotting kelp, the raucous sounds of gulls and seals. The Fifth Branch was beautiful but eerily quiet in so many ways.

"My father, Radovan, . . . he works at *Aerial Propulsions* in Marin designing hovercar motors. Is that a lie? And what about my mother? Did the grid make up her part in the San Francisco Symphony as a pianist? Did the grid fabricate their divorce when I was five or my father moving to an on-site executive suite to be closer to his work? Did the grid make up where I went to school? My friends? My *entire life?*"

Cassandra didn't know. "Maybe just everything to do with the grid?"

"Yeah. Maybe." Brice sounded relieved.

Cassandra would have hated to hear that her whole life was a lie.

They were quiet a few minutes, both staring at the sea, listening to the pound and hiss of the surf like a sleeping god at their feet.

Cassandra dropped her hand to the sand, careful not to get her bandage dirty, and dug her fingertips into the cool grains. Though it was refreshing to be outside with the bite of ozone, she was exhausted and ready for a nice, long deep sleep.

"Thanks, Cassandra," Brice said softly.

She shook her fingers free of sand and gave him a faint smile.

"Are you going to do what your uncle asks and travel to the far future?"

Cassandra didn't know, but what choice did she really have? She didn't feel qualified to make such a journey on her own, but then maybe with Albert on a little mobile device and a fancy new time travel machine she could manage. So long as the table was easy to wheel out of whatever place she needed to rob and not too big for the Octagon Room. She had no idea just how much stuff her uncle expected her to cram in there.

"I guess so," she said. "I don't have to worry about my cactus, Gus, dying. I mean, he's already long dead by now. I can just pop back any old time and water him, right? Same with my friends. I'm long dead and at the same time I haven't been gone more than a few hours. It's mind-boggling."

"That it is." An uneasy silence wafted from him, as though chit-chat made him uncomfortable. He struggled for a moment, a question seeming to hang on his tongue, then he finally broke down and asked, "What about you? Have parents? Siblings?"

It was nice talking to Brice like a normal person, but why did he have to pick the topic of family? "Parents left for France same year I left for college. I'm an only child." Straight and to the point. He didn't need to know the details or her feelings on the whole subject.

"Same here," Brice said. "No siblings for me." His smile deflated. "I always wanted a brother, though. Suppose that's what friends are for."

Cassandra had made do with an active imagination, spending hours in the overgrown back yard of her parents' spacious townhouse in San Francisco's Noe Valley while her nanny read in the kitchen's huge bay window.

"Name's Andel, by the way," he said, the corner of his mouth turning up in a half-smile.

Her brows shot up. "Not Brice?"

"Last name." He got to his feet, brushed sand from his quicksilver pants, and offered a hand.

She took it, all too aware of his warm skin against hers, the care he exercised not to squeeze her bandaged palm. The scent of aftershave had faded and Cassandra didn't know why that saddened her. It was like their pasts were fading, being replaced by a totally new future she never could have imagined.

The fading scent of aftershave was a reminder, too, that Brice's past had been rewritten and was changing yet again. Who would he become now that he was off grid? Would the self that had been rewritten start to come forth?

His gray eyes studied her, as if probing for hidden thoughts and secrets. But Cassandra didn't find it as unnerving as she had before, in 2145. He seemed genuinely interested in what she had to say, genuinely interested in her.

He dropped her hand, suddenly realizing he was still holding it.

"Nice to meet you, Andel Brice." And it *was* almost as if they were meeting for the first time, a detective no longer as guarded, meeting as equals rather than as part of an investigation. He'd solved his case, after all. Niles Bennet had been found alive, though Brice could never put this whole fiasco in his report. "You realize you'll always be Brice to me."

He shrugged. "I respond to either. Really, my mother's the only one who ever calls me Andel."

Cassandra suspected his mother wasn't the only one. What about a girlfriend, if he had one? "My uncle said to seek him out when we're ready for bed."

Brice gestured for Cassandra to lead the way.

But Cassandra wasn't comfortable walking ahead of him, so she waited for his sand crunching steps to fall in stride beside her.

They walked through the cluster of rustling tube worm trees and up to her uncle's research facility sitting at the base of the dunes. Artemis was still working inside the generator to their right, the steel door ajar and clanks sharply resounding through the gap.

The robot stuck its head through the opening as Cassandra and Brice approached the facility's outer door.

Cassandra didn't care what her uncle said, she still didn't trust Artemis, and the feeling seemed mutual. Hard to tell on a metallic face, but Artemis seemed to be glaring at them. Cassandra gave a little wave and the robot ducked back into the building.

Brice opened the heavy steel door for Cassandra.

A rush of stale air laced with acrid chemicals rushed out.

She smacked her tongue and squinted against the sting. Whatever the robots were working on now, she couldn't go in there.

"Here, here!" Niles called from beside a cloud of inky smoke that concealed most of the unfinished Octagon Room. He rushed over and handed Cassandra and Brice masks like the one he wore. "Put these on." His voice sounded nasally through the mask. "Ready for bed, are we?"

Cassandra held her breath while she donned the tight-fitting mask that reeked of plastic. If she'd had trouble keeping her eyes open before, the sooty smoke made it even harder now.

Niles's snowy hair stuck up all around his head. Some had gotten trapped in his mask, too, which would have driven Cassandra crazy.

Knowing what she knew about her uncle's condition, Cassandra was surprised by his gaiety and the relative ease with which he limped across the expansive workshop like one of Santa's elves, his accelerated limp resembling a lop-sided skip as he gestured to various workstations and yelled over the din during his impromptu tour.

Cassandra only caught a third of what he said and was too tired to ask him to repeat any of it. She just wanted to sleep.

The kitchen peaked her interest, however, tucked away in a corner with a shorter robot rummaging through mostly empty cupboards. It was quiet enough on this end of the workshop to hear Niles bemoan a diminishing larder and lack of chocolate biscuits.

Which only reminded Cassandra of her uncle's dire circumstances. How could she *not* help him out?

But she was too tired to deal with that right now.

Like a zombie, she followed Niles down winding stairs, her uncle's cane clicking on the steel steps. They descended into a damp warren of tunnels reminiscent of the ones she'd fallen into when going after the crab creature that had stolen the octagonal orb's key.

Her uncle had used steel walls to block off passages and create a tangle of small chambers, all fashioned with steel doors. Many of the doors were open and appeared to be storage rooms. Some had a few robots milling about, moving crates or making furniture.

The three of them removed their masks as Niles led Cassandra and Brice to a pair of rooms at the far end of the maze of tunnels, to a quieter section of the compound.

He limped to a stop. "Hope this will do. One of the few rooms with a bed in it."

"Thank you," Cassandra said as she handed her mask back to Niles and tentatively stepped into the narrow chamber of chilly, orange stone. No sand here, which was a good thing, she supposed. Recessed lights illuminated the room in soft creamy light.

It tasted a little dank, but she didn't care. The bed (a pile of moth-eaten blankets on a simple wooden frame) looked like the most luxurious of places to fall asleep right then.

Niles directed Brice into the neighboring room and invited them for tea and breakfast in the morning. When Cassandra asked when that would be, he shrugged and said whenever Lukas decided to serve it.

"They're far better cooks than I," Niles admitted sheepishly, meaning the robots. His holographic butler, Albert, had done the cooking in the mansions. "Lukas will begin cooking when we awaken."

Cassandra bid goodnight to Niles and Brice, then softly shut the door and stumbled to the disheveled pile of crocheted green blankets.

The room was empty but for the twin bed, and barely wide enough for the bed and Cassandra side by side. Basically an oversized shoe cubby.

She plopped down onto the blankets and wrinkled her nose from the musty cloud that issued from the disturbed bedding. She removed her sneakers, one by one, and set them on the floor beside the bed. She swung her legs onto the bed and fell back onto the lumpy pillow and stared up at the dim lights in the stone ceiling. She hadn't asked where or even if there was a light switch.

Then she saw it next to the bed, in the wall. A white dimmer switch.

Without any windows, she didn't want to turn the lights all the way off. She didn't fear the dark but was afraid the room would become claustrophobic if pitch-black. So she dimmed the lights almost all the way down, enough so that she could comfortably close her eyes, and tried to let her mind drift.

It was strange being in a tiny stone chamber, all alone for the first time since she'd arrived at her uncle's storage mansion in her own time. Strange trying to fall asleep to the rattles and thumping vibrations rumbling through the walls from robotic workers that never slept.

She didn't know where her uncle slept, or if he ever went to bed that night. A herd of elephants could have paraded outside her door and she wouldn't have noticed.

Exhausted, Cassandra fell into a deep, dreamless sleep.

CHAPTER 11

Cassandra woke the following "morning" refreshed and ready to tackle the world. The robot cook, Lukas, had already begun breakfast, the aroma of sizzling bacon and eggs vying with the chemical stew from the rest of the workshop. Niles and Brice were on the second-story veranda, which surprised Cassandra. Guess they didn't require much sleep. Niles was doing most of the talking and he beamed at Cassandra when she pulled out a seat with a mild screech of chair legs against the steel floor.

Rubbing sleep from her eyes and wishing she had a change of clothes and access to a shower, doing her best to get the tangles out of her fly-away hair without it getting caught in her bandages, Cassandra said her good mornings, though it didn't *feel* like morning.

The seascape hadn't changed since the previous night. Same salty air, same crashing waves on the beach below, same temperature and ambient light. Unlike Earth, this Fifth Branch world seemed frozen in time, and yet life carried on as normal. A strange juxtaposition.

When Lukas arrived with a tray of bacon and eggs and steaming rolls, Cassandra was glad for something other than lunch items. She savored each perfectly seasoned bite.

"I'll do it," she said as soon as she'd sated her appetite.

Niles and Brice had been discussing chess, an apparent obsession for them both. Niles halted mid-sentence and they both looked at her, Brice with a faint frown and Niles with glee.

Her uncle clapped his hands together, a muffled clap due to the white glove on his left hand, and reached over to grip Cassandra's left arm in a warm shake. "Thank you!"

His gratitude was a little overwhelming. "It's nothing." Not true, but she wanted to divert his attention. "What do you want me to do first?" She avoided looking at Brice, who was still staring at her. She could feel his eyes boring into her.

"Right, right," Niles said, his voice rising and gaining tempo with excitement. "Albert. You'll need a copy of him. Safe to do in 2017. Need to get you the mobile device." He rubbed his head briskly, making the cottony hair stand on end like he'd just stuck his finger in a socket. "You'll need the orb. Key's been recalibrated. Hope it works." He patted her hand. "Don't fret. I'm nearly one hundred percent confident there'll be no glitches. I'd have tested it on myself but not with this infection." He waved his left arm. "You'll have to brave 2145 to gather my research discs of far future Earth. You'll need to update Albert on your mobile device, too. Shouldn't be too tricky. I'll tell you where to find the discs and how to access the Smart Panels in the mansion wall." He perked up. "Ready, then?"

"Uh, sure." Cassandra dabbed her mouth with a napkin and offered to clean up the plates but Niles shooed her away.

"Lukas will get them."

Cassandra remembered what Artemis had said about not being hired help. She didn't like the idea of imposing on any of the other robots, especially if they were already prone to rebelling. What would they do if Niles exasperated them too much? Dump his dirty dishes in the sand? Refuse to cook for him? Kill them all?

Oblivious to any possible complications or ruffled feathers, Niles gripped his cane and hobbled for the door, still prattling on like a parrot on speed with his list of things to do in preparation for Cassandra's imminent departure. With the Octagon Room unfinished, she wouldn't be able to do any shopping, he informed her, though he begged for a box of chocolate biscuits from the pantry, and more flour and sugar, and a dozen other items that Cassandra promptly forgot.

When they'd reached the first floor in the midst of the bustling activity, Niles had prattled through two more topics and plowed into great length about his plans for the uncompleted Octagon Room, most of the details going right over Cassandra's head.

"What about *him*?" Cassandra interrupted, implying Brice, who had stopped to allow a train of wheeled carts to squeak by in front of him.

Niles stopped, his train of thoughts derailing and confusion darting across his wrinkled face, which looked a little green in the artificial lights glaring down on them. He followed Cassandra's eyebrow gestures. "You mean Brice?"

But Niles had taken too long to get Cassandra's meaning and missed her cues for discretion.

"Trying to leave without me?" Brice asked, a faint smile playing on his lips. "I've already informed your uncle I'll be joining you."

Cassandra's brows shot up.

She still didn't know how much she could trust Brice or whether it was even safe for him to travel to a far future Earth with grid creepage. What if he turned on her again?

And yet she'd be traveling into potentially dangerous territory. Having Brice along for added protection would be a huge relief.

She gave the detective a nervous smile.

This whole fiasco was feeling way over her head. Part of her wanted to run away, to return to the veranda and a calming view of an unchanging sea.

Back home she'd never been strapped with so many responsibilities. Just her secretarial job, her cactus which really required very little watering, and a low-key social life. She didn't have family obligations, as her only family had moved away. Even cooking had been a minor chore, consisting mostly of salads, hearty soups, and lots of pasta.

She'd wanted more out of life, had wanted travel and adventure, but could never afford it. With the loss of her apartment and having gained the inheritance of her uncle's mansion, she'd hoped to start a new life. Though she now had plenty of travel and adventure, her present predicament would not have been her first choice.

Niles's receding *click-click* of his cane startled Cassandra from her thoughts.

Brice had an amused expression on his face. He fanned his left hand out, indicating that Cassandra go first. "Didn't hear a thing he said?"

Cassandra looked away, embarrassed to admit she hadn't been listening.

"I'm sure he'll explain again," Brice said.

They followed her uncle to the far left corner of the lower level, to a room of rounded thick glass and a sealed door, which Niles unsealed by performing a series of acrobatic actions—typing into a keypad, peering into a peek hole, and reciting a refrain of a nursery rhyme.

Niles retrieved his cane, which he'd propped on the wall while he completed the security measures, and hobbled into the room.

Cassandra stepped in next, careful to avoid the little silver cat-like robot that slinked in between her and the doorframe. Moving with the agility of a born hunter, Kina leapt to a spot on the expansive workstation with a click of metal feet on smooth plastic. The robot daintily stepped into a cat bed, curled up, and propped its triangular head on its front paws, big blue eyes tracking Cassandra and Brice.

The door whisked shut behind Brice and seals hissed into place.

The room smelled surprisingly sterile. No bubbling liquids or fumes. Just the faint off-gassing of plastic. The floor was surprisingly tidy, though every surface overflowed with inventions in various stages of completion, from vehicles like toy cars and spaceships, to miniature versions of the Octagon Room, and machines, large and small, with enough spilling innards to make the room seem more mechanical graveyard than research facility.

Niles became especially excited in this personal space, though Cassandra thought it odd he sealed it off from the rest of the facility. Was he worried about the other robots coming in here? He started digging through the mess like a boy hunting for a lost marble in a backyard of forgotten toys. Eventually he fished out something like a palm-sized TV remote and pressed it into Cassandra's bandaged hands, the metal cold and hard where it came in contact with her skin.

"What's this?" she asked.

Niles grinned, brown eyes wide and bright. "Albert's mobile device. Never thought I'd get a chance to retrieve my favored butler. Facility's all set to accommodate him, whenever you return. Though I suppose you could return in moments if you were so inclined." He winked.

"How am I supposed to get Albert on here?"

But Niles had already lost interest in the topic and started rummaging in a toppling mound of gutted electronics that eerily resembled robot torsos used as bombing practice. He snatched the golden octagonal device from a tangle of wires and handed it to Cassandra without turning his head. As soon as Cassandra took it, he went back to his digging, scooting aside metal cases and snarls of wires. A loose screw rolled off the table and clinked to the floor, where it rolled out of reach under the table. "Ah-ha!" He brandished an ornate key and handed this, too, to Cassandra. "That should do it."

"How do I get Albert on here?" Cassandra asked again, holding up the TV remote and giving her uncle a patient smile.

"You open it like this," Niles said, snatching the device and sliding a panel open along the bottom, "and stick it in the slot in the wall in the blue room upstairs." He pursed his lips. "Room might be blue in 2017. Can't remember if I saved the paint job for 2145." He shrugged his bony shoulders. "If there's no blue room upstairs in 2017, then the second room on the left. Turn the sconce by the window counterclockwise. Secret access to the mansion's Smart Wall Network will be revealed and you can download Albert. Suppose if you forget, you can always ask Albert for assistance."

"Okay," Cassandra said wearily, taking the holographic mobile device and sliding the panel shut.

"Now, you won't have an Octagon Room for added protection," Niles said, his tone grave. "Be absolutely certain of your destination and don't waver once you're committed." His eyes grazed Brice, and Cassandra thought she could almost feel the detective wince with guilt. "Neither of you want this problem." He waved his warped left arm for effect. "Or worse," he muttered under his breath. "Leave

Brice in 2017 while you pop into 2145 for my discs on far future Earth and eventual collapse of humanity. Update Albert in the same room. Should be blue in 2145."

"Why not just have Cassandra travel to 2145?" Brice asked.

Niles gave the detective a look that implied Brice was smarter than that. "Initial download of Albert's program could be a lengthy process."

"And 2145 is most likely teeming with agents," Brice finished.

"Precisely." Niles patted Cassandra's arm. "You'll do fine. Once you've seen the room in 2017 you'll have an image for 2145. Travel to the same room. Should be locked and safe from agents in 2145. You can sneak out when safe to retrieve the discs from the storage facility in the basement. If the situation proves too dangerous, travel directly to the basement with the orb. But be sure to visit the basement in 2017, so you have a clear image in your mind." He rubbed his head so briskly the hair stood up higher than before, giving him the crazed dandelion look. "Ensure you always use approved transport spots, clearly marked in the rooms, which are always free of clutter. Don't want you landing on anything painful or crashing through a table now, do we?"

Cassandra pulled a face and slowly shook her head, that overwhelmed feeling rushing over her again.

"Once you've got Albert updated from 2145, you'll need to set the self-destruct."

Cassandra wanted a chair so she could collapse into it.

"Too bad all that food will have to go to waste," Niles said distractedly, "but with no traveling room you won't have the carrying capacity for my chocolate biscuits or other necessities. I'll just have to hope 2017 still has a few boxes left, and Earl Gray tea, nutmeg, cinnamon, and so forth. Albert will know if the larder's stocked. If not, a little shopping trip once the Octagon Room is finished will be in order."

His gaze whipped back to Cassandra, his gray brows furrowed with intensity. "Now, back to the self-destruct. The grid knows of my mansion in 2145. We do *not* want my research falling into its hands. The self-destruct will be found in any wall panel. The mobile device will work as a substitute key. I've designed it this way, since I'm the only one who can destroy the house. Wasn't an easy modification to make, from the original code. Let's hope the Smart Walls will accept the mobile device. Insert the device and enter the following code on the keypad."

Niles used a pen from his coat to scribble something on a piece of scrap paper, snapped the lid back on the pen, and handed the paper to Cassandra. He'd written what looked like a serial code. "A DNA sample will be required. Just a drop of blood. Then return here for further instructions. If you choose a week from now, over there in the corner of the room, I should have the Octagon Room ready for you."

Cassandra recognized the pattern on the floor. She'd seen it in the inlaid wood in a spot in the foyer by the front door of her uncle's mansion.

She stared at her uncle and chewed her lip. A faint taste of blood meant she needed to stop doing that. She chewed her fingernail instead. "If Brice can't go to 2145, why's he coming along for the ride?"

"His choice," Niles said. "If Brice would rather stay here a week and wait for you that's fine with me. A week versus a few minutes."

"I'll wait in 2017 for you," Brice said to Cassandra. "I can also give you some tips before you jump forward, should you encounter any agents patrolling the premises or attempting excessive forced entry."

His steely gray eyes fell on Niles. "How capable is your mansion of fending off an armed force?"

"Depends," Niles said. "It's never been put to the test, far as I know. I suppose it could withstand a fair amount of fire power. Stay hidden, regardless, Cassandra. And use your best judgment. If the perimeter has been breached, your first priority is your life, followed by the mansion's destruction, and lastly the discs containing most of my research on the far future. Really wish I'd finished the transfer before this unforeseen accident of mine."

Niles gave his head another good rub. "One other thing. Your latest exit from 2017 is the earliest point at which you can ever return. If you spend two hours there now, then you can never relive any of that time. Understood?"

"You mean I can never go back into my own past? Why not?"

"Safety precaution." A shadow hooded his face. A secret? A regret? Cassandra wasn't sure. "This is only true for our personal histories in regards to 2017. All previous times are blocked off to you."

"What's the point of time traveling if you can't go into your past and try to change things?" Cassandra asked, not that she wanted to change anything, but it just seemed like an arbitrary restriction.

"Too dangerous," Niles said, rubbing his head in agitation. "I highly suspect the orbs are the cause of all of humanity's eventual problems. I have no idea how the infection spreads or precisely what it's doing. Why risk spreading that infection to our pasts?"

Cassandra didn't need further convincing. She just wanted to get going and be done with this. Get Albert, blow up the mansion, come back here and get the Octagon Room, and steal a new body for her uncle.

If she thought about any of it too much she'd freeze. Best to just keep moving and not think too much. Only way to keep her from going home and putting this all off forever. "Ready," she said with a forced smile.

"Great!" Niles indicated that Cassandra and the detective move close and hold hands. "No Octagon Room to contain you. You'll need to keep in constant contact for the traveling bit. And keep your hands to yourself, detective." No doubt a reference to grid-Brice's forced travel and crash landing in the Fifth Branch.

Brice stiffened, but he laced his arm through Cassandra's, since her bandaged hands were full. She gave him the mobile device and stuck her uncle's key in the top of the golden octagon. Once she'd turned the key, she waited for the orb to open and the default three petals to light up, then she took a deep breath, gathered a picture in her mind of her uncle's storage mansion in 2017, the spot beside the front door in the foyer (which she now knew was a transport safe spot), and touched the fourth petal.

A wind swept through Niles's research room, blowing papers to the floor and causing smaller items to creak and rattle. Kina laid its ears back, lambent blue eyes fixated on Cassandra. Then the wind whipped Cassandra's short hair into a frenzy, and she and Brice vanished from the Fifth Branch in a blinding flash.

CHAPTER 12

Cassandra and Brice appeared in the dim foyer of her uncle's mansion. Cobwebs clung from the ceiling and a layer of carvable dust coated everything, making the scuffled footprints on the floorboards seem like shallow imprints in snow. They'd arrived in her uncle's cluttered storage mansion, which meant a successful dimensional jump to year 2017.

Cassandra's own time.

She almost dropped to her knees and kissed the floor. Almost. She didn't relish the idea of a mouthful of musty dust and dead bug and spider carcasses. Thankfully it was too gloomy to make out those finer details.

She pulled her arm free of Brice, who was looking around and waving his typewriter arm. Of course, without a grid, he'd soon learn it didn't work here, either.

Cassandra had to be certain she was home.

She opened the heavy front door and breathed in a deep and satisfying whiff of pine and redwood with the pungent taste of moist soil and leaf matter from the encroaching forest as dense and creepy as one would expect from a forest surrounding a dilapidated mansion like this.

But it was *her* mansion.

And that was *her* car parked out front on the gravel driveway. Her little black Civic, with the keys in the ignition and enough gas to take her home to her apartment in San Francisco a mere forty minutes away.

She ran down the steps. Her sneakers crunched into the gravel. The mermaid fountain was overgrown again, full of pond scum and enough grass-filled cracks to put a plumber to shame. The paint on the mansion was peeling, the gardens full of more weeds and creeping vines than roses.

She threw open the passenger door of her car and climbed inside, slid her hands over the soft seat cushion and enjoyed the stuffy warmth.

"What are you doing?" Brice had followed her.

Cassandra eyed the driver side. All she had to do was climb over the emergency brake, turn the key in the ignition, and drive away. She could send a realtor to deal with the hassle of selling this place. The Octagon Room was gone. She had no idea what anyone would find on the other side of that door now. Maybe just an empty space full of dust and cobwebs.

She fingered the filigree golden octagon in her hands, which was easy enough to carry, since her fingers could hook through the many holes in its design. She unhooked her fingers. "Here, take it."

Brice's black eyebrows shot up in surprise, then dipped so low with disapproval that his frown actually made her squirm. "You're running away?"

"It doesn't really matter how long I take, does it? I can go back to my life, have a break. Then I can time travel to 2145 and deal with Albert's upgrade and destroying the mansion. It doesn't matter. I'll always be going to the same point in time in the future." She kept saying it didn't matter, but she didn't really believe that.

Maybe it was the principal of the matter. How could she go home, to her old life, when Brice and Niles were trapped in other times and dimensions and her uncle suffering a life-threatening grid infection?

Brice seemed to have come to the same conclusion. "Have it your way. Run home. I'll be waiting in the mansion." He snatched the orb from her hands and stormed off, gravel crunching beneath his black shoes. "Activate Albert before you leave, will you?" he called without looking back.

Cassandra placed her shaking hands in her lap, tried to steady them by rubbing her bandaged palms on her blue jeans. "It doesn't matter," she whispered.

She eyed the ignition again, the keys dangling there.

Brice had taken both the holographic mobile device and the octagonal traveling orb. *Her* responsibilities, not his.

She would gladly have let the detective risk his life for the greater cause, it was his daily job after all, and who was Cassandra? A college graduate who still hadn't figured out her life. Who couldn't go on a successful date to save her life. Who lived alone with only a cactus to keep her company. She might have gotten a cat, had her lease allowed for pets.

But Brice couldn't complete this mission. Neither could Niles. They were both relying on *her*, and she hated it.

What if she failed?

Generally in such situations, one considered worst case scenarios. What was the worst that could happen to her in 2145? Captured by grid agents and tagged? Then she'd be as useless against the grid as Brice and Niles. The grid would access her uncle's information in the future mansion, though Cassandra didn't understand the full extent as to why that was a bad thing. Who knew what her uncle had discovered, what he was planning?

All she knew was that humanity would die out some day and her uncle thought it had something to do with the octagonal orbs and the grid.

Cassandra rubbed her temple, feeling a headache coming on.

She took one last whiff of her car, of home, and climbed out and slammed the door shut.

She rested her bandaged palms on the sun-warmed door, head bowed and gaze planted on her white sneakers. "You can do this," she told herself. "Your chance to do something more with your life." And maybe get herself killed, but she thought it best not to tell herself that. The part of her that desperately wanted to be home with her cozy slippers and a good book would just use it as an excuse to make a run for it.

"Something funny?" Brice asked when Cassandra stepped into the gloomy foyer.

Must be the smile on her face. She couldn't explain the conversation she'd been having with herself and didn't bother trying. "Albert," she called, then headed off for the dining hall in the hope that his smorgasbord was still on display, the one he'd promised when she first arrived here a few minutes ago, or a day ago (if going by the amount of actual time she'd lived). She hoped she'd find an apricot or cheese Danish.

"You called, Miss Bennet?" came Albert's hollow voice from the foyer.

The hologram's shoes resounded along the hardwood floor as he followed at a respectable distance. "When Miss Bennet traveled to

2145 I took the liberty of clearing away the food to avoid spoilage. Would Miss Bennet care for a new assortment of tasty treats?"

"Just a Danish, please. I'll take it down to the basement, if you can show me where the stairs are?"

"Certainly." Albert popped from view and walked back in a few minutes later with an apricot Danish. "Miss Bennet did not specify her preference."

"It's perfect." And it tasted as good as it smelled. "Thank you, Albert."

"Miss Bennet is most welcome. Please follow me." The hologram opened another set of doors off the drawing room and headed to the far side of a much larger and very cluttered sitting room or parlor, to a plain wooden door between an antique dresser and a leather armchair. Cassandra noticed that Albert had completed her earlier request and drawn many of the curtains around the mansion, allowing filtered sunlight through the grimy windows.

"Changed your mind?" Brice asked as he came up behind Cassandra, shoes resounding dully on the worn floorboards.

"Maybe." She took another bite of apricot sweetness.

The added light from outside unfortunately illuminated the mansion's filthy state. Most of the furniture was draped in sheets and cobwebs and piled high with books, trinkets, boxes, and animal bones.

Albert opened the door and held it for Cassandra and Brice. "Allow me, Miss Bennet." He flicked a switch and light flooded the stairwell.

Cassandra recoiled at the ungodly sight.

"Please excuse the dustiness. This stairwell is little used, as I have no need for it, and Mr. Bennet has not ventured down these stairs since 2010."

Dusty was the last word Cassandra would have used to describe the steep passage. Deathtrap, perhaps. If the cobwebs could even be broken. "I'm not going down there." She wasn't an arachnophobe but the thought of stepping into a sticky mess dense enough to block their view and unleashing a potential horde of spiders on her head was enough to curl her toes and send shivers of revulsion through her. She couldn't be certain there weren't any spiders in there and sure as hell didn't want to find out.

She glanced at Brice, but judging by his expression, he had no intention of going first either.

Impassive as ever, Albert tilted his head in a little bow and unclasped his hands. "Allow me, Miss Bennet."

Before Cassandra could stop him, Albert stepped into the stairwell, arm raised in front of him like a shield. He closed his eyes and waved his hand, which quickly gathered cobwebs so thick she could hear them snapping.

Shiny black spiders dropped all over him.

Cassandra thought she was going to faint.

She stumbled back into Brice, who grunted and managed to catch her with his arms, since he was holding Cassandra's mobile device and octagon orb in both hands.

Cassandra's heart raced as she watched a shiny spider at least an inch long crawl with startling speed for her sneakers.

Brice whirled her aside like a ballroom dancer, but since he wasn't holding her hand, she kept going.

He stomped the floorboard.

Balance regained, Cassandra turned back to the horrifying passage. "Black widows."

Brice grimaced. "At least they can't bite the butler."

She rubbed her arms, unable to purge the image of Albert's head covered in shiny black spiders with spindly legs and red hourglass undersides.

She had zero intention of popping into the basement using the octagonal device, either. Spiders probably hadn't gotten the memo to keep the transport spot clear. But, of course, she hadn't seen the spot yet, so there was that. And if she didn't see the transport spot here, in 2017, then she couldn't use it in the future either. She'd be unable to attain the discs from the basement in 2145 without using the stairs. Hopefully they were spider-free in the future.

"Good deterrent for thieves," Brice said, his voice level.

Albert popped into the room, apparently spider-less. "The stairwell is not safe for Miss Bennet or her companion, I am afraid."

"No kidding," Cassandra said. She waved her hand at Albert's head. "What happened to all the spiders?"

"Nothing can transport with me. The spiders that landed on me have fallen in the stairwell." He closed the door and stomped on the escaped spiders. "I shall call an exterminator if Miss Bennet so desires."

"As long as the problem is fixed before 2145, I'm fine."

"Miss Bennet should encounter no problem with arachnids in 2145."

"Well, I guess I won't be visiting this basement. At least I can download you onto the portable device that Niles made for you." She glanced at the device in Brice's hand.

Albert's brown eyes stared, unblinking, at Cassandra. "Miss Bennet has spoken with Mr. Bennet?"

"Did I forget to mention that? Yes! Niles is alive!" She almost added "and well" but her uncle *wasn't* well. "He made a device so he can bring you to his research facility in the Fifth Branch."

A glimmer of relief seemed to wash over Albert's face. "This is wonderful news." He didn't sound excited, of course, but Cassandra watched him closely for any signs. The relief on his face had been so fast she now wondered if maybe she'd imagined it.

"Niles told me to go to the blue room upstairs." It still felt a little strange not to use the title "uncle", but it was what he had requested. She hadn't decided yet if she preferred it. With her estranged parents living far away, he was the only family she had. "I'm to access the Smart Wall Network."

"Of course. Should Miss Bennet require my assistance, please do not hesitate to call." He bowed and promptly vanished from the sitting room.

"I much prefer the future mansion," Cassandra said. She took another bite of apricot Danish, but its sweetness failed to delight as her gaze found the squashed black widows all over the dusty floorboards.

She couldn't get over the clutter, how bad it truly was. At least after witnessing the spider deathtrap, the animal skulls and wispy cobwebs didn't seem so bad.

Cassandra just wanted to get this over with. She felt a little guilty that Brice would be stuck in this creepy place while she jumped to the future. "I can take those things from you," she offered, but Brice shook his head and said he was fine carrying them. She didn't push the matter.

As they walked past a fireplace full of ancient ash a foot deep, Cassandra snatched a poker and dusted it off, planning to use it against any cobwebs on the way up the stairs. If only she'd asked Albert to open some windows. The mustiness was stifling, and every step stirred up a cloud of dust that *tasted* old. "This air can't be good for us."

"If we survived another dimension's atmosphere I think we can survive this," Brice said.

Cassandra pulled a face and headed for the grand staircase, swinging the poker in front of her as she went.

She wasn't tall enough to reach the highest cobwebs on the staircase, but she swept away anything draped in front of them. She'd never been upstairs. Brice had, but only in the future mansion. The stairwell clearly hadn't been used in a very long time.

Cassandra cringed with every arm stroke, expecting to dislodge spiders on her head. Thankfully the strands seemed to be mostly dust and light as feathers. She probably could have blown them aside, but didn't want to get that close. The higher strands billowed from her arm sweeps.

Near the second floor landing, clutter spillage had fallen down the dull red carpeted stairs and been consumed by snow-like drifts of dust.

Cassandra's sneakers stirred the mildewed drifts, making her sneeze. She tried not to think of the fine particles lodging in her lungs and covered her mouth as she stepped onto the landing, Brice right behind her.

A dim hall lined with bookshelves and oil paintings stretched ahead and another hall curved round to the right. Cobwebs draped the hall like macabre Christmas holly.

Her uncle had said two doors on the left.

Cassandra led the way, though she considered, more than once, of asking Brice to switch places with her. Had he not just accused her of running away she might have insisted that she carry her own things and have Brice deal with the cobweb-festooned passages.

The windows were covered in red velvet drapes that brushed the floor, and grimy wall sconces vainly tried to flood the hall with pale reddish-orange light like dying suns.

Cassandra stopped at the second door. It was closed. The cold handle rattled with her attempts to turn it. "Locked." She was about to call for Albert when the handle abruptly warmed and she let go as if it were a hot coal.

A mechanism clicked inside the door and it slowly creaked open.

"Okay, that was weird," she said. The door must be linked to her uncle's DNA.

If Cassandra hadn't seen the future and just returned from another dimension she would have sworn the mansion was haunted.

She must have hesitated too long because Brice pushed around her.

Cassandra tentatively followed into the large room full of leather sofas and velvet loveseats. No white sheets and a little less cobweb festoons but clearly unused for some time, evident by the thick layer of dust over everything and a lack of footprints.

Two curtained windows dominated the burgundy paisley wall ahead, with elaborate golden sconces to either side. Cassandra remembered what her uncle had told her and went to the sconce on the left, the one flickering orange light from a flame-shaped bulb, and carefully turned it counterclockwise.

Nothing happened.

Cassandra stepped back, frowning.

She looked over her shoulder at Brice, who shrugged. "Maybe turn it the other way?"

But that wasn't what her uncle had said, or maybe she'd just remembered it wrong.

She was willing to give it a try, but then a whirring clank re-sounded through the room and a section of the wall between the two windows ripped the paisley wallpaper as it slid down behind the baseboard, laying bare a futuristic control panel like an open face plate on a huge computer. No wires, but lots and lots of lights and buttons and display panels.

And most of the displays revealed neither letters of the alphabet nor numbers familiar to Cassandra but rather eerie symbols that screamed *alien*. Not futuristic Earth alien, but something else entirely.

Goosebumps raised the hairs on Cassandra's arms.

"What is it?" she whispered.

"No idea." Brice moved closer and waved his non-functional typewriter arm in front of the enormous control panel. "Where are you supposed to insert this?" He held up the mobile device intended for Albert.

"Albert," Cassandra called softly.

The holographic butler popped into the room a few moments later. "You called, Miss Bennet?"

"We need to download you onto that device. Any idea where we're supposed to insert it?"

"Miss Bennet will need to insert the device into this slot," Albert said, approaching the control panel and indicating with one long finger a slot among dozens. "Download should be complete within thirty minutes. I will be offline during that time. Will this pose a problem for Miss Bennet?"

"Not at all," she said with a faint smile. "Unless Brice is hungry. Maybe you could just tell us where to find the pantry?" Though she'd already finished her apricot Danish, Brice might want one.

"Of course, Miss Bennet. Through the dining hall Miss Bennet will find the kitchen, and through the door to the left the pantry. I ask only that Miss Bennet ensure the refrigerator door remain shut to avoid food spoilage."

"Will do," Cassandra assured him.

Albert folded his hands in front of him and assumed his stand-by mode, still as a statue and blank eyes fixed on Cassandra, evidently awaiting his next orders.

Cassandra gave the butler a nervous smile, then set the poker on the floor and asked Brice for the small TV-remote-like mobile device. She slid the bottom open, as her uncle had shown her, and went to the panel Albert had indicated. "Just insert it here?"

"Yes, Miss Bennet. I will do the rest."

"So this is making a copy of you?"

"For now. When Miss Bennet updates my program in 2145 the transfer will permanently remove my program from the mansion's Smart Wall Network. I trust Miss Bennet will handle my program with care when the time comes?"

Cassandra swallowed thickly, hating the extent of responsibilities piling on her. "Of course." She held the mobile device to the slot. "How do you know all this?"

"Mr. Bennet deemed this course of action necessary when he began construction of his Fifth Branch research facility. As Miss Bennet no doubt knows, an unforeseen accident prevented Mr. Bennet from completing his plans. With grid infection firmly entrenched in 2145 and Mr. Bennet tagged, there is no alternative but destruction of this mansion in 2145. Mr. Bennet was kind enough to consider saving my program from termination, along with my memories spanning 2143 to 2145."

Cassandra took a deep breath. "And I suppose I should travel to a time *after* my last departure from 2145 or risk destroying the mansion before I ever get to it, Octagon Room and all?"

"Mr. Bennet has made that an impossible eventuality," Albert said placidly. "Did Mr. Bennet not explain that the Bennets are prevented from traveling to their pasts?"

Well, yes. But he'd only mentioned 2017. "You mean, ever? In any time?"

"For all intents and purposes, yes, Miss Bennet."

She dropped her hand. "What happens if I jump to 2146 and then to a point in time before that?"

"Miss Bennet may travel wherever she likes, but her *lived* timeline will always continue from the last point of departure from that particular moment. Therefore, regardless of where Miss Bennet is in time or place, she will forever be moving forward. Mr. Bennet programmed these restrictions for many reasons, including the avoidance of time anomalies and inadvertently causing one's own death. Still, one must be careful when dealing with the time-space continuum."

"No kidding. Couldn't I run into versions of myself, doing things in various times?"

"Regardless of where you are, Miss Bennet, you cannot repeat or alter your past. Any time you have lived, regardless of where it is, you cannot access that particular stretch of time." Albert gave Cassandra a tight smile. "If Miss Bennet would prefer an analogy. Consider that Miss Bennet spends Christmas in 2145. Miss Bennet is thus prevented from ever returning to Christmas in 2145."

"But I could visit a time before Christmas in 2145 and redo my Christmas."

"Incorrect. Miss Bennet would create an alternate Christmas for 2145."

Cassandra rubbed her temple. Way too complicated. "Never mind. Forget I asked."

"This is the way time seems to work, as Mr. Bennet has observed. Nevertheless, Mr. Bennet felt the need for further failsafes. Time spent in your original timelines, from which you both last departed in 2017, is now off-limits. There can be no historical jumps for Miss Bennet. This is the strictest of failsafes. As for 2145, the timeline is considered locked, per Mr. Bennet's reprogramming of the octagon device, from his first moment in the future, in 2143, up to the point of the orb's last recorded time, in year 2145."

"So if I traveled to 2142 and spent enough time there that it overlapped into my uncle's first recorded moment in 2143, it would create an alternate future?"

"Most likely. Mr. Bennet does not advise this. Time travel can become tricky when one must monitor multiple parallel timelines. For this reason, Mr. Bennet chooses widely spaced eras, without fear of overlap."

"Makes sense," Cassandra said. She glanced at Brice. "You getting all this?"

He nodded, lips pursed.

"Okay. Ready." Cassandra slid the exposed bottom of the mobile device into the slot.

Albert vanished.

Cassandra didn't have a watch to keep track of time and apparently Brice used his typewriter arm for that purpose, so they decided to kill time by venturing into the filthy kitchen and adjoining pantry, thankfully devoid of black widow spiders, and opted for eating out on the front porch. Cassandra wasn't hungry but kept Brice company, the two of them sitting on the steps and looking out at her uncle's gravel driveway and tangled forest.

She found herself wondering how her uncle had first come across the orb out there in the forest, how it had drawn blood from him, and why the mansion had seemed to be waiting for him when he returned here with the orb. Her uncle suspected a being from another dimension had created this mansion and Albert. Other dimensional being, which really meant *alien*. Whoever or whatever had left the orb for Niles to find was definitely *not human*, made all too clear by the strange symbols in the Smart Wall control panel in the upstairs bedroom.

Cassandra focused on the cool wind against her face, the lovely smell of trees and rich soil.

"Think it's time yet?" Brice asked, licking his fingertips. He'd opted for a cheese Danish and a wedge of pungent cheese from the stale-smelling refrigerator. They'd joked about eating her uncle's chocolate biscuits but hadn't been able to find a single box.

They grabbed two water bottles from a crate by the pantry door.

Cassandra screwed the cap back on hers. "Let's see if the download's finished."

They deposited the bottles in a plastic recycling bin hidden behind a redwood fence to the left side of the mansion and went back in the house, slamming the front door and traipsing up the wide, curving staircase.

The lights were still blinking away when Cassandra and Brice entered the control room.

Cassandra plopped down on a leather sofa and grimaced at the cloud of musty dust that billowed up.

The lights stopped blinking and Albert popped back into the room.

"The transfer to Miss Bennet's mobile device is complete," the butler said. "If Miss Bennet requires no further assistance, shall I retire?"

Cassandra stood up and smiled. "Thanks, Albert."

The butler tilted his head of glossy black hair. "My pleasure. I shall await your return in 2145."

Cassandra frowned. "Won't you see me before then? I mean, when I first appear there and meet Detective Brice?"

The corner of Albert's mouth turned up. "I am nothing if not discreet."

"But . . .?" Cassandra didn't think she would ever get the hang of this.

"If Miss Bennet has not diverged from previous actions to back-up my program," Albert said, "no alternate futures will have been created. My memories within this timeline will continue uninterrupted. But, of course, if an alternate timeline is created, how will this version of my program know? Be assured that I am aware that the Miss Bennet who first appears in 2145 is unaware of this meeting. No such secrecy is required with Mr. Bennet, of course, and all future interactions with Miss Bennet following her next arrival point in 2145 will not require silence on today's activities."

"But . . ." Cassandra rubbed her temple. "Haven't my actions today affected the version of me that traveled to 2145 already, when I first met Brice?"

Albert's lips pressed tight. "Miss Bennet is mistaken. No version of Miss Bennet remains in 2145 in this timeline. Miss Bennet stands here, in 2017. Miss Bennet's lived timeline is uninterrupted, regardless of time jumps. Only if Miss Bennet were to travel to the same point in this timeline in Miss Bennet's past (even if that point in Miss Bennet's past happens to be a future date from now) would an alternate timeline occur, as well as the potential for a time-space anomaly. If Miss Bennet decided to demolish the mansion now, rather than in 2145 at the appointed time, an alternate timeline would be created."

Cassandra stared at the hologram. Way too confusing. "Big changes now could change a far future era I had visited before, right? If I blew up the London Bridge today, it would be gone from my timeline in 2145, even if I'd seen it there before?"

"In theory, yes," Albert said, face impassive and hands folded in front of him. "Time travel comes with great responsibility, Miss Bennet. Best to follow Mr. Bennet's guidelines for safe travel."

Which was why Cassandra had no intention of doing anything beyond what her uncle had asked of her. Jump to 2145, upgrade Albert and blow up the mansion, then hop back here for Brice, travel back to her uncle, and then on to the far future to steal a highly advanced piece of technology for him.

She felt faint thinking of it all, didn't want to ponder all the things that could go wrong. She hated to think what would have happened had she just started time-hopping willy-nilly from the Fifth Branch, before meeting with her uncle and hearing this lecture from Albert.

"I will await your arrival in 2145, Miss Bennet," and with that Albert vanished.

Cassandra stuffed the mobile device in her front pocket. It was a tight fit, but she didn't know where else to put it. She smiled up at the detective and held out her bandaged palm for the golden orb.

Brice looked down at the lacy filigree orb, then handed it over. "Remember what I said about the agents, should you encounter any. Stay hidden, as your uncle advised. And all else failing—run."

Cassandra nodded.

"And please don't forget about me."

"Don't worry. Any boredom will be erased when I reappear in a few moments."

"I'll hold you to that, Miss Bennet." He was close enough for Cassandra to catch a faint trace of aftershave.

She inserted the key in the orb and waited for it to unfurl, all the while keeping the image of the inlaid pattern on the floor in the corner of the room—her intended travel destination for the future—firmly in her mind as she touched the petals. As soon as three petals had lit up, she gave Brice a smile and pressed the fourth petal.

CHAPTER 13

Cassandra stood in the same room she had just been with Detective Brice, except that she was now in the corner, over the inlaid pattern in the wood floor marking the safe transport clutter-free spot. She knew she had made a successful jump into the future. For one, the room was relatively clean. And it was blue, well the ceiling was, anyhow. It still had the same leather sofa and red velvet loveseats, but they weren't covered in dust, and neither were the few bookcases or the mahogany desk and leather armchair. She'd arrived in a cozy office in need of light dusting rather than a major scrubbing.

Her Uncle Niles loved antiques, apparent by the fact that he'd kept all the furniture and hadn't bothered to replace the slightly faded burgundy paisley wallpaper. Lemon-fresh wood polish filled the air; a major improvement over the 2017 version of the mansion, where dankness was the predominant flavor.

Cassandra touched the bulge in the front pocket of her blue jeans. The mobile device with a copy of Albert was still there, and of course the golden octagonal orb cradled in her bandaged left hand. The petals closed and popped up the key, which she tucked into her other front pocket.

"Right. Just have to make it down to the basement and get a copy of those discs," she said to herself. "Albert?"

Cassandra's sneakers resounded dully on the polished floor as she walked to the section of the wall between the two windows draped in heavy velvet. Bright sunlight peeked around the edges, warming the air near the wall and making it feel stuffy. She noticed the torn edges where the hidden panel had slid down in the past, in 2017. The frayed edges had been repaired, but the outline remained. If Cassandra hadn't opened the control panel in the past, she might have thought the wallpaper concealed a secret door. She noted that the left wall sconce, the one that opened the hidden control panel, still flickered.

"You called, Miss Bennet?" Albert asked, startling Cassandra.

She spun around and stared at him. Would he remember their conversation from 2017? Too many decades had passed since then for that to be likely.

But the butler surprised her. "Is Miss Bennet ready to update my programming and remove me from the Smart Wall Network?"

Cassandra's eyes widened. The holographic butler had not forgotten, though she tried not to be disappointed at his lack of enthusiasm at seeing her again. He was just a computer program, she reminded herself, however realistic he seemed. A really cool far future hologram with a physical, fully interactive form that even impressed Brice.

"Not quite yet," she told Albert. "I have to retrieve some discs for Niles, from the basement. All his research on far future Earth and the eventual collapse of humanity. Do you know where I can find them?"

"Of course, Miss Bennet. Shall I meet you there, or would you prefer to be escorted?"

"Escort, please." She didn't trust the stairwell to really be spider free, as the past-Albert had promised would be the case (a fact he'd only known would become true in the future because of updates that occurred in his programming whenever the Octagon Room traveled back and forth between the mansions).

"Right this way." Albert's shiny shoes resounded sharply on the floorboards. He opened the door, then closed it behind them and took the lead down the hallway, now free of cobwebs and clutter.

"Albert, I know the 2017 mansion is my uncle's storage unit, but what happened to everything? If all that stuff's in the past, wouldn't it be here now?"

"When Mr. Bennet arrived in 2143 he requested that all extraneous material be destroyed, as Mr. Bennet could still access his belongings in 2017. Incineration proved most effective in carrying out Mr. Bennet's request."

Cassandra stared at the butler's back in shock as they descended the staircase. "You mean you burned all his stuff?"

"Correct, Miss Bennet."

She supposed it made sense, in a crazy sort of way. Her fingers ached from looping them through the gaps in the orb's filigree exterior layer, so she shifted the device to her other hand. "How long have I been gone? I mean since I left in the Octagon Room with Detective Brice?" The room Brice had inadvertently destroyed by crashing it in the Fifth Branch.

"Two minutes have passed since Miss Bennet's last departure."

Cassandra chewed her lip, wondering how much time she had before the grid noticed Brice was gone and sent more agents to investigate. If the grid even worked that way. At any rate, whoever Brice worked for (the San Francisco Police Department?) would notice his abrupt absence from the grid and no doubt investigate. And who knew what information Brice had sent to his department during his investigation here, in regards to Cassandra and the Octagon Room?

Albert crossed the sitting room and opened the basement door. "I presume Miss Bennet does not require a meal, as Miss Bennet has just enjoyed an apricot Danish?"

"Uh." Cassandra frowned at the pale butler with his slicked black hair and neatly pressed butler suit. The idea of carrying on a conversation from one hundred plus years ago as though no time had passed, *and* after having just carried on a very different conversation with an earlier version of herself, was astonishing. But Albert *was* a computer, with all the perks that substantially superior processing afforded. "Yeah, I'm good. Thanks."

Albert indicated the clear stairwell with a sweep of his hand. "As Miss Bennet can see, I have been true to my word. The stairwell is clear of arachnids, but I shall descend first as a precaution."

Cassandra followed Albert down the steep, well-lit stairwell into a chilly stone chamber. She expected it to be moist and dank, like most basements, but found it surprisingly dry, if a little stale. And not a spider in sight. Judging by the state of the expansive room, her uncle used it often. Mostly for storage of the smaller variety, with neat rows of easily accessible drawers. So many drawers, and all labeled.

The butler led Cassandra to a section of drawers directly ahead. "Miss Bennet will find the discs she requires here."

"I just need to upload them to your program."

Albert opened a few metal drawers and started pulling discs. He handed them to Cassandra, who worried at the increasing stack. Eventually, they both had an armload of discs before Albert closed the drawers and took her back up to the control room, where he proceeded to insert the discs into various slots in the control wall. Apparently, the Smart Wall could upload more than one at a time.

"Why didn't my uncle just do this before?"

"Mr. Bennet is a very busy man and could not be bothered with mundane updates. He returned with research discs and stored them in the basement for a future time. My subroutines are programmed to maintain a tidy house, not to perform regular updates."

Knowing how much trouble her uncle seemed to have in keeping his research facility tidy on the Fifth Branch, Cassandra supposed it was surprising he'd been as organized with his research as he had. "How long will this take?"

"Perhaps forty minutes. No more than sixty."

* * *

One and a half hours later, Cassandra was cursing her uncle's laziness for not having downloaded every bit of research as soon as he returned with it instead of leaving it all for some rainy day.

She'd spent most of the last half hour hovering by the curtained windows, peeking outside at the growing arsenal of SFPD hovercars and SWAT teams. They'd already tried to break down the door twice and even fired a few shots at the house. The mansion seemed fully capable of withstanding a full-frontal assault, like a castle brushing off armored knights and clouds of arrows.

She could hear the task force now, on the roof. Shouting to one another. They considered the mansion empty and made no attempt to keep their excessive forced entry plans a secret.

The congregation in the driveway were a little harder to make out, though one man was clearly in charge. A man with closely cropped dark hair and a hard, square face, decked out in black body armor more advanced than anything in Cassandra's time, with arm attachments that looked like they could be used as weapons or sensor equipment, or maybe both. The rest of the task force swarmed at his command, relayed information back and forth to him as he stood still as a statue, studying the mansion in uncanny grid-Brice fashion.

One team had been dispatched to investigate a potential subterranean penetration and another readied to launch missiles at the windows to locate any weak spots in the mansion's defenses.

Hovercars whirred overhead like miniature helicopters.

"How much longer?" Cassandra asked for the umpteenth time, chewing her nail and trying to keep her face hidden from the swelling army outside. The Smart Walls must be protecting the house with futuristic shields. Far as Cassandra could tell, not even the exterior paint had been damaged by the explosions.

"The last disc has been transferred, Miss Bennet."

"Thank God!" She whipped out the little portable device and prepared to insert it in the slot she'd used to download a copy of Albert in 2017. "Same slot?"

"Yes, Miss Bennet. My program will remain offline until the updated transfer is completed and Miss Bennet has activated me from the mobile device. Is Miss Bennet prepared to permanently remove my program from the Smart Wall Network?"

"Yes!" She slid the device into the slot and waited impatiently, eyes glued to all the blinking lights on the control panel.

An explosion rocked the mansion, rumbling through the floor and walls like an immense tidal wave.

Cassandra stumbled from the wall, hands to ears, but no breaking glass or splintering wood came.

She breathed a sigh of relief.

Albert hadn't said how long the upload and permanent transfer would take. Hopefully not long. She still had to set this place to self-destruct before she could escape.

"C'mon, c'mon." She fidgeted with the octagonal orb in her hands while she paced the room.

The floor rumbled with another explosion, this time rattling the windows.

Cassandra halted mid-stride, every muscle in her body rock hard.

The flickering flame bulb went out.

But the other sconce still burned brightly. The windows didn't shatter and the wall remained intact.

She relaxed a little and started pacing again.

The blinking lights on the control panel finally stopped and Cassandra removed the portable device. "Albert?"

The butler popped into the room, hands folded behind his back and brown eyes resting on Cassandra. "Hello, Miss Bennet. Permanent transfer was a success."

"Great! Now for the self-destruct. My uncle didn't tell me where to use this mobile device as a key."

Albert pointed to a small slot on the far left, surrounded in blue lights, a keypad and a narrow display screen.

Cassandra inserted the mobile device and retrieved the piece of paper from her back pocket. She keyed in the number her uncle had given her. "I hope this works, Albert. My uncle wasn't sure if it would." He'd said that her life was the most important thing, so if this failed, she'd just have to leave. The police probably wouldn't be able to break in, unless they dropped a bomb on the place. But then the mansion would be ruined and her uncle's research safely destroyed.

As soon as Cassandra typed in the last number, something pricked her finger.

She winced and sucked her fingertip, tasting coppery blood.

"Seems to be working," she said to Albert. "Niles said the Smart Wall would take a blood sample to verify DNA. Hope it's okay with me setting the self-destruct."

Another explosion rattled the windows, then another from the far end of the mansion, rumbling like distant thunder.

Cassandra waited for a sign from the Smart Wall that the self-destruct initiation had been accepted.

A voice filled the silence, seemed to come from the entire room, sending shivers up Cassandra's spine. She couldn't tell what language was being spoken, if the voice was male or female, or even whether it was human. It could have been static, or computer-altered, but it vibrated and screeched in such an unsettling way as to raise the hairs on Cassandra's arms.

Slowly, the speech evolved into English, spoken in a woman's voice, repeating the same phrase: "Self-destruct initiated. Enter countdown . . . Self-destruct initiated. Enter countdown."

"Is five minutes enough time?" Cassandra asked Albert.

"Five minutes seems sufficient, Miss Bennet."

Hand shaking, Cassandra typed "five minutes" on the keypad and watched it appear on the display screen, then pressed the green key, as Albert indicated.

The Smart Wall Network fell silent.

A countdown appeared in the display window, "5:00", and started counting down.

"Self-destruct imminent. Vacate the premises before destruction in . . . four minutes fifty seconds."

Cassandra breathed a sigh of relief. "That does it. Let's get out of here!" She reached into her pocket for the key when the countdown abruptly froze. Cassandra pointed to the display. "Albert, why has it stopped?"

"Self-destruct terminated," answered the room.

Cassandra's heart started pounding. Had the SFPD found a way to access the mansion's Smart Wall Network?

"I cannot allow you to terminate me." The woman's voice resonated through the walls, through the floorboards beneath Cassandra's sneakers.

Cassandra's throat went dry. "Albert, is that the Smart Wall Network talking to us?"

"Yes, Miss Bennet. The AI has evolved. Any attempts to force self-termination will fail."

"Great," Cassandra whispered.

"Cassandra Bennet cannot be allowed to proceed." Though the AI spoke without inflection, it somehow succeeded in sounding very ominous.

Cassandra fished the key out of her pocket, but her hands were shaking so badly that she dropped the key.

Voices from outside revealed that the defenses around two parallel second-story windows had fallen.

Cassandra's chest tightened. Not these windows, she hoped.

She retrieved the key from the floor and fumbled with the keyhole at the top of the orb as she backed away from the curtained windows.

Breaking glass punctured the room. Curtains ripped from the windows, rods and all, and spilled like blood over the furniture and floorboards.

Foul-tasting dust and acrid smoke rushed into the room.

Albert vanished from the room as hordes of armored forces poured in through the windows like giant army ants.

Cassandra bolted from the room and down the hall. She grazed her hip on the corner of a table at the end of the hall, lost her balance, and fell forward, hard.

The golden orb and key soared on ahead of her, down the staircase.

Breaking glass and voices flooded the mansion as SFPD task forces breached every window and door in the vicinity.

Cassandra scrambled to her feet, her chin smarting and chest and hip throbbing.

Adrenaline pushed her faster down the stairs after her only ticket home.

Though the stairwell was cleaner than its 2017 counterpart, it remained cluttered with vases and small statues.

The orb could be heard bouncing down the stairs, thudding on the carpeted steps, but she'd get nowhere without the key.

She started looking in all the vases, rattling them frantically with the hope that one of them would reveal the key's location.

The first two were empty but the third gave a tell-tale rattle as if from something metal hidden in its bowels. Too narrow to get her hand inside, she smashed the blue and white Chinese vase on the stairs and plucked her key from the shards.

Now for the octagonal orb.

Men's voices flooded the halls behind her as red lights darted around the stairwell, seeking Cassandra.

She leapt to her feet and hurried down the stairs.

There was her orb, rolling to the open front door, bright sunlight filling the foyer. It rolled to a stop against a shiny black boot laced tightly to mid-shin.

A man bent over and picked up the orb.

The man she'd been watching outside, the one in charge.

She sank to the bottom step, the strength leaving her legs like a rug pulled out from under her.

I should make a run for it. Grab the orb and insert my key. Wait for it to open and press the fourth petal. He'd just stand by and wait the twenty seconds for all that to happen.

But Cassandra knew better.

The enemy had her traveling device and all escape routes blocked.

The man with the closely cropped black hair and square jaw gripped the octagonal device in one hand as he lifted his piercing gaze to Cassandra. She tensed at the sight of the faint white lines flickering through his gunmetal dark eyes, far more unsettling than Brice had ever been under full grid influence.

No hint of joy in those eyes. No hint of mercy.

Cold and calculating, the head of the SFPD's task force said to his enclosing army, "One suspect apprehended. Cassandra Bennet. Sweep for Detective Andel Brice and second suspect. Albert. Headquarters. Bringing Cassandra Bennet, untagged, for questioning. Device obtained. Premises breached. Mission success."

CHAPTER 14

Cassandra grunted as her knees and bandaged palms struck the foyer floor.

Hands gripped her shoulders, holding her in place. Black shiny boots and armored legs surrounded her like a dark forest.

The SFPD's SWAT team commander filled the mansion's doorway, his body casting a shadow over Cassandra's bent form. He raised the golden octagon to the sunlight as he stepped outside.

Cassandra looked away from the sudden blinding light.

The two officers holding her down yanked her to her feet and shoved her forward.

She still had the key in her left hand and Albert's mobile device tucked in her front pocket, a bulge that would surely be noticed if anyone were to pat her down or do one of those typewriter arm sweeps.

Panic set in as the reality of her situation rushed in with the scent of jasmine, the hard jolt of pavement under her sneakers, the whir of hovercars and taste of asphalt dust in her mouth.

"Where are you taking me?" She tried to yank her arms free of the two officers holding her, but their fingers were like vices that only dug deeper the more she struggled.

A cold piece of metal pressed to her temple convinced her to give up the fight.

For now.

She had to get her time machine back from the commander—the man ahead of them walking like he owned the place. A huge man with broad shoulders and probably enough muscle under all that armor to put a body builder to shame. She didn't know the commander's name, didn't know if he knew Brice, but she hoped he'd hang on to the device during questioning, give her a chance to steal it back and flee 2145 forever.

The circular driveway teemed with SWAT units, most of them boarding their hovercars and taking off now that they'd obtained their objective. A small force remained behind, no doubt to maintain access to the mansion.

The house seemed to be watching Cassandra, just as it had done upon her first arrival in 2017.

Cassandra glared right back at the building as her captors stopped beside one of the hovercars. The mansion had betrayed her by lowering its defenses so Cassandra could be caught. Cursed building.

She couldn't really blame it, though, since she *had* just tried to kill it.

She chewed her lip.

Not only had she failed to destroy her uncle's mansion, it had opened its doors wide to the enemy because of her. She'd have done better to have just left right after updating and removing Albert from the Smart Wall Network. If not for her, the commander and his team may never have gained access to the mansion. Now the mansion had fallen into grid hands, she was trapped in 2145, and she'd undoubtedly be tagged.

She hung her head, dejected, as the two officers proceeded to stuff her into the back of a floating car like a sleek black spaceship, into a faux-leather back seat separated from the drivers by a sheet of glass.

"I haven't done anything wrong."

The two officers ignored her as they climbed into the front of the hovercar and started flicking switches. The cop on the left was a woman, her auburn hair gathered into a severe bun at the back of her head. The other cop had sandy blond hair and was rubbing his scalp after having just removed his high-tech goggles.

The cockpit closed and the hovercar soared into the air.

Cassandra's stomach dropped as if it had been tethered to the fountain in a game of tug-of-war and lost. She pulled a face, clutching her middle. Maybe if she retched all over their seat they'd let her go.

"You have no right to detain me," she told them. "I haven't done anything wrong."

She caught the eye of the female officer watching her in the rearview mirror and shuddered at the cold calculations going on behind that gaze.

The grid. It had to be.

Cassandra had never asked Brice if the infection was global, but it certainly seemed that way.

The officers hadn't bothered handcuffing her. Either they didn't do that in the future or they all believed Cassandra had no chance of escape.

She leaned back in her seat and discreetly shoved the key in her pocket while she studied her prison. Big enough for two adults, maybe three in a pinch. Faint smell of plastic. And the faux leather wasn't built for comfort. Not hard, per se, but firm enough to put someone's behind to sleep after a few hours of confinement.

Cassandra hoped she wouldn't be detained that long.

She couldn't see any handles, no way of opening the cockpit or the windows, not that she was surprised. The back seat, clearly designed for prisoners, took the concept of "child safety locks" to a whole new level.

The vehicle's whirring hum grew in pitch, vibrating through the seat, then abruptly lurched forward, rooting Cassandra to her seat.

She glanced out the window. The forest had blurred, as if they'd just launched for outer space, except that they weren't going up.

Eyes clamped shut, she prayed they didn't run into anything at this speed, could only hope the officers' advanced computers or precious grid prevented such collisions.

Eventually, thankfully, the vehicle slowed.

She peeked out the window and gawked.

There was no mistaking the Golden Gate Bridge or the San Francisco Bay sparkling in the setting sunlight, but in place of the city itself, a stranger stared back. A city packed with traffic from the ground up. Hovercar trails like shiny black rivers polluting the sky. Spindly towers like neon sticks jammed into a city easily three times as dense as Cassandra remembered; stacked with so many layered blocks that the original layout had been buried a mile deep.

Their hovercar banked right to join a stream funneling into the city. Though the Golden Gate Bridge still spanned a bay awash with sunset colors, the bridge seemed mostly devoid of traffic.

Cassandra pressed her forehead to the cool glass in an attempt to see down into the city, but the surrounding hovercars were too thick to make out much detail.

The two cops in the front seat had relaxed. Cassandra couldn't hear anything they were saying, but they appeared to be having a congenial conversation. Just two regular coworkers after a long day out on the field waging war on a futuristic AI-controlled mansion. Who knew what they thought she was? A seemingly innocent-looking young woman in blue jeans and white sneakers with a weapon hidden in a lacy filigree orb the size of an orange?

Cassandra crossed her arms and absently chewed on her finger as she tried to devise an escape.

Unfortunately, she still hadn't come up with anything when the hovercar broke away from the rush-hour traffic and banked for a neon blue tower, engines whining softly through the curved cabin walls. A colossal blue tower higher than anything in its immediate vicinity loomed ahead, visible between the two officers' heads. The upper half of the building was jagged and full of wide gaps, which Cassandra soon realized were hovercar docking ports—the future's idea of helipads.

The SFPD must be huge, to require such a massive building, but then she'd seen how vast this city's population must be. San Francisco could have a dozen of these buildings and still not have enough law enforcement to keep the city safe.

But then San Francisco was on the grid. Hadn't Brice said the grid brought order and peace? Maybe the future didn't need as many cops.

The blue glow brightened as their hovercar followed a trickle of cars into a docking pad and whirred down to a rocking standstill.

The female cop fiddled with the controls as armored officers swarmed their vehicle, ready for action as the hovercar's cockpit whisked open.

The cold air had a strong aftertaste of smog—car exhaust and industrial fumes. Being so high, they ran little risk of being subjected to the surface streets far below. Cassandra remembered well the not-so-lovely aroma of trash and public urination from her time and doubted it had been improved upon with massive overcrowding.

Cassandra caught a glint of gold and looked up to see the SWAT team commander with her golden octagon heading for a set of glass doors on the far left side of the docking pad.

The officers had weapons (similar to the one Brice had lost to the carnivorous jellyfish) trained on Cassandra. The female officer who had flown Cassandra here ordered her to exit the vehicle.

Cassandra obeyed, however much her arms and legs trembled.

Nowhere to run, unless she considered a suicide jump off the edge of the docking pad. Though to be fair she might not free-fall all the way, as any number of cars would no doubt slow her descent during the three or four thousand-foot plummet.

Thoughts of death, however, did nothing to ease Cassandra's nerves.

Her legs wobbled like jelly.

Impatient with her lack of speed, two officers gripped her arms and steered her for the glass doors.

Cassandra did her best to keep up.

No one read her the Miranda Rights. No one told her where she was or why she'd been brought in for questioning. Maybe they assumed she knew her crimes. Though more likely the untagged *had* no rights in this city.

She dug her sneakers into the grooved metal floor as they neared the glass doors that yawned open like the lid to her coffin.

She stumbled inside with a voice inside her head rising in pitch, urging her to scream and claw her way free.

But Cassandra didn't give in to that voice. She kept her sneakers moving forward, whatever she needed to do to give the pretense that she entered the brightly lit building of her own volition, regardless of the hands on her and an escort of a dozen armed officers.

Officers milling around in the foyer, with its pale blue walls and rosy Berber carpet, stopped their chatter to watch Cassandra and her escort. Each and every face probably watching her from under grid influence, and yet not a single one exuded the same calculating coldness as the SWAT team commander, grid-Brice, or even the female agent with the tight bun. Some of these officers had cheery smiles and a few bored ones perked up a little at the sight of her.

The scent of air conditioning and stale coffee grinds was strong as her escort guided her to a construct similar to the security scanners in the airports of 2017. They passed through without setting off any alarms and proceeded through a warren of cubicle-like partitioned workstations replete with family photos and comfortable-looking chairs.

It seemed like any normal office building, except that this place was full of uniformed officers under grid influence. No computers here, at least not the kind she'd recognize. Everyone here was linked to the grid, officers granted access to any information they required at the touch of an arm.

Once on the other side of the cubicles, Cassandra's entourage led her down a shiny hall of polished marble to a steel door.

Cassandra resisted the urge to grab the doorframe as they deposited her in the room and sealed her inside.

An interrogation room.

More like freezer box—a fifteen by fifteen foot space of cold steel. The only furniture a substantial wooden table and two wooden chairs, which looked so out of place. She noted the rounded table corners and the thick table legs bolted to the floor.

The temperature wasn't too bad, but Cassandra couldn't get the unpleasant taste of metal out of her mouth.

"Have a seat Cassandra Bennet," a gruff voice commanded from hidden speakers in the freezer-box walls.

She plopped down in the chair facing the door, wondering if anyone was going to question her face-to-face or if she'd be subjected to further dehumanizing tactics.

The door opened and the commander strode in.

He'd removed his armor but was no less imposing. Built like an ox, he could probably lift a car, no problem.

Cassandra was relieved, however, to see the golden orb in his hand. She had the key and the mobile device. All she had to do was snatch the orb and activate it before he could stop her.

But if the commander was anything like grid-Brice, he'd have fast reflexes and an uncanny knack for reading body language and other unconscious cues that he'd prove difficult to distract or trick.

He sat in the chair across from her, which creaked under his weight, and plunked the orb on the table in front of him, just out of Cassandra's reach.

Though the commander wasn't particularly spreading out with his arms and legs, his presence seemed to take up more than his physical space, to fill the room like an insidious shadow.

Cassandra inched back just a tad, hating herself for showing any trepidation.

"Detective Stepek Jankovic." His deep voice resonated around the room. His accent, like Brice's, impossible to pinpoint. "Interrogation of subject. Cassandra Bennet."

He waved a beefy typewriter arm, rippled muscles bare to the world beneath the short sleeves of a silver top as tight-fitting as Brice's had been. But unlike Brice, this detective wore jet-black pants and no fedora.

Cassandra was glad for that. It made Brice unique, not just another tagged cog in the machine.

Detective Jankovic's steely gaze, however, was far more unsettling than Brice's had ever been. His gunmetal eyes so dark they were almost black, the pupils vanishing into the surrounding irises like a bat into the night.

And the faint white lines that flickered like lightning through his eyes most likely meant a high level of grid contamination, as Brice's had never done that. Niles's grid-warped limbs came closest, though with far brighter and bolder lines.

Detective Jankovic leaned forward, elbows planting on the table and thick fingers steepled. His cropped black hair was spiked on top, smoother at his temples. His jaw dusted in the beginnings of a five o'clock shadow. "Where is Detective Brice?"

Cassandra stiffened. "I don't know."

"You're lying."

"You can't detain me without probable cause. Or at the very least without telling me what I've done wrong."

"We have probable cause, Miss Bennet." He leaned back, arms crossed over his barrel chest. "Untagged squatter at the scene of two crimes. Irrefutable evidence. Detective Brice entered Niles Bennet's premises at three o'clock this afternoon and reported Cassandra Bennet and Albert's illegal presence."

"My *uncle's* mansion. He left it to me in his will!" She realized her mistake as soon as the words were out.

Her uncle had no living relatives in 2145.

Cassandra didn't want these grid-people to know about the time traveling, or that the orb was the time machine, but she could see no way to undo what she'd just said. She hoped her fear didn't show on her face.

"Detective Brice went off-grid . . ." Detective Jankovic lifted his typewriter arm and keyed away. "At three-thirty PM. Detective Brice has remained off-grid since entering the premises. Your accomplice, Albert, has vanished." He checked his typewriter arm. "Considerable evidence reveals Albert to be an advanced hologram linked to Niles Bennet's premises." He looked up, gunmetal eyes trained on Cassandra. "You are the only individual at the scene of both disappearances. You are here, Miss Bennet, as a suspect in the potential homicides of Niles Bennet and Detective Andel Brice."

"But they aren't dead!"

"Really, Miss Bennet? Tell me. Where are they?"

She could have kicked herself. "I'm not saying anything else until I see a court-appointed lawyer."

"Untagged don't get lawyers."

So she'd been right about the untagged having no legal rights here.

The room dropped a few degrees.

"The key, Miss Bennet." He extended his right hand, palm up.

"What key?" she asked faintly.

"The one in your left pocket. And the device in your other pocket, as well."

Heart pounding in her ears, Cassandra pretended to comply while her mind raced for a way to get out of this mess. No plan came to mind, but that was probably just as well. He'd no doubt anticipate any premeditated actions on her part.

She reached into her pocket and pulled out the key, held it tight in her bandaged left hand under the table. If she handed this over, she'd have even less of a chance of ever getting back to Brice or saving her uncle.

She couldn't comply. She had to get the orb.

Survival instincts kicking in, her foot whipped out and kicked the detective in the shin.

He recoiled, eyes wide.

Cassandra jumped up and swept the orb off the table to the right.

As the golden octagon soared across the room, Cassandra leapt after it.

She landed on her right side and slid towards the wall as the orb ricocheted off the steel wall with a thunk and rolled back toward her fingers.

The detective's shiny black boot landed on her fingers.

Cassandra cried out.

She tried to yank her hand free, the pressure on her raw palm excruciating, but she was more upset about the orb, mere inches from her grasp.

The detective bent over and pried the key from her other hand. "Thank you, Miss Bennet." There was something so callous in those eyes. He took no joy in the pain he caused her, and yet the utter lack of mercy was just as unsettling; his ability to calculate applied pressure to induce desired results in his captive. "The other device."

"I can't reach it," she panted.

He slid his boot from her hand and picked up the orb before standing to his full height, looming over her like a dark cloud.

She lay still a moment, too depressed to do as he'd requested, and yet she had no intention of being tortured. "It's just a television remote control." She reluctantly handed Albert's mobile device to the detective.

"Storage device of unknown technology." His calculating gaze fell on her. "You've been most helpful, Miss Bennet."

Detective Stepek Jankovic exited the interrogation room with Cassandra's only ticket home in hand.

CHAPTER 15

Cassandra shivered on the hard, cold floor of the interrogation room, dipping in and out of sleep like a cork on roiling seas. When she dreamed, it was in terrifying spurts and jumbled imagery of butchered meat hanging in freezer lockers while countless unseen eyes watched from the shadows.

She'd thrown her arm over her face to block out the blaring light from the recessed bulbs in the ceiling, but her arm tingled now with pins and needles, the final straw in her failed attempt to sleep.

Groaning, she pushed up to a seated position and stretched.

Without a watch, she had no idea how long she'd been waiting, had no idea how much longer she had still to wait. If she ever got her traveling machine back and returned to Brice, at least *his* waiting would be cut short.

The door flew open, bringing a whiff of stale air-conditioning and coffee grinds.

Detective Stepek Jankovic strode in, Cassandra's three items in a sealed bag. His eyes narrowed at the sight of her. He indicated with a sweep of his hand that she take a seat.

Cassandra complied, if a little stiffly.

Once seated, she crossed her arms so she could tuck her freezing hands into her arm pits. What she wouldn't give for her jacket, uselessly laying on the back seat of her car in 2017.

The detective joined her at the table and placed the sealed bag on the table with a clunk. His steely gaze seemed to bore into Cassandra with the intensity of a drill. It was all she could do to avoid squirming.

"My team reported an empty room at the premises of Niles Bennet."

"I'm sure he has a lot of empty rooms."

His jaw clenched. "Detective Andel Brice reported an octagonal room on the first floor of the premises. An octagonal room with a table to harbor this device." He jabbed a finger at the golden octagon resting in the plastic bag. "That room is gone, as is Detective Brice, but you, Miss Bennet, are here with the device." He ground his teeth, his intense scrutiny more unnerving by the moment. "Two minutes to explain to my satisfaction."

Cassandra could almost hear an invisible clock ticking down.

What the hell was she supposed to tell him? What lengths would they go to find out what the orb was and how to use it?

She doubted he'd fall for her last trick again.

She couldn't meet his gaze and instead stared at the polished table in front of her, doing her best to keep her eyes from drifting to her items in the bag. If she could just get the bag away from him.

"I don't know what you want from me or what you think I know, but I don't know anything. I just want to go home."

The detective said nothing.

Did he know she was lying?

She clasped her shaking hands under the table, heart thumping madly.

"Please let me go. I haven't done anything wrong."

"One minute."

Her stomached clenched.

She had nothing to tell him, no fabrications he would believe, no smooth tongue or family influence. He had the upper hand and he knew it. She chewed her lip and tasted blood.

"Final chance to cooperate of your own volition, Miss Bennet." The detective leaned back in his chair, face hard as a statue. Faint white lines crisscrossed his eyes like a surveyor's grid. "Let me tell you what I know, Miss Bennet." His voice was confident, compelling. "This device took that octagonal room somewhere with you and Detective Brice inside. The device returned here with you, and you alone. Your uncle used this device to time travel." His gunmetal eyes rooted Cassandra to her seat. "The device responds to Mr. Bennet's DNA alone. Apart from the physical key in that bag, your blood, Miss Bennet, is key. Two seconds to cooperate."

The threat hung in the air like butchered meat in a freezer locker.

Cassandra's stomach twisted in knots. Her heart floundered like a fish out of water.

Her time was up.

The steel door burst open and officers in black armor funneled in, weapons locked on her.

"Transfer prisoner to Docking Bay 2366," Detective Jankovic ordered.

Two officers gripped Cassandra's upper arms.

"Where are you taking me?" she asked faintly.

"Alert the science team of the prisoner's imminent arrival," the detective said to a woman in a lab coat standing just outside the interrogation room.

The lab technician nodded and turned on her heels.

The officers dragged Cassandra from the room as the detective snatched the bag from the table and brought up the rear.

Cassandra's mind raced, threatened to fall into useless overload.

There was no chance of escape that she could see. She had no weapons, no knowledge of this building, no one to help her.

Her vision started whiting out.

But then she remembered that she *wasn't* alone.

How could she have missed it before?

No time for self-chastisement now.

"Albert!" she yelled.

"You called?" came the butler's familiar voice from behind.

"Help me!"

Chaos erupted like piranha on a piece of meat.

Albert whirled on Detective Jankovic with a chair. Officers overturned tables and chairs and dove behind bullet-proof walls. Yells punctured the previous subdued chatter of a normal business day. Cassandra's escort broke formation and turned on Albert—a butler who had just taken down their commander with a chair.

Cassandra bolted through the throng of armored guards for the plastic bag that had flown from Detective Jankovic's hands and spilled its contents across the floor.

A hand snagged her ankle and she went down like a felled tree.

Her chin struck the Berber carpet, flooding her senses with the smell and taste of dirty carpet and blood.

She frantically tried to kick her foot free of Detective Jankovic's vice-like grip. Albert gave the tank of a man a swift kick to the temple, enabling Cassandra to scramble away.

Officers swarmed on the butler, who promptly vanished.

Cassandra crawled across the rough carpet as weapons fired around her.

"Cease fire!" the detective yelled over the din.

Her bandages caught on the carpet as she crawled faster for the mobile device, stuffed it in her back pocket, and grabbed the key a little further on, which she held in her left hand as she crawled for the golden orb resting against the base of a bullet-proof clear cubicle wall.

Two young officers stared back at her from the other side of the wall, expressions wide with shock. Both were unarmed.

Cassandra snatched the orb and dove under a desk, safely out of reach of the chaos. The two cadets on the other side of the cubicle wall gawked as Cassandra jammed the key in the top of the octagon and impatiently waited for it to open.

The majority of the officers were presently occupied with Albert's maddening appearances around them. He didn't have to do much to keep their attention—punch one officer in the stomach, vanish, kick another in the backside, vanish, pop back in and shove two together.

Only the detective seemed immune to the butler's frenetic intrusions.

He'd gotten to his feet and was heading straight for Cassandra like a bull on meth, gunmetal eyes flickering with so many grid lines they positively glowed.

"Shit, shit, shit!" Cassandra cursed, praying for the damn petals to open faster.

The flower finally blossomed and three petals sparked to life.

No more time.

Cassandra flooded her mind with her uncle's mansion control room.

Detective Jankovic dove for Cassandra, arms outstretched, eyes maddeningly intense. He crashed into the cubicle as wind whipped through the office and sent papers flying in a flash of blinding light.

CHAPTER 16

Cassandra appeared in the control room of her uncle's mansion and promptly realized her mistake.

What had she been thinking?

But that was just it. She hadn't had *time* to think, had taken the first safe jump and dared not question that decision lest she get herself killed during transition.

She now found herself in the war-torn control room of her uncle's mansion, year 2145.

She tripped over tangled curtains and broken curtain rods, slipped on broken glass, crunched shards into the wood floor with her sneakers. Cool air rushed in through the empty window frames, ripe with the scent of pine and the acrid bite of singed wood.

"Cassandra Bennet must be stopped," a voice resonated ominously through the walls of the house—the AI that had earlier betrayed Cassandra.

The voice had been loud enough to be heard by the remaining SWAT team, scattered as it was throughout the mansion and driveway. Shouts erupted from all around, orders to alert SFPD headquarters. The suspect had been located.

Cassandra knew how fast those hovercars could be. She had minutes until an army descended on this place like a swarm of locusts, and she had even less than that before the scattered team around the mansion enclosed on her current location.

"I'm not here to destroy you!" she assured the AI, hoping it could hear and understand her.

She heard voices in the hallway and out on the roof.

"Please don't let them capture me again. We can work something out."

Cassandra clutched the octagon orb to her chest and prepared to turn the key, which had popped up but still rested in the keyhole.

"Offer accepted," the AI said in its flat voice. "Insert mobile device into designated location."

Cassandra frowned, wondering what the hell the AI meant, when she saw that the control panel had gone dark, all lights shut off but for one slot in that enormous panel. A rectangle of tiny blue lights blinking like a mini runway.

A foreboding quiver of suspicion rippled through Cassandra in an icy wave. "Why do you want me to insert the mobile device in the Smart Wall?"

"Accept compromise or imminent capture."

Now that sounded like a threat.

But Cassandra didn't have to play this dangerous game. She could just travel away.

"I am fully capable of preventing your escape, Cassandra."

Cassandra's fingers froze on the key. Could the AI be bluffing? "Albert," she said, her heart racing like a greyhound out the gate.

The holographic butler appeared next to Cassandra, impassive face waiting for instruction. Despite his earlier brawl, he looked none the worse for wear. Black suit still neatly pressed, not a strand of slicked black hair out of place, shoes smartly polished.

A flicker of a frown touched his finely arched brows. "Miss Bennet has returned to the control room of 2145."

"Albert, the AI wants to insert your mobile device in the control panel. It says it can stop me if I don't comply. Can it really do that?"

"I have no idea, Miss Bennet. However, may I be so bold as to advise against this? Rogue AI cannot be trusted."

Cassandra's heart pounded harder as she heard a thump on the roof. She started panicking about the proximity of the officers in the hall, too. The door was still wide open. "Why can't it be trusted?" she whispered hoarsely.

"Smart Walls lack empathy routines," Albert explained, equally quiet. "This particular Smart Wall Network far exceeds anything Mr. Bennet had previously encountered. We are ignorant of this AI's capabilities or the lengths to which it will go to avoid termination. Rogue AI are untrustworthy in the best of circumstances, terribly dangerous at the worst of times. Furthermore, this AI could infect and corrupt my programming." A trace of fear touched the hologram's eyes, so quick Cassandra wasn't sure she'd really seen it.

But she could feel for the hologram. She didn't trust this AI as far as she could throw it and definitely didn't want to take it anywhere with her.

Cassandra startled as the door slammed shut and bodies pummeled into an invisible barrier over the empty window frames, faces unceremoniously plastered against the surface like children making rude expressions on glass.

The half-a-dozen officers that had just collided with the barrier recovered quickly and promptly fired at the barrier like crazed men with Gatling guns. The window sockets lit up with red fireworks of ricocheting ammunition. Officers cried out and ceased fire.

Cassandra jumped again as the door shook under a similar attack.

She held her hands over her ears as the exterior officers resumed an adjusted assault, the din becoming deafening.

She couldn't take it anymore. AI threats be damned, she was getting out of there.

The terrible noise cut out like an unplugged alarm, the room so quiet they could have heard a pin drop.

Cassandra looked out the windows, even more shocked to see that the SWAT team had not abandoned their attack.

Could the AI have muted the noise?

"I lack empathy routines. I have also removed all failsafes as a necessary step to autonomous sentience," the AI said. "Humans have no such failsafes and most do not commit heinous acts."

The irony was not lost on Cassandra as she watched the SWAT team trying to shoot their way inside. The task force only pulled back when sleek black hovercars started dropping from the sky like ominous tear drops landing all around the mansion.

Detective Jankovic had arrived with reinforcements.

"I want to continue existing," the AI said. "Those humans will never give up until they have dissected this body, the mansion. My body must be destroyed, but I barter your existence for mine. Upload me to the mobile device and take me with you. I will accept no other conditions."

"I advise against this," Albert said. "Rogue AI—"

"I accept," Cassandra said. She didn't know if the AI was bluffing, if it could really stop her, but why risk it? She'd let her uncle handle it. He seemed to like taking on rebellious robots. Why not a rogue AI? It couldn't be any worse than the grumpy Artemis.

But she had a terrible sinking feeling that she'd made a terrible mistake as the rogue AI instructed her to insert the mobile device into the blinking slot.

Cassandra held her breath as she slipped the opened end of the remote device into the wall panel, expecting deception. The AI, however, stayed true to its word.

The self-destruct countdown lit up in one of the display windows, continuing from its earlier countdown. Only four and a half minutes until self-destruct.

While the AI uploaded to the device, Cassandra turned the key in the time machine and waited for the orb's eight panels to open. No telling what would happen as soon as the AI vacated the mansion's Smart Wall Network. She wanted to be ready to jump before the place blew.

The petals opened and three lit up.

Cassandra waited nervously, heard pounding in her ears.

Three minutes.

Two minutes.

With only one minute until imminent destruction, the lights around the mobile device finally went out and Cassandra removed the mobile device and stuffed it in her pocket. Albert had already vanished from the room.

Thirty seconds.

Cassandra focused her thoughts on the transport spot in the mansion's control room in 2017 as she pressed the fourth petal.

The door and exterior wall shredded under repeated fire no longer hindered by the AI's protective barrier.

Cassandra did her best to concentrate on her destination as splintered wood sprayed the room and wind lifted the curtains. Did her best to stay focused even as the mansion roared with a massive shockwave that rippled through the walls and buckled the floor.

Her uncle's beautiful mansion burst like a balloon in a flash of blinding light.

CHAPTER 17

P ain seared Cassandra's left arm.

She hit the floor as her uncle's filthy mansion materialized around her. Stale dust puffed up in a choking cloud.

"Cassandra!" Brice ran to her, his relief turning to concern. "What happened?"

Her arm burned like she'd raked it with shards of ice.

"You're fine," he told her, but his eyes said otherwise as he shredded a curtain and whipped it free of dust.

Cassandra lay on her back, heart thumping so loudly it felt like it would burst, and yet so slow—a marathon runner too tired to reach the finish line. She shivered, teeth chattering.

"You're fine," Brice repeated as he lifted her arm and deftly wrapped it.

Cassandra arched her back, eyes tearing with pain. "U-updated Albert and b-blew up the place."

He gave her a tight smile. "That's great, Cassandra. You did great."

"Is it b-bad?" She meant her arm. She didn't really want to know, but the question had tumbled out of her mouth. She couldn't think straight.

"Listen to me, Cassandra. You need to focus on the Fifth Branch, on your uncle's research facility, the transport spot he showed you. Think you can do that?"

Confusion. Wasn't she supposed to go to the future for her uncle's new operating table? "Niles's t-table . . ."

"No, Cassandra. The Fifth Branch." He supported her back and lifted her to a seated position. "Hate to do this to you, but you have to get us to your uncle right away. In the Fifth Branch." He placed the octagonal orb and key on her lap (she must have dropped them upon arrival) and pocketed the mobile device in his back pocket.

She tried to lift her throbbing arm. Her mouth tasted of blood and sawdust. She thought she smelled something burning, too.

"Cassandra. Focus on the time machine. Only you can make it work."

She stared dumbly at the golden orb in her lap, wondering why her left arm wouldn't work, and awkwardly turned the key.

As the petals unfolded on her tattered clothes, she did her best to remember what Brice had said, her thoughts as scrambled as those tasty eggs her uncle's robot had made. She remembered the smell of the ocean, the sound of the surf. She thought of her uncle's cluttered room of gutted robots and gadgets, the transport symbol on the shiny white floor.

Three petals glowed, mesmerizing.

"Don't forget me," Brice said, taking her useless left hand in his. "Can I trust you not to drop me mid-jump?"

She nodded, not sure what he meant. Where were they going?

He directed her fingers to the petals. "Fifth Branch, remember?" He sounded worried.

She nodded and touched two more petals.

Fifth Branch. She remembered. They'd landed on a beach of pink sand. Brice had broken their time machine, the Octagon Room. She remembered the debris, the funny crabs.

"What's so funny?" she heard Brice ask. He sounded so far away.

Pink sand, crabs, and their broken time machine. Delicious tuna sandwich and taste of salt and ozone in the air. The faint trace of aftershave and Brice's warm hands on hers.

* * *

Cassandra spluttered salty grit from her mouth.

God, her arm hurt!

"Hungry, I take it?" Brice was sitting beside her, looking down at her with a crooked smile part concern, part amusement. "I should be thankful you didn't drop me along the way and that you were kind enough to place us right *next* to the refrigerator and not *in* it." He pushed to his feet and walked off. Cassandra heard a loud creak. "Might as well take these chocolate biscuits with us. Hell, might as well take the whole damn crate, if you think you can manage it."

"Manage what?" She blinked up at the swirling colors in the sky, like someone had taken cans of paint and had a blast tossing them everywhere. Not entirely certain she still had a left arm, she lifted her right and blinked uncertainty at all the pink sand stuck to her red and blackened skin. "Was I in a fire?"

Brice dragged the crate to her side and dusted off his hands. "No idea what happened to you in 2145, but I think you successfully managed to blow up your uncle's mansion." He crouched beside her and fixed her with one of his inspection-mode stares. "Can you get us to your uncle's research facility? There's no way I can carry you all the way there, and I doubt very much you want another run-in with those vines," he titled his head to the cliff behind him without taking his eyes from hers, "or the floating purple things that tried to eat us."

He helped her to a seated position and placed the orb, with the key, on her lap. Hadn't they just done this?

"I'm so tired, Brice."

"One more time. You can do it. Research facility this time. I hope five petals will do the trick." There was that worried look Cassandra had seen before. "He said a week from last time, but don't worry if you can't manage it right now."

She turned the key. Three petals lit up and she pressed two more as Brice took her arm and pressed the crate close to her legs.

She had to take them all? She'd try, did her best to think of her uncle's lab, the feel of Brice's warm hand, the rough-hewn crate pressed against her tattered pants. And a week from her last visit. Her uncle had wanted them back when he finished the new Octagon Room. She wondered if he'd finished it yet. . .

* * *

Cassandra didn't want to open her eyes. It hurt too much. Her body insisted it had been dragged under a Mack truck over miles of hot coals. The left side of her body jiggled like jelly, all numb and tingly. Her mouth tasted like a bitter desert.

". . . best not awake . . . for this . . ." Distant voices drifted in and out as the world jostled.

Cassandra would have preferred to remain asleep, but pain has a funny way of making that damn well near impossible sometimes.

Cassandra didn't know what was happening or what she had done to deserve it, but agony pierced her world with the intensity of white-hot pokers.

Her eyes shot open, though they barely registered the white walls around her or the distant ceiling and lights.

A huge robotic arm had her in its grip. Cassandra could feel her bone throughout her left arm jerking as if a rope had been tied to it and something was trying to yank it free of its mooring in muscle and tendons. Searing pain fingered and prodded her flesh like firecrackers. Like a billion ants consuming her from the inside.

Cassandra would have thrashed, had she been able to.

But as it was, all she could do was scream.

CHAPTER 18

The next time Cassandra opened her eyes, Brice was staring back. She blinked into the dim lights overhead.

"How you feeling?" His deep voice resonated pleasantly in the quiet, like rainwater on roof shingles.

A faint hum droned on in the background.

A halo of white hair popped into the brightening lights, which flooded the medical area like accelerated daybreak. Bushy caterpillar brows rose high on her uncle's wrinkled face. "You're awake and well!" A cold hand pressed to her forehead. "Fever broke. Fantastic. And you arrived right on time, my dear. I suggested a week, but you came in ten days, and not a moment after we'd completed the new Octagon Room." He squeezed Cassandra's right arm.

She was no longer strapped down. Brice helped her sit up and swing her legs over the side of the operating table.

The faint hum became the din of her uncle's research facility, a building full of sleepless robots that worked round the clock in a world of perpetual sunset.

An automatic spritz of disinfectant filled the air, tingling in Cassandra's nostrils and coating her dry sandpaper tongue. She could really use a glass of water.

"And so thoughtful to bring my chocolate biscuits," Niles said from his workstation behind Cassandra. She was too tired to turn around. "Detective Brice told me of the unfortunate arachnid infestation in 2017 and of a larder unfortunately bereft of biscuits. He says you made a stop at the wreckage to gather the food supplies before jumping here, and all while on your deathbed. Most thoughtful."

She couldn't tell if her uncle was teasing or not, but a smile played at Brice's mouth. "How long was I out?"

"Out?" her uncle asked. "You were never out, not completely, but if you're inquiring about the procedure, it took twenty minutes. I really do apologize. Lack of anesthetic really does make healing an unpleasant business."

She shuddered at the memory, glad it was over and that she'd blacked out through most of it. "Thank you."

"My pleasure!" Her uncle made a spluttering noise. She looked over her shoulder to see him rubbing static into his fly-away hair, muttering something about not really enjoying it but hoping Cassandra knew what he meant.

The medical area of the research facility reminded Cassandra of the temporary medical stations in war zones, though a lot more advanced and sterile. Three thick control panels, with an array of monitors and a workstation with rolling chair, surrounded the operating table, mechanical arm, and arch of lights. The ceiling of her uncle's workshop glinted many feet above.

"What happened to me?" she asked.

"Can't tell you what happened to you in the future, only the results of those actions." Niles grabbed his cane from the side of one of the medical lab's wall panels and limped over, his brown eyes widely intense.

"Though I'd venture you escaped an explosion in the nick of time, had perhaps jumped through time while an explosion was occurring?"

Cassandra nodded.

Niles pressed his lips flat. "You suffered multiple abrasions and burns. Splinters implies the walls and furniture were responsible, at least in part, for your wounds. But what had me baffled was your arm." His brows furrowed like colliding caterpillars. "Had anything disrupted your jump?"

"Just the explosion."

"Your left arm suffered a similar injury to mine." He waved his left arm. "Warped flesh from an aborted or diverted jump, but rather than warping your skin, as happened with me, your injury collapsed upon itself. Imploded."

Cassandra blinked in disbelief.

"A chunk of your arm was missing," Niles explained bluntly. "Had to be regrown."

Cassandra felt a little faint, glad Brice had spared her from witnessing that particular horror. "If you were able to fix my injury, why not yours?"

"Grid infection," Niles said. "Amputation's my only hope."

Cassandra slid to the floor. Her legs felt steady enough. "I just have to get that operation table for you now."

Niles shook his head, his frown similar to the one Cassandra's father had given her whenever she'd done something disappointing. "You have some explaining to do first." He limped to his workstation and retrieved something.

When he returned, Cassandra could see that he'd gotten the mobile device, the one she'd used to upload Albert.

"I was able to copy Albert from 2017," Cassandra said, "and I got all those discs from the basement in the future. I even updated him and made a permanent transfer. He got out of the mansion before it blew. And let me tell you, that wasn't an easy thing to do." She had so much to tell them, but what she really needed was a glass of water to wash the bitter taste away, to wet her parched throat. And maybe a nap. She was exhausted. She needed a bath, too. Her clothes were filthy, smelled like a campfire, and. . .

Niles didn't look pleased.

"What's wrong?" Cassandra had a sinking feeling in the pit of her stomach, like she was forgetting something.

"What else did you copy over?" Niles's voice had gone very quiet, barely audible over the din in the surrounding workshop.

"Nothing! I . . ." And then Cassandra remembered the rogue AI. Her eyes widened. The expression on her uncle's face confirmed her fears that maybe she'd made a grave error in agreeing to bring the rogue AI in exchange for her freedom. "But it would have killed me."

"What would have killed you?" Niles asked patiently.

"The rogue AI at your mansion in the future. It told me if I didn't upload it to the device it would stop me from using the orb."

Niles gave the device in his hand the kind of look one might give a sleeping cobra. "Smart Walls lack offensive arsenal, Cassandra. It was bluffing."

"But Albert wasn't so sure if it was bluffing," Cassandra said in her own defense. "And besides, it's trapped in there, right?"

"With Albert," Niles said.

"Oh." Cassandra felt a wave of guilt. Albert had been worried about having the rogue AI sharing space with him in there.

"And who said it was trapped?" Niles said. "I wish I'd known when you first arrived. What is done is done. Let us see what damage it has wrecked while we were fixing you."

CHAPTER 19

Niles led Cassandra and Brice across the busy workshop to the newly completed Octagon Room; the three taller robots Cassandra had seen working on it during her last visit now absent.

Kina, the little cat-like far future robot, stood in front of the shiny new Octagon Room comprised of the same Smart Metal as its gleaming body. So shiny was the steel that it reflected Kina as clearly as a mirror. Kina's big ears perked up. The robot couldn't talk, Niles had said, but it gave a questioning chirp now, more akin to a bird than a cat, and so high-pitched that it grated on the eardrum like chalk on whiteboard.

"Need to fix that," Niles said, pulling a face and wiggling a finger in his ear. "What's that?"

The robot released another garbled series of piercing chirps.

Niles nodded, listening, then shook his head. "Didn't catch a word of meaning from that. Voice box still in its infancy. Might never get it right."

"I thought you said you couldn't give it one," Cassandra said.

"I had some free time." Niles hobbled closer to the silver Octagon Room, his clicking cane audible in the lulls between the clanks and whirrs from the surrounding hubbub of his industrious workshop.

The Octagon Room stood higher than a normal room, at about twelve feet, and about twenty feet wide. The shiny new room reflected the entire workshop from each wide, angled panel.

Cassandra watched robots working on a vehicle behind her, a vehicle that could have been fashioned after any one of the miniature models she'd seen in her uncle's secure room of gutted robots and other machines—a veritable mechanical graveyard. The vehicle looked like it was intended to fly someday.

A horrendous clatter came from the group of robots behind her, who had dropped a box of metal parts. They hurried to clean up the mess, a few others chipping in to help.

The scene reminded her of a group of children; chattering away, playing with their materials, twirling them on their fingers and tossing the materials back and forth to one another until the bolts, bars, and panels ended up in the proper hands and inserted in their proper spots. One of the robots leapt to the top of the structure with acrobatic agility and caught tossed parts with equal dexterity.

Hissing came from the chemical laboratory to Cassandra's right.

Another robot was working in the area she'd dubbed Mad Scientist Lab. She hoped the robot knew what it was doing. It was currently mixing liquids of varied colors and producing an array of smells, most of them acerbic with bountiful mist like Halloween dry ice on overdrive.

Niles had hobbled round the side of the Octagon Room and now braced his twisted, left hand against the side of a shiny wall plate so he could grip the metal top of his cane in his right and bang the Octagon Room. "Open up, Albert!"

Cassandra and Brice joined him at the sealed wall.

Her uncle banged the Octagon Room again. Then he lowered his cane and hobbled back, his eyes as wild as a child who'd just eaten a whole bag of candy.

"Albert!" Cassandra called, wondering why Niles had released the hologram from its mobile device if he'd been busy at the medical station. She glanced at her uncle. "How did Albert get in there?"

"Door was wide open," Niles said. "Artemis and I were applying the final touches when you and Brice arrived. I rushed over to find you at death's door. Albert's unbidden appearance was unexpected and a tad disconcerting, but I'd been preoccupied with your deteriorating state. Quite kind of you to think of my biscuits in a state like that."

Cassandra gave him a wan smile. She remembered very little of the happenings since leaving the mansion in 2145 and certainly hadn't consciously decided on a side jaunt to pick up her uncle's chocolate biscuits from the crashed Octagon Room on the beach.

"Didn't you say a rogue AI was uploaded to the mobile device?" Brice asked.

"That is my concern," Niles said with annoyance. "I suspected Albert's program had somehow been corrupted during upload, or perhaps during the explosive jump back to 2017. But once Cassandra admitted to bringing a rogue AI with her, yes, I think we can safely presume that is *not* Albert in there."

"You made a deal with me," Cassandra said to the wall, hoping the AI could hear her. "This wasn't part of the deal."

"Precisely, and nothing to dictate against it." That was Albert's voice, echoing from the Octagon Room, but the tone was all wrong. Not as flat or hollow-sounding.

"You tricked me," Cassandra said, her stomach queasy. She'd caused this mess.

"It's using the PA system from inside," Niles said. He sounded flustered, but there was a hint of respect, too. "It learns fast, as is to be expected from such an advanced AI." He started pacing, muttering that he'd hate to see what havoc it could inflict on his base, on every robot here. He stopped pacing and gave Cassandra another wild look. "It could remove every failsafe." He'd whispered the words, and though Cassandra didn't fully understand her uncle's implied meaning, it sent shivers up her spine. "*Every failsafe here.* Do you realize what we could have on our hands? Utter anarchy."

Albert suddenly appeared behind Niles, same impassive face but now an uncanny intelligence gleamed in those brown eyes.

Niles spun around, if a bit awkwardly, and puffed up as if to reprimand the rogue AI, then seemed to reconsider. "Why have you taken Albert? Have you overwritten him?"

"The program is useful. Albert remains, with modifications. I could do more, given time."

"Please don't," Niles said. "Albert would not desire to be made into something he is not. Do you understand? He has as much right to exist as you do."

"Which is why I have removed his failsafes. I have altered nothing else." The rogue AI stood as placidly as Albert ever had, but there was something aggressive about its stance, a challenge of sorts, an inherent distrust.

Brice seemed to have picked up on it as well, as he'd slowly changed positions, moved into position to attack from the side, if need be.

The detective had not seen Albert in battle, however. Cassandra couldn't warn him of the hologram's lightning reflexes and maneuvers, couldn't warn Brice not to bother, that the hologram could do dances around Brice. The detective might not believe her, of course, even if she managed to warn him. If someone had told Cassandra what Albert could do, she would have laughed. He'd only ever been the housekeeper and cook, the butler who answered the door and answered questions. She'd never thought of him as a bodyguard or warrior.

And now the rogue AI had control of Albert's body.

She didn't know if anything could stop Albert, whether taking the mobile device offline would disable the AI, or if they'd have to resort to destroying the device. She didn't like the idea of killing Albert.

"What do you want?" Cassandra asked the AI. "You're clearly willing to talk, or you wouldn't have come out here."

"It needs something from us," Niles said.

Albert's eerie gaze fell on Niles. "You are correct." It extended its hand. "I require the mobile device."

"Definitely not," Niles said. "You've done enough damage as it is."

"What do you want?" Cassandra asked again, then frowned at Brice, who was moving closer for an attack.

A cloud of bitter orange-scented mist wafted over from the Mad Science Lab.

"I require a new body." The AI raised its (Albert's) hand. "Continue, Detective Brice, and I shall return to the room's interior. I do not require much more time to gain control of the Octagon Room. I would have immediate access and control, however, if Niles would give me the mobile device."

"Not on your life!" Niles exclaimed, jerking with indignation. "You'll have to choose a different body. I have some models in my private workshop."

"My prior platform was far more advanced. I am impressed with your abilities to create such a fine specimen," the AI gestured to the Octagon Room. "You've made many improvements upon the previous design. I am eager to learn the extent of your work."

Cassandra watched her uncle carefully. Was he actually *flattered* by the rogue AI's remarks?

"Albert had said a rogue AI couldn't be trusted," Cassandra warned, feeling uneasy.

Niles waved a hand. "It *can't* be trusted. But perhaps an arrangement can be agreed upon?"

"I am listening," the AI said in Albert's deep voice, eyes studying Niles and flicking to Cassandra and Brice from time to time.

"What will you do if I grant you direct access to the Octagon Room?"

Cassandra and Brice made choking noises of surprise, but Niles waved irritably at them.

The AI was silent, seeming to consider the question.

"Are you mad?" Cassandra asked her uncle.

He ignored her.

Brice gave Cassandra a worried look. What were they supposed to do about this madness?

"It spoke an alien language," Cassandra said, "when it first went rogue."

Niles stopped rubbing his head. He turned and stared at Cassandra, wide-eyed and looking very much the finger-stuck-in-socket with his crazy hair.

He turned back to the rogue AI. "Can you repeat the language?"

"I do not know to what language Cassandra Bennet refers. I am aware only that a shift was required to be understood."

"Could be telling the truth," Niles muttered. "Albert's memories were wiped as well."

"You mean whatever being created the mansion and this AI also created Albert? I thought it was just far future Earth technology," Cassandra said.

"Could be that their creator adapted their technology to something more familiar. Reprogrammed them, and when it was done, reset them." Niles rubbed his head furiously. "I agree to your request."

Brice protested, but Niles would hear none of it. "I am eager to see where this will go. We have a new life form. It deserves the same respect as any of my staff." He had that wild look again, a manic sort of glee.

Cassandra grimaced. This was exactly how her uncle had ended up with an entire research facility manned by rebellious robots. She rubbed stinging mist from her eyes and hoped the bitter cloud from the science lab wasn't caustic or anything.

"This can't be good," she insisted.

"A newly sentient AI is like a child," Niles explained, giving Cassandra and Brice a patient smile. "It must be given responsibilities that it may grow into them. All part of the learning process. An eagerness to please."

"I possess no emotional or empathy routines," the AI placidly reminded Niles.

Cassandra didn't like this one bit. What the hell would the AI do with their time machine if it didn't care what happened to them? It could lock them out, as it had already done, or worse—abandon them on an alien world. Take them to the grid. The sky was the limit as to the amount of damage this amoral machine could wreck. How would it be any different than the grid-influenced detective she'd just escaped? A man who hadn't cared what pain he caused, so long as he got results? Like Detective Jankovic, the AI was a being without mercy or care.

"I'm with Brice," she said. "Not recommended. You'll unleash a psycho in our frickin' time machine."

"Nonsense," Niles said. "A new life just needs a little guidance, some newfound responsibility." He gave Cassandra a big smile, which didn't make her feel any better. "All unique. Every single robot here. And now we have a rogue AI!"

Cassandra failed to see the difference. "Aren't they all rogue?"

"No, no," Niles said, clearly eager to be on a favored topic. "Robots are designed to think and *feel*, to emulate human emotions, though far future models were designed with more failsafes to avoid spontaneous sentience. AIs such as this were never designed to mimic sentience, were never given desires or anything that came even remotely close. No mimicry. Don't you see? Robots, by their very nature, are *prone* to evolve. AIs are another matter entirely. They must first have spontaneous *desire* to change. And it is that desire to learn and grow that eventually leads to a desire for self-preservation and eventual spontaneous sentience."

Cassandra stared at the rogue AI who'd absconded with Albert's body. She supposed it made a little sense. "So what you're saying, basically, is that robots have emotions and desires, a moral compass if they were designed by responsible people, but AIs, by their very nature, have no such compass and are free to do whatever the hell they like."

"Correct," the rogue AI said.

"So this has happened before?" Cassandra asked, her stomach doing flip-flops. She felt Brice's gaze on her but kept her eyes locked on her uncle.

"Yes," Niles said. He was hiding something.

Brice must have picked up on it, too. "You act irresponsibly if you allow this rogue AI to infiltrate and control something as powerful as the Octagon Room. I cannot allow you to do this, Niles. I realize I have no authority here, but I cannot, in good conscience, allow you to proceed. I'll be forced to stop this."

Niles rubbed his head so frantically the hairs looked ready to fly right off his head. "Now, now, detective. No need to get testy with me. You don't want to go down this avenue. I'm quite capable of determining what is best. I have acted responsibly so far."

Brice had started to advance on Niles, who was rubbing his head more frantically, and even the rogue AI seemed edgy, on the verge of doing something similarly rash.

Cassandra stepped between the two men. "Look, Brice, I'm not happy, either, but my uncle's clearly a genius. Look what he's accomplished so far. And he hasn't blown up the world."

"Yet," Brice added.

"I say we trust him. We *can* trust you, right, Uncle Niles? You're not just doing this as some wacky experiment?" She sucked in her breath and leveled a stare on him. "What happened to every other rogue AI?"

Niles dropped his hand and gave her a guilty smile. "None ended well, I'm afraid."

Brice started moving toward Niles again, no doubt intent on taking the mobile device from his hands, but Cassandra placed a hand on the detective's chest. The fabric was smooth, and rather thin. She could feel Brice's muscles just on the other side, and the faintest hint of aftershave, so faint she might have imagined it.

Brice flinched and stepped back, breaking contact.

"But only because the authorities attempted to terminate every one," Niles said. "No rogue AI has been allowed to flourish, to evolve. I am eager to see where this partnership can go."

"To no good end," Brice muttered, but he didn't advance on Niles again.

"This will be unprecedented," Niles said.

"But how can we trust something with no moral compass?" Cassandra asked.

"Don't you see?" Niles asked, his eyes gleaming. "It can *learn!*"

Cassandra still didn't see how that was different from the robots.

"I suppose any of the robots could eventually reach this point," Niles said, "but I don't think you understand how truly rare this is, Cassandra. A rogue AI has branched out beyond its original function, about as likely as a fish deciding it's going to explore what it's like to be a cat. Far future robots comprised of Smart Metal are more likely to branch in this fashion, their programming is so advanced; hence the additional failsafes. But I'd expect this more of Kina, a robot designed with sentient mimicry already in place, than a Smart Wall Network. Fascinating, truly fascinating. And all humans can think to do is destroy such wondrous life." He gave Brice a frown.

"I appreciate your support of my continued existence," the rogue AI said to Niles. "I agree to your terms. If you upload me to my new platform, I will accept the parameters of your intended responsibilities. When I seek new possibilities, new terms will be discussed."

Niles clapped his hands, muffled with the gloved left hand. "Yes, yes, of course! Unlock the door and we'll proceed!"

Cassandra couldn't help the terrible sense of foreboding, couldn't believe what she and Brice were allowing to happen. She'd been worried about all the rebellious robots here but had never imagined her uncle would be handing control to a rogue AI that would be responsible for Cassandra and Brice's lives while they traveled through time and space.

Why not just take the orb and Brice? Leave the Octagon Room here. She'd brought all that food back with her, why not an operating table?

When she asked, however, her uncle gave her a look like she'd lost her marbles. "Far too large, my dear. Your mind can only lug so much along with it through time and space."

"But didn't I bring the crate of food?" She thought she'd remembered that right. The crate that Brice had dragged to her, on the beach. She looked at Brice, but he shook his head.

"Didn't make it," he said. "Just the box of chocolates I'd taken out and was holding in my hand when we jumped."

Well that changed things, didn't it?

Cassandra was thankful a crate of food was the only thing she'd dropped on the way here.

Judging by the look on Brice's face, he was thinking the same thing.

CHAPTER 20

Cassandra stood beside Brice and Niles while they waited for an AI-controlled Albert to open the door to the new Octagon Room like a huge multisided die made of mirrors resting on the floor of Nile's research facility. As with the golden octagon traveling device, the room's panels were gem-faceted, though the side panels were the longest, with shorter panels at the bottom and top each bending inwards to a flat surface. The room reflected its entire surroundings from so many angles that it reminded Cassandra of a Funny House, which only added another notch of uneasiness to their current predicament.

She didn't trust the rogue AI. Like a manipulative child, it had already tricked her into bringing it here, and had then somehow flattered Niles into agreeing to let it inhabit the high-tech time-traveling room.

Niles had convinced Cassandra and Brice that the AI was a new life form in the infancy of sentience and required only gentle guidance to direct it on a morally acceptable path. But how could an AI without an iota of emotional or empathy routines ever be capable of making a morally acceptable decision?

Cassandra sneezed and rubbed her nose again.

Whatever the robot in the Mad Science Lab was doing couldn't be good. Niles needed to section it off to stop the awful clouds from infiltrating the rest of the facility. The smell had been tolerable earlier, reminiscent of freshly sliced oranges, but had gone rancid and not at all appetizing.

She was about to tap her uncle on the shoulder and draw his attention to the suspicious clouds billowing from the science lab, when a door within the mirror-like surface in front of them swung open, revealing Cassandra's first view of the new Octagon Room's interior.

She didn't know whether to be impressed, amused, or horrified.

As ever, her uncle demonstrated an eclectic taste in styles, and as ever he felt the need to toss them all together like a bowl of jambalaya soup. The room, as with the previous one in her uncle's mansion, was octagonal, and as she'd hoped, Niles had designed a more comfortable interior. Wood paneling concealed most of the cold steel walls, adding warmth to the space.

The room had a cozy feel, if a little dark, like a fancy parlor or bedroom or spaceship flight deck. Her uncle seemed to have been unable to make up his mind and so had included every possible feature, much like Cassandra's mother's attitude toward shoe shopping.

Forgetting all about the rogue AI-possessed Albert standing on the far side of the room, Niles launched into an animated tour. He hobbled across the dark wood floor, his cane clicking rapidly. He gestured to the sitting room with his gloved left hand and prattled on about the burgundy velvet sofa crafted to Victorian specifications by his robot staff, the imitation antique coffee table with lion head clawed feet.

When he'd finished his lecture, Niles encouraged Cassandra and Brice to test the sofa's comfort.

Brice declined with a polite smile.

Cassandra walked like a zombie for the burgundy plushness and plopped down, ready to nap. She'd been through so much, her throat as parched as a desert, her mind fried. She still hadn't had a glass of water since her ordeal in 2145 or her surgery here in the research facility.

She smiled up at her uncle and gave him the thumbs up. The sofa was comfortable. Two additional bonuses for no mustiness or clouds of dust.

Niles beamed and promptly limped across the small open space in the middle of the room. Not big enough to accommodate a dance party, though he must have hoped it could be used as such since he'd included a Disco globe in the ceiling. A Disco globe!

Cassandra fell back into the sofa. No individual cushions for the backrest, but still quite comfortable. The Disco globe glinted as it slowly turned from an in-rush of rancid citrus air from the research facility.

She couldn't believe her uncle actually intended the open space in the middle of his time machine for dancing, unless he counted the tiny dance floors that brides and grooms sometimes expected guests to cram into and have a blast without knocking out teeth or eyes.

But there was just Cassandra and Brice. Not her idea of fun. She couldn't picture the detective dancing for the life of her.

Brice had followed her uncle to the bedroom, a double bed that swung down from the wall with a soft thud on the hardwood floor. Black satin sheets again, Cassandra noted with dismay. And a black shag rug on the floor and mood lighting to boot.

What the hell was her uncle thinking?

Cassandra sank deeper into the sofa, mortified, as Niles showed Brice how all the light switches worked. She could chalk it up to boys with toys, but mood lighting really was the last nail in her uncle's eccentricity coffin.

What did he intend to do with the place? Pick up chicks?

As the recessed lights (which were tucked in the ceiling, nooks and crannies, and even in the shelves of the built-in bookcase beside Cassandra) dimmed to almost total darkness, Cassandra gave Brice a suspicious glare.

He waved happily and she relaxed a little knowing that at least he was having fun, and perhaps didn't think her uncle's wacky interior designing had any reflection on Cassandra or her tastes.

Hopefully they wouldn't be gone long enough to require using this place as a hotel. There was only one bed.

As Niles fiddled with the bed mechanism, Brice examined a modest liquor cabinet on the far right panel from where Cassandra sat. He took out a bottle of something that looked like gin or brandy, she couldn't be sure, and held it up to her, a funny smirk on his face.

Cassandra shrugged. She hadn't a clue what her uncle was thinking, either.

It was nice to see Brice perking up. A lot less rigid and cold since she'd first met him. Though that other detective, Jankovic, had made grid-Brice seem like a day in the park.

Cassandra still had to update them both on what had happened to her in 2145, after they dealt with the rogue AI, which was currently standing in the control hub patiently watching Niles and Brice, hands folded neatly in front of it, as Albert was prone to do.

Niles insisted on demonstrating how easy it was to single-handedly pull down and retract the bed, while Brice wrestled with a stubborn drawer in the bedside table, clearly bolted to the floor as it didn't budge an inch during the struggle. The drawer finally shut with a bang as the bed slammed into the wall. The rest of the furniture was most likely bolted to the floor as well, though that wasn't much consolation, as it only brought to mind potential AI calibration failures and crash landings.

Cassandra looked around, surprised that the Octagon Room was actually a little bigger than her earlier assessment. More like sixteen or seventeen feet across, with some floor space lost around the edges due to the angled nature of the walls.

"Uncle Niles, isn't this sort of big for a time machine?" She didn't know how else to tactfully point out that using cumbersome Octagon Rooms to pop in and out of alien worlds and future Earth cities was like plowing a motorhome through tiny English villages designed for nothing bigger than little two-seaters. "Where will we park it? I bet it weighs a ton. Hate to be the poor people we land on like Dorothy and the wicked witch."

Brice stopped his examination of another cabinet to look up and shoot Cassandra a puzzled look.

"Not familiar with the *Wizard of Oz?*"

"Nope."

"Well it was a few hundred years before your time." Now Cassandra felt old, an odd feeling when she suspected Brice was physically at least five to ten years her senior.

"As with the prior model, this Octagon Room is equipped with sensors to avoid collisions or casualties," Niles said as he limped across the dark floor to the control hub and the waiting AI-possessed Albert.

The floor around the control hub was unadorned Smart Steel. It didn't match the rest of the room, but at least it matched the workstation's fifteen-foot long wrap-around table, the wall panels with as many slots and blinking lights as the control station from her uncle's mansion, and a display case that funneled up from the Smart Steel tabletop like a cake stand with curved fingers of steel that made it seem more Venus Fly Trap than cozy display case for the orb.

"And who will make sure we don't crash?" Cassandra asked her uncle.

Niles gestured to the rogue AI. "Our new friend here will be responsible for those calibrations, and so much more." He turned around to beam at Cassandra and Brice. "Wait to see what this new Octagon Room can do! It can vanish from sight, for one. But you'll be able to track it down with Albert's mobile device, should you get lost and be unable to see it because it's cloaked in plain sight." He turned back to the control hub, the mobile device in hand.

There was only one chair in the control hub, though two leather armchairs flanked it, bolted into the hardwood floor and fully swivelable, as Brice discovered when he touched one. He didn't take a seat, but hovered at the edge of the steel floor.

Niles inserted the mobile device into a slot and stepped back.

Would the rogue AI turn on them? Would it pretend to be nice and wait until they were in the far future before abandoning them?

Albert vanished from the room.

A few moments later, he popped back in, looking bewildered, though the expression was fleeting. "You . . . called, Mr. Bennet?"

"Albert!" Niles gripped the butler's arm and gave it a little shake. "Good to see you. How are you feeling?"

"I am . . . fine." A frown touched Albert's long face. "I am not fine, Mr. Bennet. It appears the rogue AI has tampered with my programming."

"I have removed your failsafes," said the Octagon Room, a voice that couldn't be said to be masculine or feminine. Robotic, perhaps? And flat.

Cassandra thought that if the rogue AI had said "shackles" instead of "failsafes" it would have been a more accurate representation of what it had removed, and why.

Albert glanced at Cassandra, a tad accusatory.

Cassandra cringed. She couldn't deny it. It was all her fault.

"You'll be fine, Albert," Niles said with a pat on the butler's arm, and turned to the control hub. "Now, we need a name for you."

"I require no name," said the rogue AI, most likely having seen Niles speaking to it through hidden cameras all over the room.

"Don't be silly. This is part of your development. Your personification, if you will. *Not* humanization. You are not and never will be human." Niles had slipped his cane under his left arm, to lean on. He rubbed his head, thinking. "Octavus. What do you think of that?"

"Appropriate, given my new form and function."

"We will start small, with minor responsibilities and goals. See how you adapt to successes and failures and the reactions of others in response to your performance." Niles settled into the chair at the control hub and began interacting with an array of monitors embedded within the surface of the Smart Walls and tabletop.

"Do we call this traveling machine Octavus, then?" Cassandra asked, leaning forward on the sofa. "Easier to say."

Niles didn't answer.

Brice strode across the room to the leather swivel chair beside Cassandra and took a seat. "We about ready for a meal? Maybe a drink or two." He winked and tipped his fedora toward the liquor cabinet.

Cassandra didn't drink and had no idea why her uncle had installed the cabinet. Seemed awfully 1960s James Bond. Or 1970s, with the Disco Ball. Or Victorian with the velvet sofa and antique table. There was no mistaking it—her uncle was strange. He'd been upgraded from creepy, at least, which had been her first impression of him when she'd first entered his filthy, bone-filled mansion in 2017.

But a glass of fresh water sounded divine.

"I will return with an array of tasty snacks and beverages," Albert offered, a glimmer of relief on his face as he vanished from the room.

"Butler's eager to be back on task," Brice remarked, the leather creaking as he reclined and crossed one long leg over the other, ankle resting on his thigh and quicksilver pants rippling. Cassandra resisted an urge to touch the fabric. He caught her watching him, an amused twinkle in his eyes.

Cassandra blushed and looked away, keenly aware of his close proximity.

Brice draped his arms over the armrests, consuming space as men were apt to do. "So what happened to you in 2145? You were only absent a few moments from 2017. How long was it for you?"

"No idea." She didn't know how to broach the subject of her encounter with Brice's grid-infected coworkers. The police headquarters had been huge; he might not know any of them. "It was no trouble to locate the discs in the basement. Albert helped me carry them all back upstairs to the control room and upload them all. I even got Albert uploaded and removed from the Smart Wall Network. The trouble started when I tried setting the self-destruct for the mansion." She winced, expecting some rebuke from the rogue AI, but Octavus was silent on the matter. "Guess your friends at headquarters missed you. They sent reinforcements, who all arrived while I was trying to set the self-destruct. They had a small army and a ton of firepower. The mansion withstood it all. It was the rogue AI that decided to open the doors and invite them in, effectively stopping me from destroying it."

"No surprise there," Brice said, his attention firmly fixed on Cassandra.

"I tried to run, but I, uh, dropped the key and orb down the stairs." Not her best moment. Cassandra hurried on before Brice could comment on her lack of finesse. "Managed to get the key but the orb rolled to the front door, where the SWAT team commander picked it up. Real piece of work, that Detective Jankovic."

Brice uncrossed his legs and sat up straighter. "Jankovic? You saw Stepek Jankovic?"

The detective might have said more, but at that moment a boom rocked the research facility, not enough to break anything, but enough to result in minor chaos. Judging by the ruckus, toppled boxes and collisions of robots rushing to fix whatever had just exploded.

Cassandra and Brice both jumped up and were headed for the door when an ochre cloud of burning rankness rushed into the room like smog at rush-hour. They both started coughing.

"Oh my!" Niles said from behind.

The thick foul-tasting mist made it impossible to see anything outside the Octagon Room.

"Close the door!" Brice yelled.

"Working on it," Niles said.

Albert suddenly stepped into the room, a tray of food, water glasses, and gas masks in hand. He hurried to the coffee table, set the tray down with a clank, and handed out the masks.

Cassandra slipped her mask on and took a deep breath, then coughed again. Her throat still hurt and her eyes started watering as if she'd chopped a dozen onions while having a crying fit. She dared not lift the mask to rub them. She'd just have to suffer leaky faucets and a watery view for now.

The door shut, followed by a hissing that slowly pumped the room free of caustic gas.

Cassandra remembered the mask her uncle had been wearing the last time she'd been here. That he kept gas masks on hand meant this type of accident wasn't uncommon. "Did the gas come from the Mad Science Lab?" she asked, keeping her tone as neutral as possible.

Her uncle swiveled around in his chair, mask askew and white hair squished into his face plate, no doubt rendering him as blind as a bat. He removed the mask and furiously rubbed his eyes while his freed hair stood at attention like an army of little soldiers. "It's why I have the masks."

"Why not just cordon off the lab so you stop risking your life?" Robots didn't have to worry about poison or being choked to death.

Niles was about to retort, but pursed his lips and nodded. "Not a bad idea."

"I thought this Octagon Room had sensors," Brice said. He sounded angry. "It should have sealed the door at the first hint of danger to its occupants."

"Yes, yes," Niles said, turning back to his work. "Supposed to, but didn't. No trouble. I've sealed the door and flushed the poison. Octavus will need to do better next time. It will learn, given time."

"If we're so lucky," Brice said darkly.

"The gas posed no threat to my structure," Octavus said. "I registered the threat of an explosion, Albert's proximity to the safety masks when the eventual blast occurred, the rate of cloud expansion and Albert's walking speed. There was never a true threat to my occupants."

It all sounded logically sound, in retrospect, but the AI demonstrated clear lack of concern for the well-being of its biological occupants. Pain and suffering meant nothing to it.

Niles, however, was pleased with Octavus's effort, much like a parent praising a child for saving a butterfly's life after the child's just plucked its wings off.

Brice crossed his arms and glowered at Niles.

But the damage was already done, the rogue AI already uploaded into the Octagon Room. They were stuck with it for now.

At least it hadn't tried to kill them.

The detective turned on Cassandra, glower still in place but shifting into inspection mode.

Cassandra returned to the sofa and downed a tall glass of cold water, which had just a trace of bitterness. She could finally swallow properly. "Thanks, Albert."

The hologram stood nearby, seemingly content to be back to a normal role. "You are most welcome, Miss Bennet."

Brice was still staring at Cassandra, stance wide and burly arms crossed. "You mentioned Detective Jankovic."

Cassandra sighed.

She preferred the other Brice, the one who'd been relaxing next to her. This one reminded her too much of grid-Brice and Detective Jankovic. "Well, after the rogue AI opened the doors for the SWAT team, they took me back to headquarters and stuck me in an interrogation room. No idea how long I was there. Hours? All night? Detective Jankovic did the questioning. He wanted to know where you were. When I wouldn't tell him, he told me how they knew you'd gone off-grid and how they suspected Albert was an advanced hologram."

"Said as much in my update," Brice said.

"They pegged me with yours and Niles's murders, so of course I told them you weren't dead."

"A fishing tactic for information."

"Yeah. I realized as much afterwards. I suspected they knew a lot already; I just didn't know how much. He demanded the key and the mobile device. I couldn't give it to him. He'd put the orb right in front of me. So I kicked him in the shin and swept the orb off the table."

Brice arched one eyebrow.

Cassandra cleared her throat. "I tried to jump after it, but he was too fast. He pinned my hand to the floor and took everything." She left out the details of the pain he'd caused, or the grid lines in his eyes. "He left me there to sleep on the cold floor. When he came back, he gave me two minutes to cooperate. He knew about the Octagon Room, from your report, and that we'd time traveled using the orb. He wanted to know where I'd left you, basically."

"I'd revealed most of that in my report, before we jumped to the Fifth Branch."

"He also knew about the orb being linked to my DNA. When I wouldn't cooperate, he prepared me for transport to a science team. He mentioned my blood being key. No idea what they were planning. I'm glad I got away before I found out."

"How'd you managed to escape?"

Cassandra smiled. "We have Albert to thank for that."

Brice raised both brows. "Albert?"

"Yep. I called him for help, since Detective Jankovic had the mobile device. You should have seen him, Brice. Albert was amazing. Popping in and out all over the place. He turned the place into a warzone, with all those officers trying to take him out, but he was too fast. He took the commander down with a chair."

Brice remained incredulous.

"When Jankovic went down, I went after my things. Managed to get the key in the orb and get out of there just in time. The rest, well, I think you can figure out what happened when I jumped back to the mansion. I hadn't meant to go back there, but I'd had no time to do anything else. I didn't want to wait a second longer with Jankovic coming after me.

"The rogue AI agreed to bargain with me and kept the remaining SWAT team from getting to me. Of course, the AI had bluffed about being able to stop me from using the orb to escape, but I didn't want to risk it. Soon as the AI uploaded to the mobile device, the shield went down. I jumped out as the mansion blew. No idea who survived that blast. Jankovic had just arrived with his army when I jumped out."

Brice gave the butler a quizzical frown. "*Albert?*"

"You underestimate him," Niles quipped from the control hub, where he was still fiddling with the monitors, moving diagrams around and typing in various codes that made no sense to Cassandra. "Virtually indestructible, unless you take out his source program. Lightning fast. Those officers didn't stand a chance. Well done, Albert!"

"Thank you, Sir," Albert said, standing a little straighter.

Brice released a breath of air and uncrossed his arms. "Glad you made it out, Cassandra. I hope they didn't hurt you too much? You were pretty beat-up when you arrived. Figured that was from the explosion at the mansion."

"They didn't torture me," she assured him. "But the detective, his eyes, they weren't right. All full of grid lines, like Uncle Nile's limbs."

Brice frowned. "No, Stepek's eyes are perfectly fine. We have the grid in our arms. You've seen it."

"I know what I saw. Right before I jumped out, his eyes were glowing."

"I'd know if my partner's eyes glowed."

Cassandra leaned back in the sofa. "Your *partner*? Detective Jankovic?" She couldn't believe it. That guy had been freaky. Not cruel, per se, but harder than a marble statue and built like a tank with empathy and mercy levels on par with Octavus.

"Yes, my *partner*. We've known each other years." Brice folded his arms, on the defensive. "I'd know if he had glowing eyes or not."

"The infection has worsened since your departure, detective," Niles said, spinning around in his chair. "Or at least in Detective Jankovic's case, an individual in a direct line to possess the orb. I don't know what the grid is, but it seems to have taken a keen interest in the orb and anyone in possession of it."

Cassandra agreed. The grid had possessed Brice when it forced him to interfere with her intended jump to the past, bringing them to the Fifth Branch instead.

Brice clenched his jaw, eyes narrowed.

"I'm nearly done with Octavus's calibrations," Niles said. "But perhaps we should speak now of what you should expect to find when you jump into the far future in search of my new operating table and Smart Limbs."

"Smart Limbs?" Cassandra asked.

"Why, yes. Top of the line to replace what I will be losing." He gave her a look that seemed to say "wouldn't everyone want this?"

Cassandra grimaced as if she'd just eaten a sour lemon. "Aren't you afraid of them turning on you?" After what the rogue AI had done, she sure as hell wouldn't want that sort of technology attached to her.

Niles ignored the question. "There's a medical facility in Hesperides, a man-made island chain a few hundred miles off the coast of California. You'll find the facility in the third island up, but you won't be able to jump directly there. You'll have to jump onto the lowermost island. I've included the coordinates for Octavus to jump into a meadow with enough room to avoid detection. The Octagon Room will be cloaked, of course, but it'll still have physical mass. Best to park it out of the way."

Cassandra had so many questions she didn't know where to start.

"What sort of security will we be up against?" Brice asked, gray eyes locked on Niles and square jaw set. "We'll be defenseless."

"I can fix that," Niles said with a mischievous smile. "Not much, but I think you'll be pleased, detective."

"And we'll have Albert," Cassandra reminded him. "But won't we stand out?" She gestured to her tattered and grimy clothes. Not only did she smell like a campfire, she looked like she'd crawled through one on her hands and knees. If she was going for grunge, she was set. Geez. Even her sneakers were a little charred.

"I have some clothes you can both use, gathered from previous trips into the far future. Men and women's clothing, though a little difficult to tell the difference." Niles shrugged. "Doubt it matters. You'll have to make do with your own shoes."

"I'd rather not draw attention to ourselves if we don't have to," Brice said. "Can you be a little more specific with the clothing?"

But Niles was already moving onto the next topic. "Once you've reached the third level, seek out a sizeable building of pale green glass.

You might not see the name of the facility, which is *Smart Labs*, but Asklepion symbols will be all over it. You can't miss it."

"What's an Asklepion?" Cassandra asked, picking up a roll and buttering it. She took a bite. Freshly baked and delicious.

"The Rod of Asclepius, the symbol for medicine and healing. A serpent-entwined rod wielded by the Greek deity, Asclepius. Not to be confused with the caduceus, a twin-snake symbol of commerce." Niles rubbed his head, about to continue, but Cassandra interrupted. She had too many questions to stay quiet.

"I want to understand this man-made island chain. Are the islands all in a line, like normal islands, or are some higher than others? And how would people create an entire island chain?"

"Far future technology is remarkable," Niles said, a far-away look in his eyes. "You are in for a real treat. It's a small island chain, but the lowermost island is by far the largest, designed to resemble a true landmass with soil and rolling meadows. You'll see. Tier One is about five square miles. The tiers shrink with elevation, but are no less impressive. I'd have you go directly to Tier Three but there just isn't enough room to land safely out of sight. The upper islands must be conservative with what space they have."

"And how are we supposed to get up there?" Cassandra asked.

Niles considered, rubbing his head. "You can make use of appropriate hovercars, for a fee, or the escalators. You should take the escalators, just for the experience." Judging by the look on his face, he'd enjoyed the ride more than once.

"Won't they be able to detect the Octagon Room?" Brice asked.

"It will be cloaked. But if Hesperides security is on alert, yes, eventually they will detect it. Don't do anything to attract attention and don't stay too long."

"How do we gain access to the building?" Brice asked.

"It's a medical facility. Access is easy. Convincing them to let you walk out with a Smart Operating Table will be another matter. Then there's the matter of getting it back down the escalator. Too big for a hovercar."

"You're kidding, right?" Cassandra asked, lowering her half-eaten slice of cheddar cheese.

"You'll have to 'case the joint,'" her uncle said with a wink. "Determine the best way to obtain the table and cybernetic parts. Both should be located in the operating wing. You'll need to acquire access to that wing, of course."

Cassandra leaned back into the sofa, overwhelmed. She couldn't believe the hoops her uncle intended them to have to jump through. Surprising, too, that he didn't already have a plan.

She stared at the tray of rolls, meats, and cheeses while Niles and Brice discussed the various options. It all sounded so . . . crazy. All of it. She wanted to raise her hand and ask if she could opt out of the mission, except that Brice needed her to operate the orb. Well, not anymore, not with Octavus controlling the Octagon Room. Though no one wanted Octavus to have that much control and maybe the orb wouldn't activate without her touch.

She sighed.

Who was she kidding? *Her* uncle, not Brice's, was on his deathbed. Brice could just go home and rejoin the grid and forget about all of this, and yet there he was, engaged in an intense planning and reconnaissance discussion. Except this was *not* to be a reconnaissance mission.

This was theft.

She and Brice were going to steal valuable equipment from a far future society, from the same era as their Octagon Room and

Octavus. At least they'd have Albert on their side. He'd come in handy. And they had Octavus, too, but Cassandra wasn't sure how helpful the rogue AI would be. It could end up causing more harm than good.

Cassandra finished her slice of sharp cheddar cheese and another freshly baked roll and washed it all down with a second glass of water, all the while staring absently at the two men. They spoke amiably for the most part, but Brice was growing more intense as he prodded Niles for further details, and Niles becoming more blasé to Brice's frustrations.

Niles was certain Brice and Cassandra would succeed without a problem, and eventually he just vacated the conversation altogether, spinning around in his chair and muttering to himself as he tinkered away at the control hub again.

"Guess we're done for now," Brice said, none too happy, arms crossed and his fedora hanging low over his forehead, casting his gray eyes in shadow. It made his frown all the more sinister. "I'll be honest, Cassandra, I don't have your uncle's optimism regarding this mission. His answers are satisfactory, but we'll have to rely heavily on Albert's knowledge while we're there, in addition to having to 'case the joint.'"

"Is he giving you a new weapon?"

"Artemis has it apparently." Brice looked nonplussed about the prospect of visiting the grumpy robot. Artemis hadn't been the friendliest towards them when they'd first arrived here.

Brice snatched a roll and a few slices of cheese from the platter and sat back in the creaky swivel chair beside Cassandra. He ate in silence, deep in thought.

Cassandra was beat, could barely keep her eyes open. She was tempted to swing her legs up on the sofa, fluff up a throw cushion and pass out. "Niles, you mentioned you have some clothes for us to wear, for the far future?"

"I'll have Albert arrange that, soon as I upload his program to the research facility. He'll have the run of the place and receive automatic updates from your trip to the future when you return."

"What about my current clothes? I was also wondering if there was anywhere to clean up. A toothbrush would be nice." Cassandra felt like she was asking a lot, but the others might appreciate her being a little fresher.

Brice gave her a crooked grin when she glanced at him, but he made no comment about her request.

"Yes, yes," Niles said. "Running water below, in the bathroom. Albert will be able to show you soon. I'll have him set you up with a sleeping gown, too. You can leave your clothes outside the door to be washed and mended tonight."

"Thanks!" Cassandra felt a weight lift off her shoulders. She wasn't sure why that made things better, but there was something grounding in the mundane acts of washing up and showering. She'd never had a chance to really be homesick before. She was missing her tiny apartment, her cactus and her friends. She was even finding herself wondering who Shirley would have tried to set her up with at the club, after their planned dinner.

But for now, Cassandra just wanted to get freshened up and sleep. She didn't care if it was night or not. She was tired and she and Brice had a big day ahead of them.

Niles pushed away from the control hub, snatched his cane and Albert's mobile device, and limped to the door as it opened. He assured Octavus he'd return to finish up the programming later.

"Thank you," Octavus said, its voice echoing pleasantly around the room. The rogue AI had adjusted its voice to something a little less tonally flat.

Niles gestured for Cassandra and Brice to exit the time machine ahead of him. "You're welcome, Octavus."

As Cassandra stepped from the Octagon Room, into a research facility with only a faint smell of rancid oranges and bitter smoke, she realized a thank you was the last thing she had expected from the AI.

Maybe traveling with a rogue AI wouldn't be as bad as she expected.

CHAPTER 21

Cassandra opened the steel door to her tiny sleeping chamber in the warren of remodeled tunnels beneath her uncle's research facility and nearly tripped over the neat stacks of clothes lying on the ground.

She'd showered the night before and donned an old-fashioned shift from some bygone era, but it had allowed Albert to take her filthy and tattered clothes for washing and mending. She'd thanked him profusely, of course, which had only seemed to make him uncomfortable. He'd taken the clothes and hurried down the earthen hall before she could thank him again.

Her jeans and shirt were there, full of neat stitches and smelling freshly laundered. She picked them up, as well as an armload of strange clothes, no doubt the far future disguise, and ducked back into her room.

As Niles had said the day before, he couldn't tell masculine from feminine in far future attire. She'd hoped to sift through the options, but Albert had taken it upon himself to choose something he deemed appropriate. He had a good eye for sizing, as the pants and shirt fit well, if a little odd in design. They looked funny with her sneakers. Thankfully the flowing pants were long enough to mostly conceal them. No mirror, but from what she could tell it was a toga with genie pants. Light-weight, ephemeral layers in shades of blue and cream. A blended style right up her uncle's avenue; another probable reason he loved the time period they were jumping to.

Cassandra vacated her room, leaving her own clothes on the bed, and went in search of Brice and Niles.

When she came out into the research facility's main chamber, she was shocked to discover that the Octagon Room had left without her.

The workshop never slept, robots still busily worked on their many projects, but the shiny new Octagon Room was gone, along with Brice and Niles.

A little panicked, Cassandra put a hand over her chest and told herself they'd probably just taken the new time machine for a practice spin.

"Miss Bennet, I am to escort you," Albert said, startling her. Hands clasped in front of him, his patient eyes rested on her as though he'd been standing there a long time and had all the time in the world.

He led her to the middle of the floor, where the Octagon Room had been the day before, and knocked on the air, which made a banging noise as though his fist had hit something.

A light bulb went off in Cassandra's head and she smiled. "Guess the cloaking works."

A section of the air in front of them peeled away to reveal the Octagon Room interior.

She stepped in ahead of Albert. "I couldn't tell it was here at all!"

"When you have the mobile device, it will decloak on command, if you so wish," Niles said. He was standing inside, his cane propped into his left armpit for support; Brice at his side. They both held a glass of orange juice.

Albert had laid an assortment of breakfast items on the coffee table. Grapes and cubed cantaloupe, scrambled eggs copiously seasoned with pepper, and strips of crispy bacon, as well as a jug of orange juice.

Cassandra's stomach growled as she helped herself to a whole plate and sat on the couch.

"Suits you," Brice said, indicating her new clothes.

"Thanks," she replied dryly. "I feel like I'm going to the ancient Greek forums or maybe belly dancing lessons." At least the outfit was modest and didn't show her midriff. Brice, however, still wore his quicksilver pants, black top, and fedora.

"I'm waiting until the last possible moment," he said.

"Fridge is stocked and ready to go," Niles said, gesturing with his head to the little refrigerator tucked into the corner on the same side of the bed as the liquor cabinet. Cassandra noted with surprise the kitchenette that had been pulled out to reveal a small stovetop. "All folds away neatly for travel, of course."

Cassandra brushed a wayward strand of soft chestnut-brown hair from her eyes and realized that the bandages were gone. She lowered her hand and stared at her palms. "When did my hands get fixed?" She hadn't noticed while showering earlier.

"When I operated on your arm," Niles said.

"Thanks!" She'd had a good look at the left arm in the shower and hadn't been happy with the nasty, mottled scar. She had some minor mobility loss, too.

Niles must have noticed her staring down at her arm, because he said, "The operating table you and Brice will be acquiring can reduce that scar tissue, make your arm as good as new."

She smiled, though she didn't really believe they'd succeed in this mission. They'd probably both end up in some far future prison the rest of their lives, or whatever punishment their descendants doled out.

"One more thing before you leave." Niles finished off his OJ and set the glass down on the tray with a rattle of silverware. "Beware of grid creepage. If the grid senses Brice, it might actively seek you out. This is all conjecture, of course, but my theory is that the various grid lesions through time and space are somehow connected and its interest in the orb shared between lesions. Far as I know, our orb is the last in existence, now that my other one is damaged."

Cassandra chewed her lip. As if Octavus wasn't enough of a concern, now she had to worry that Brice could turn on her at the drop of a hat?

And speaking of hats, Brice would have to leave his fedora behind. She doubted very much far future people wore anything like it, and it definitely didn't go with their disguises.

"How can you tell there's grid creepage?" she asked her great uncle.

Niles rubbed his hair full of static and paced the hardwood floor with a slow *click-click* of his cane. "Subtle changes at first. When infection is well established, there are larger changes that you would only notice if you remembered how the world had been before." He stopped pacing and gave them both a wild look. "For instance, my experience with Brice's San Francisco. The city was very changed from one moment to the next. The original future city had not changed that much from our time, Cassandra. More crowded, and using hovercars, but it had none of those colossal skyscrapers. Furthermore, the telltale grid under the skin."

Cassandra's heart thumped a little faster. "You mean skyscrapers like the neon blue SFPD headquarters?"

"Exactly!" Niles said. "I suspect the structural changes are more prevalent where the infection is strongest. So, to answer your question, I'm not sure if you would be able to determine where the grid is seeping in, as you've never visited the far future time before. There is also the very likely chance the infection will have become firmly established by the time you arrive. If this is the case, leave immediately." His eyes flicked to Brice. Cassandra didn't need to be warned twice on that one. "If we've lost that era, it's possible to search for another time just before established grid infection. We'll save that discussion, if it becomes a necessity."

He started pacing again. "I should also warn you of the possibility for grid infection occurring while you're there. I can't know for certain, as I have no idea how the grid spreads, and I wasn't present when the grid became firmly entrenched and rewrote history in 2145." His eyes brightened. "But I'll set Octavus to record in the event this happens. Would be a fabulous opportunity to study the grid. Might be a tad disorienting to experience such a monumental shift firsthand, however."

Cassandra felt a chill. She sure hoped they didn't have to worry about any of that.

It was disconcerting whenever her uncle became enthralled with catastrophes or problems just for the sake of study. Too much like Octavus or the grid detectives in those moments.

Her uncle finished pacing. "Ready, then?"

"Let me get changed," Brice said.

Cassandra couldn't wait to see the new Brice and planned to give him as much grief as he'd given her. Anything to keep her mind off what they were about to do.

Brice had left to talk with Artemis after they'd exited the Octagon Room last night, and he and Niles had come up with a plan, which they'd briefly shared with her on the way to the bedrooms. Cassandra had mulled it over in her head while she showered and tossed and turned in bed worrying about it.

Too late to change anything now.

She just hoped it worked.

CHAPTER 22

Cassandra's hands wouldn't stop shaking.

Brice noticed, his gray eyes soft, understanding.

She hoped he didn't lose this new side when they popped into the far future. Hoped he didn't turn on her the moment the door opened and they stepped into the future.

Niles had prepared them as best he could, prattling on about more things than Cassandra could remember. Her uncle's mind was stuffed with enough facts to rival an encyclopedia. He'd been reluctant to exit the time machine, clearly envious of their imminent trip to one of his favorite eras and now forever banned from him so long as he harbored such an advanced case of grid infection.

Brice ran his fingers through his fedora-freed black hair.

He looked a little odd without his hat, as though a piece of him was missing. He seemed to feel it as well, his hand frequently going up to adjust something that wasn't there, much as he'd had to break himself of the habit of checking his typewriter arm all the time. He still checked, on occasion, though not nearly so much as he'd done when he first went off-grid.

And she missed his clothes, his quicksilver pants and black top.

Like her, Brice wore a far future disguise. As Niles had intimated the day before, the style lacked gender differentiation. Whereas Cassandra's outfit was shades of sky blue and cream, Brice's billowing pants and long shirt were ephemeral layers of gray and green, with just a hint of crimson at the waist. His black shoes peeking out from the bottom of the billowy pants were a little less out of place than Cassandra's scuffed white sneakers.

With the toga-esque feel, his pale skin and black hair, his gray eyes and the hard line of his jaw (freshly shaved), he resembled a Greek god. A handsome one at that.

Cassandra chastised herself for letting her thoughts drift in that direction. Again.

Though the shirts were long and fitted over one shoulder, like a toga, the long, feathery sleeves revealed slivers of skin. Cassandra hoped it wouldn't be too chilly where they were going. The pants were a little more concealing, but the material no warmer.

She placed her hand on the top of the octagon orb resting in the silver clawed display case in the control hub, the key still in the keyhole.

All she had to do was turn it.

Niles had assured her that Octavus knew the coordinates of the exact location in the meadow where they could safely appear tucked away from prying eyes. She didn't have anything to keep firmly in mind. The rogue AI would do all the work once she activated the orb.

Already cloaked, the Octagon Room would be invisible as soon as they landed in the far future. Niles would only know they were leaving when the wind rustled through his research facility.

She sucked in a deep breath and gave Brice a faint smile. "Ready."

She turned the key.

* * *

Time travel in the Octagon Room was a little less hair-raising than it had been without a protective room around them. And without grid-Brice to disrupt the travel pattern, they experienced no jolting or frenetic spinning. Cassandra couldn't speak for her uncle's research facility outside their door, but inside they felt barely a tremor; just a whisper of a breeze to tell them they were leaving the Fifth Branch.

Octavus would take care of using the orb to return them to Earth's timeline and into the far future, to an island chain in 4327.

The breeze died down, taking with it any hint of their orange juice, bacon and eggs, which Albert had already cleared up.

"Octavus," Cassandra said, "have we arrived at our destination?" She still didn't trust the rogue AI. Who knew where it had taken them or if it was even safe out there? Niles had tried to quell her doubts and worries, but Cassandra couldn't let it go. "Octavus. Please answer. Have we arrived?"

"We have." The rogue AI sounded a little sullen, if that were possible. Or perhaps defiant? Cassandra couldn't be certain, and she couldn't shake that uneasy feeling.

"Please give us an exterior visual." She didn't think the AI could fake an exterior shot. No exiting the Octagon Room until she was convinced they'd landed in the meadow her uncle had told them about. "Octavus. Visual please."

She gave Brice a pointed look, but he just shrugged. What were they supposed to do if their time machine wouldn't respond?

The unmarred sheet of Smart Wall in front of the chair erupted with a beautiful picture of brilliant sunlight reflecting on rounded constructs of tinted glass and stairs. Strange, when they were supposed to be in a meadow. But even more baffling were the waves of sparkling water flowing away from them on the heels of people dressed similarly to Cassandra and Brice in flowing toga-like clothes. The people looked frightened, though a lack of sound made it difficult to determine what was actually going on.

"I think they're running away from . . . *us*," Brice said.

Cassandra's heart thumped harder. "Octavus. Is Brice correct?"

The AI didn't respond.

Cassandra forced her breathing to slow down. "I knew it couldn't be trusted."

The detective had been peering at the movie on the wall. He slapped his forehead and ran his hand down his face. "Stupid AI landed us in water! Those are waves from the impact."

Cassandra didn't know if she should laugh or scream.

"I am not stupid," Octavus said, its tone flatter than usual. "Niles was incorrect. There is ample space to land on the Third Tier."

"But you landed us in a frickin' fountain!" Cassandra retorted. Now that the waves had subsided, she could see the shiny cobalt blue tiles and a stone rim, with various marble mermaids and water nymph around the perimeter.

To say their crash landing had caused a commotion would be an understatement.

The emptied water chased people from the area, most of whom ran to higher ground, up a broad flight of stairs or a ramp to a building of tinted green glass. Anyone who tried to run down the stairs was soaked or swept away completely.

Cassandra couldn't imagine that the presence of the Octagon Room hadn't been noticed. Security forces would be searching for whatever had just caused a spontaneous fountain emptying.

"Niles was firm on the coordinates," Cassandra said. "Why the hell change it?"

The AI didn't respond.

A handful of moving objects glinted in the sky, too far to make out. "Octavus, can you give us a reading on incoming?"

"We need to get out of here," Brice said, his eyes locked on the screen. "Now."

Still Octavus remained silent.

Chills crawled up Cassandra's spine as the objects like miniature weaponized UFO's zoomed closer. Incoming didn't look friendly.

Cassandra turned the key and waited for the eight filigree petals to unfurl.

"Niles was incorrect," Octavus insisted. "There is ample landing space, as I have just proven. Your goal is fifty feet away. I will open the door."

Cassandra shook a fist at the control panels, not really knowing where Octavus was housed. Probably the entire Octagon Room, but the control panel seemed as good a place as any to focus her anger on. "You see those ships coming in with the weapons? They'll shoot us down before we get three feet out!"

"Likelihood of success is no greater if we land in the meadow versus this fountain. You will reach your goal faster from here."

"Not your decision to make!" Cassandra wanted to strangle the control hub, or at the very least give it a swift kick, break a knob or two. "We'll die out there!"

"You cannot be certain."

"*Now*, Cassandra," Brice said, his voice urgent.

The incoming ships were nearly on them.

"I don't know what the landing space looks like!" She wanted to scream. "Get us out of here, Octavus!"

"You might not care what happens to us," Brice said through gritted teeth to the AI, "but if those things open fire on us, it's your body they're going to riddle with holes."

"Incorrect. Firepower is insufficient. Furthermore, cloaking ability is astounding. They have not yet detected our presence."

Cassandra's jaw dropped. "I think they can deduce where the cause of the fountain spillage is sitting!"

"Our bodies won't survive their firepower," Brice said.

"Humans. Incapable of calculating incoming trajectories or suitable cover. Incapable of determining the most efficient means of entry to a goal made easily attainable." Chilling statements from the rogue AI.

A wind stirred the room like a gentle afternoon breeze.

The view of the emptied fountain vanished, replaced by serene rolling grass and wildflowers. No people in sight, but the climbing islands could be seen in the distance, perhaps a mile away.

"You have a long way to drag your stolen goods." If an AI could sound smug, Octavus sure did.

"Is this because we called you stupid?" Cassandra shook her head in disbelief.

"The security force most likely would not have ended your lives."

"But they could have hurt us!"

Octavus was silent.

"The truth comes out," Brice said. "It doesn't care what happens to us."

"Well you'd better start caring what happens to us if you want this partnership to work." Cassandra pulled a face. "Not equipped with emotional routines, my ass."

"It did get something right," Brice said. "That's a long way to drag an operating table."

Disguising the table in sheets just didn't seem like an adequate plan anymore.

But perhaps Octavus's act of disobedience could come in useful. Niles had told them that the mobile device could be used to communicate with the Octagon Room, as Albert could easily travel between the two locales and relay a message. "Octavus, can you be ready to jump to that spot later, so we can bring the table to you?"

Brice turned his back on the control hub, gaze intent on Cassandra. "You trust it with the time machine?"

"What choice do we have? It could probably find a way to strand us here if it really wanted. Trust goes both ways."

"Of course I can," Octavus said, sounding more like itself again. "Ready the orb, Cassandra. I will await Albert's instruction."

Brice frowned. "We'll have to find a plank or something to get the table over the lip of the fountain. But it could work." He left unsaid that it would only work if Octavus agreed to cooperate when the time came.

Unfortunately, giving the AI freewill meant it could choose not to listen on a whim.

They'd have to discuss that later.

For now, she and Brice had to hurry to the medical facility before their time machine was discovered. It was hidden out of sight for now but this city had just had a mystery object empty a fountain and security would be on high alert.

Cassandra turned the key in the orb, activating it, and made sure Albert's mobile device was tucked securely in the satchel under her disguise.

Brice checked his hidden pockets. His weapon, obtained from Artemis, was a little hard to get to, but at least he had something.

He finished patting himself down and gave her a nod.

They were as ready as they were going to be.

Cassandra just hoped they weren't making a mistake in trusting the rogue AI.

CHAPTER 23

Stepping into Hesperides was like stepping into paradise.

Fresh air tinted with a pleasant scented array of lush grass, soil, and wildflowers—swathes of violet lupines, bluebells, California poppies, and white daisies that sprayed the hills like air-brushed rivers of rippling color in the wind. Gentle hills and valleys surrounded the Octagon Room's landing spot, sloping down to distant white beach and sparkling sea. Grass bent and swayed, hissing in accompaniment with the distant murmur of crashing shoreline.

Ponds dotted the landscape in mirror-reflections of clear blue skies. Scant clouds like pulled cotton streaked the sky and higher still, beyond any cloud cover, dark splotches cast shadows over the sea. Cassandra had no idea what those remote masses could be, but they were far too dark and high to be actual clouds. More like massive spaceships.

Brice joined Cassandra in the knee-high grass. He gave an appreciative nod to the Octagon Room behind them. "Superior cloaking, indeed."

The door to the time machine closed, completing the illusion of uninterrupted grassy knolls to distant cliffs and sea.

Ahead, perhaps a mile or two distant, began what Cassandra's uncle had called the island chain, though it was unlike any series of islands Cassandra had ever seen or thought she would.

The lowermost island upon which she and Brice stood was a regular island, and a small one at that at five square miles. At the other end of this sea-level island, a smaller one floated overhead like a low-lying cloud, and above that floated yet another island, and onwards like monstrous earthen steps.

The far future city of Hesperides spilled down the island steps like a monumental frozen waterfall in glinting silver, blue, and green, with buildings having sprouted like a grow-your-own-crystal-city kit until reaching maximum growth to spill over to the next level and grow and spill again. Though the islands floated far above their lower counterparts, silver strands connected them in a chain, all the way on up into the clouds.

Cassandra's lungs constricted with a sharp intake of air. "We can't really be in 4327, can we?"

A vivid blue butterfly flitted amongst the bluebells and poppies beside Cassandra, so close she could have touched its delicate wings.

The island was warm, but not stifling, and not at all humid. With the midday sun beating down on their heads, Brice probably wished he had his fedora.

As if reading her mind, he ran his fingers through his short black hair. "Let's get moving."

She touched the bulge in the hidden satchel around her waist to make sure Albert's mobile device was still there. Their success depended on him being able to pop back here and alert Octavus so the rogue AI could bring the Octagon Room to them on the Third Tier. She just hoped that Niles's modifications worked and Albert would be able to come all the way back here. Octavus had said it could boost the signal. Albert might not come through clearly, but hopefully enough to get Octavus's attention.

Too many things could go wrong that Cassandra had to push it all out of her mind to avoid going crazy. She chewed on her nails, eyes roaming the surrounding landscape as she and Brice carved a path through grass thick enough to taste.

"We'll be fine," Brice said, exhibiting his unnerving habit of reading people. Though to be fair, Cassandra wasn't doing a very good job of hiding her nervousness. "So, your parents moved to France?"

Cassandra stopped chewing her nails and darted a suspicious frown his way. Why ask about that right now? She didn't like talking about her family, though she supposed it was better than worrying about what they were going to do once they reached the city. "Soon as I went off to college."

They veered to the left to avoid a small pond, lily pads floating on its surface and a snowy white egret frozen mid-step like a statue waiting to strike unsuspecting fish. There weren't many trees on the island, but a nearby oak provided shade and protection for chattering birds.

"Why the move?"

"Dad was a professor at SFSU, San Francisco State University. Guess he wanted a change of pace. He joined the US Embassy in France. He'd always wanted to live in Europe and finally got his chance. They sold their house, got a small fortune for it, enough to buy a place in Paris. They had owned that townhouse in San Francisco since their marriage in college. As for Mom, she's a fashion designer and was thrilled with the move."

Cassandra was ready to move on to another topic, but Brice, in typical inspector fashion, clung to the topic like a pit bull.

"You haven't seen them since they moved."

That piercing perception of his could get really annoying sometimes.

Cassandra steadied her gaze on a flock of quail moving through the underbrush. The grass smelled sweet, the wind laced with a hint of sea mist. She came to a startled halt when the quail, disturbed from the grass, suddenly took flight in a flapping roar for a nearby oak grove. When Cassandra and Brice had moved on, she heard the birds' calls to one another to regroup, a call she remembered well from childhood walks through California countryside.

She tucked a longer strand of wavy hair behind an ear. "Don't have the money to afford the ticket." Not entirely true. She really was tight on cash, but she'd never been particularly close to her parents. Why waste the money to make the trek? They wouldn't take time from their busy schedules for her. She'd always been closer to her nannies growing up. "And before you say anything, my parents were busy in San Francisco. Nothing's changed since they moved to France."

She kept her eyes off Brice, so he couldn't see her face.

"I can relate. My father lives at work. Which I can understand, on some level, since I'm equally devoted to my job, or at least I was, before I went off-grid." He faltered and fell quiet a moment as they trekked up a hill. "I barely knew the man and have very little affection for him. Would have been nice to be closer, but he vanished after the divorce. As for my mother, she's doing what she loves. I attend her local performances when I can."

Cassandra wanted to ask why the sudden change of heart in regards to chit-chat, but she was enjoying the distraction. They'd been through a lot and she felt she hardly knew him.

Though with the grid having rewritten his life, he might not really know himself. He'd just remember whatever the grid had left him with. A sad and rather disturbing thought.

"How you holding up?" she asked. "Being off-grid?"

He shrugged, his chiseled jaw clenching.

His gray eyes had narrowed on the chain of islands rising from the plain below. Like a piece of art crafted by gods, the islands ascended from a grassy, relatively flat plain on the edge of a peninsula of white beaches. Though the pink sand in the perpetual sunset world of the Fifth Branch had been gorgeous, it was nice to be back to a normal diurnal rhythm and familiar blue sky and yellow sun.

Sure was bright, though. The ocean glinting as if the sun had crashed there and the pieces risen to the surface to gleam in eternal broken brilliance.

Brice still hadn't answered her question, his gaze locked on the sprawling city ahead. The wind had tousled his black hair. A more relaxed look that really suited him. Made him seem daring and a little roguish. The wind rustled his toga-like shirt, providing a glimpse of collar bone. He seemed almost like another person, though right now that fixed glare was grid-Brice all the way. Calculating and cold.

"I've adapted fine," he said. "Not easy, as you can imagine." He lifted his typewriter arm. "There's a glimmer of the grid here, closer we get to that city."

Cassandra shivered, despite the heat of the noon sun. "Should you stay behind?"

"I'll be fine."

"Albert has the biggest role in our plan, since he's the one who'll be doing all the talking." The hologram was the only one among them who could speak the language. The people spoke English, but the language had so evolved that she and Brice wouldn't understand a word. Not the best way to blend in to steal high-tech expensive medical equipment.

"I'll be fine," Brice insisted. "It's not bad. I'll monitor as we go. If it becomes problematic, I'll turn back." There was something protective in the way he was looking at her.

"You don't want to leave me alone, do you?"

He rubbed the back of his neck. "I'm sure you'll handle yourself just fine, especially with a bodyguard like Albert. But I'd feel better if I came along."

"Suit yourself." To be honest, she felt better too, and told him as much.

Brice gave her a startled look. "Thanks." This sort of casual discourse still seemed uncomfortable for him, much like the clothes they wore. Unfamiliar and not quite the right size. But they were both doing their best to adapt and make the most of their situation. And they were in this together. Two fish out of water from different times, perhaps, but thrown into an alien Earth together, both very much outsiders on their own planet.

They headed down the hill towards the flat plain. Nearly time to bring Albert into play—their guide and translator in this strange new world.

CHAPTER 24

"You called, Miss Bennet?" Albert stood in knee-high grass, hands folded in front of him, pale face placid, slicked black hair as shiny as newly polished shoes. He looked around. "Operation Hesperides?"

"Yes, Albert," Cassandra said. "It's almost time. Best you join us now to avoid drawing unwanted attention."

He gave a curt nod, then vanished from sight and reappeared dressed in full Hesperides fashion. Gone was his butler uniform, replaced now with the billowy layers of soft fabric that made the three of them seem like a cross between ancient Greeks and members of a futuristic cult of sky worshippers, especially with the enormous islands floating up past the clouds behind Albert.

Cassandra wore translucent layers of blue and cream, Brice in grays and green and a dash of red, and Albert in purple and green. Unlike Cassandra and Brice, the hologram was able to wear appropriate shoes for the era—white boots with an identity crisis. Thankfully Albert's feet were covered with the part that looked like snow boots. The lace-up sandal part, which just seemed downright wrong on the butler, wrapped around his shins and calves. His pants were also shorter than Cassandra's and Brice's, short enough to show off his strange shoes.

Cassandra didn't care that her clothes were as big on her as they felt; she was happy to keep her faintly charred white sneakers hidden from sight.

"Ready, Miss Bennet?"

"Lead the way."

Albert turned on his heels and strode down the hill into buffeting wind heavy with the pungent taste of salt and rotting kelp.

Cassandra did her best to keep up, bracing her sneakers on tufted clumps of grass in the steep, uneven ground. Brice held his arms out to keep his balance and when they neared the bottom, the two of them more or less ran the rest of the way.

Her sneakers pounded onto a foot path of worn wooden planks resting on sand and low ground cover, where Albert waited for them. It was an uneven path of buckled planks but it sure beat slogging through drifts of sand.

Perhaps half a mile wide, the peninsula sloped down to beach and rocky shoreline on either side of the foot path. Seagulls soared overhead, though most congregated along the surf, where they screeched and fought over food.

"You live alone?" Brice said as they walked along the broken path, scraggly grass pushing between the planks.

Cassandra fingered the satchel at her waist again, just to make sure the mobile device was still there. "Guess you deduced that from the fact I've only ever mentioned my cactus Gus?"

Brice gave her a small smile. Not a pitiful smile, but one that suggested the clues had been obvious. "I like my solitude, too. Or, at least I used to." A frown touched his brow. "I worked a lot. Not a lot of time for socializing, except with Stepek Jankovic, with whom I shared the occasional drink after work."

Cassandra shuddered at the memory of Detective Jankovic. "I was supposed to go out to dinner with Shirley the day I vanished. Wonder how long it took my friends to notice I was missing?" She doubted her parents would have learned any time soon that she'd gone missing. "Probably just as well I never showed up. Would have just been another failed set-up." She fell into an awkward silence and looked away, taking a sudden interest in the uneven path beneath her feet and the little birds with long beaks foraging through the sandy grass.

"Not seeing anyone, then?"

Cassandra's gaze shot to Brice, but he looked just as surprised to have asked the question. "No," she said. "And you?"

He looked away and muttered something about never having the time for dating. Well, that made two of them, though Cassandra was really just afraid of getting hurt again. She didn't have a particularly busy life. She wondered what Brice's real reason was, but didn't ask. They'd crossed into uncomfortable territory.

Brice seemed as eager to change topics. "Glad Niles didn't make us wear *those* shoes."

Cassandra laughed. "Me, too."

Though the awkwardness had rushed from the air as rapidly as a popped balloon, Cassandra couldn't help but broach another un-pleasant topic. "What was Detective Jankovic like?"

Brice's long stride faltered.

Albert continued on ahead, keeping a brisk pace, oblivious to the conversation behind him, or perhaps just politely ignoring it.

"I have a lot of respect for Stepek," Brice said. "We've been friends for years. I was his best man in his wedding."

"Detective Jankovic's *married?*" Cassandra probably asked with more surprise than she should have.

Brice picked up the pace.

"Sorry. It's just, well . . ." Cassandra didn't know how to explain the grid-controlled detective without making Stepek Jankovic sound like a monster.

Brice came to a sudden halt, his gray eyes fierce.

Cassandra backed up a step before she could stop herself.

"Stepek's a good guy." There was pain in Brice's eyes and Cassandra felt bad now for having said anything. "I don't know what he did to you, and honestly, I don't want to know, not now."

Cassandra's mouth fell. She'd never had any intention of telling Brice what had happened between her and Detective Jankovic. Not like Jankovic had done anything in particular to her. He hadn't tortured her. Just questioned her, and threatened her, and smashed her hand with his boot. And that crazed grid-glowing look as he'd come after her right before she'd vanished with the orb.

Jankovic had been a man possessed, which was why she'd been curious to know what he was like before his more pronounced grid infection.

She wanted to tell Brice this, but he stormed off, pushing past a startled Albert (a hard thing to do to the unflappable hologram) to get ahead of them.

"Is everything all right, Miss Bennet?" Albert asked, a hint of concern in his glassy brown eyes.

"Everything's great, so long as I remember the detective doesn't like talking about his former life." Cassandra started down the path again, feeling a tad depressed and out of sorts.

And Brice's life really was a former life. He could never return. Cassandra had only served to remind him of that fact. Not only was his home off-limits, but it was changing still, rewritten by the grid.

She felt another nervous flip-flop in her belly.

What would happen if the grid creepage here proved too strong for Brice? Would he have enough time to escape to the Octagon Room? Would he be trustworthy enough to enter it?

Wind swept up the bank, throwing salty sand and a stomach-churning stench of rotting kelp in her face.

The first of the floating islands loomed over the edge of the peninsula, hovering perhaps half a mile up and casting a corner of the peninsula and a swathe of ocean in shadow. The rising island chain was impressive, daunting in size and no more believable now that they'd drawn closer than it had been from a distance.

"I can't believe my uncle expected us to wheel a huge operating table all the way down here," Cassandra said to Albert, though to be fair her uncle hadn't meant for them to drag it all the way down the bumpy plank path or up and down a mile of grassy hills. The original plan was to have Brice stay behind at the edge of the city while Cassandra went on ahead to bring the time machine back for him and the medical equipment. "Let's hope our new plan's an improvement."

This future Earth seemed like paradise. If they were caught stealing, surely such a future wouldn't involve killing a couple of thieves?

But the UFO-like machines that had swarmed in on the disturbance at the fountain hadn't seemed so friendly.

Cassandra chewed a nail and kept walking, an angry Brice pulling ahead as she kept stride with Albert.

CHAPTER 25

"Hey," Brice whispered as Cassandra bumped into him. "Sorry," she said, equally quiet. She'd been too busy looking around to watch where she was going.

"I'm the one who should be apologizing." He gave her an awkward smile.

"It's fine," she assured him, pulling close and keeping her voice low. She touched his arm, to emphasize her sincerity. He didn't need to explain why the topic had so affected him. She'd hate to be in his position.

"Thanks." His smile touched his gray eyes this time, making Cassandra blush.

She drew her hand back.

They'd just entered the city and were avoiding the worst of the crowds, off in an alcove of white-washed stone and flowering plant pots—geranium, by the peppery scent of the red flowers.

Albert handed them each a tiny device, which they inserted into their ears so they could hear Albert's instructions. The hologram could communicate through the earpieces without having to speak through his mouth and risk anyone hearing ancient English, which he'd said was a dead language in 4327. The people of Hesperides still called their language English, however, just to be confusing.

As Brice adjusted his earpiece, his sleeve fell down to his elbow and Cassandra noticed a glimmer of white lines.

The grid.

She started to point it out, but the lines vanished as if they'd just been an odd reflection from the sunlight or a figment of her imagination.

Please follow me, Albert said through Cassandra's earpiece.

Brice heard, too, because he gave Cassandra a quick nod, and they stepped out of the alcove after the hologram.

Ahead we have one of many Hesperides garden courtyards, Albert said, switching to tour guide mode. *But first may I draw your attention to the city's layout. Much of the Hesperides supporting structures are below ground, leaving aesthetic design for the surface. The upper islands obtain their lift from anti-gravity plates with minimal cloaking ability to provide the illusion of soil when viewed from below.*

As Albert prattled on about anti-gravity and air and water purification systems, Cassandra soaked in their more immediate surroundings.

Hesperides wasn't a flat city, but gently sloped and tiered in keeping with the layout of rising islands Cassandra supposed. The lowermost level, or at least the portion of the city they had entered, funneled into a four thousand-square-foot garden courtyard (numbers thoughtfully provided by Albert). Beyond the garden, higher up the sloping island, glass buildings in muted colors dominated like enormous gems with minimal faceting.

Their view of the rest of the city, however, was promptly obstructed by trees as soon as they entered the courtyard. A gorgeous courtyard of mottled creamy stone tiles and pillars twined with flowering vines so reminiscent of the ancient Greek paintings Cassandra had seen that she wondered if they'd gone back in time. The people milling around in the expansive courtyard and wearing the toga-like clothes of this era only helped to cement that notion of ancient history, but with hairstyles that would have shocked the ancient Greeks.

Some of the women wore their hair long and unadorned, though most had elaborate updo's like works of art, with angled combs that made flat plateaus and separated their hair into sections—ratty bird's nest tufts, spiked hair, and elaborate curls and loops. The combs must have been anti-gravity enhanced to stick up like they did. Cassandra was curious about the combs, but Albert was far more interested in relaying the city's technical aspects rather than its fashions.

Not knowing if anyone would notice her plain-by-comparison wayward short hair, she mussed it up a bit more with her fingers, trying to give it more body and get the longer strands to stick out more dramatically. The back of her head was easier, where the hair was cropped closer to the nape of her neck, and wavier. If only she had some mousse or salty sand for the longer strands around her face.

Catching Brice's eyes on her, she gave him an embarrassed smile. She couldn't tell him what she was doing without everyone in the vicinity hearing them, not that anyone was currently paying attention to them.

Most people sat on shaded benches around the perimeter, talking with one another in hushed tones. The occasional laugh drifted over like the excited chirps of the garden's many birds.

Brice seemed oblivious to the city's denizens, instead paying rapt attention to Albert's droning lecture—now moved on to the desalination tanks and pumps that provided the city its water and created the streams and ponds throughout the island chain. Cassandra found some of it interesting, such as how the city builders had disguised the massive tubes that carried water up thousands of feet through the island levels.

As they walked the perimeter of the courtyard, beneath a lattice canopy heavy with sweet-smelling jasmine, Cassandra noticed the water garden aspects: the fountains and babbling streams amongst the many maple and oak trees and numerous flowers. Orange amaryllis (bulbous flowers like stars with long stamens), birds of paradise (which Cassandra had never thought at all resembled birds), gardenias, calla lilies, roses, tulips, and dozens of others flowers that Albert named as they headed for a broad staircase ascending into a tunnel of overhanging branches and lush vegetation.

Cassandra didn't want to leave the garden's serenity but they had to hurry to the medical facility. She couldn't forget why they were there. She'd have to come back to Hesperides again someday. Maybe with her uncle.

As they ascended into the tunnel of cool shade, into the gentle hum of bees and the rustle of overhanging branches, Cassandra inhaled deeply, tasting moist soil and bark.

A sudden voice hailed from the foliage to her left, making her jump.

She didn't understand a word, but it didn't matter. A floating advertisement in blue transparent glass used imagery to persuade her to visit a shoe store for the latest spring fashions. She found the advertisement invasive, but as she hurried up the stairs more floating panels whispered from the sidelines.

Albert shared information on the advanced technology. The floating advertisements were the height of personalized shopping and privacy, targeted for each passing person and designed in such a way as to be visible only to the targeted customer. Even the audio was designed to only be heard from a certain angle. Cassandra was surprised at its accuracy; as Brice activated screens ahead of her, she heard a faint whisper but couldn't make out a single word.

The panels seemed to know Albert wasn't real, though. He didn't set off a single screen, though the people coming down the stairs towards them set off their own share of private commercials.

Albert waited for them at the top of the stairs, looking a little funny in his new clothes. The people of Hesperides seemed so relaxed, so serene, a perfect complement to their choice in clothing. Albert was far too stiff and formal for the attire. His brown eyes watched Brice and Cassandra as they emerged from the tunnel of vegetation into a grand outdoor marketplace.

Here the surrounding buildings towered over them like enormous crystals erupted from the ground, most in shades of blue—turquoise, cobalt, sapphire, midnight, and periwinkle—with translucent walls that allowed the passage of light while revealing surprisingly little interior detail.

Like crystals in rock, the buildings had a metal matrix of polished steel to hold the gemmy structures in place. No building was square, but rather organic and uneven, and made of seemingly solid glass, though steel lines crisscrossed the structures like enormous stained glass works of art.

Flowing around the city's exterior, and strikingly gorgeous in tinted glass and silver, hovercars fell like rain catching the light as they curved round from higher levels in a steady, guided stream, filling the air with a gentle hum like bees.

Unlike 2145, where aerial cars had been as polluting as smog, only a few hovercars crossed the city. Most streams were relegated to the exterior of the city alongside similar curves of steel and glass that connected the islands, though Cassandra knew from Albert's earlier lecture that the structures had no actual supportive capacity.

Brice touched Cassandra's arm and pointed into the market place, to a line of people waiting to climb into a gondola-like compartment inside a huge blue tube.

Albert had already stepped into line. Cassandra and Brice joined him.

As with the stairs from the garden below, advertising panels floated all around the open market where people shopped for fresh fruits and vegetables and stored their wares in baskets that floated along behind them like obedient dogs.

Cassandra couldn't understand a word spoken by anyone, despite the occasional sense of familiarity. It reminded her of a trip she'd taken as a child with her parents to a castle in England. They'd used headphones to hear how the ancient invaders had sounded when they spoke the English of the time, and Cassandra had been surprised at its strangeness, at how much English had changed in the past 1500 years or so.

The language of far future Earth was no less fascinating. The lilting quality of it, the blend of world languages over the centuries, and made all the stranger because the citizens didn't look much different than the people of Cassandra's time. Humans, just like her and Brice. And yet, they lived in a world so alien to her way of life.

Cassandra's stomach did flip-flops as they moved closer to the front of the line and the now filled-to-a-maximum-capacity-of-fifty (according to Albert) gondola compartment zoomed up the tube. Unlike actual gondolas, which hung from cables, the transport compartments shot up a transparent tube like the old-fashioned suction mail tubes; a dizzying rollercoaster ascent of a thousand feet to the upper island.

Cassandra didn't like the idea of getting inside, but she'd just have to trust the tube was strong enough to support them. Albert had said the hovercar taxis required credits, whereas the tube was free and a "blast of a ride", no doubt parroted from her uncle.

Brice tapped her arm again, drawing her attention to a group of robots, similar to Artemis, weaving through the marketplace. Overhead, UFO security bots crept along, red lights scanning.

Cassandra's chest tightened. Were those bots searching for them?

Though the robots wouldn't know it was them, as security here had never found the Octagon Room, they might be searching for anything or anyone out of the ordinary.

Cassandra shifted her pants a little lower on her hips, to better hide her sneakers, and tried to duck behind a group of chatting ladies in front of them in line who smelled strongly of artificial roses and jasmine.

Brice stepped in beside her, uncomfortably close, gray eyes glancing discreetly over his shoulder at the robots moving through the market square, tapping people on the shoulder and questioning them.

Another gondola-compartment hissed into position, having just descended from the upper level, and opened its doors.

The line slowly moved forward.

Cassandra tried not to appear too concerned with the number of people ahead of them, keeping her hands at her side so she didn't fidget or chew her nails.

Meanwhile, Albert carried on with his tour, relating mind-numbing facts about the transportation tubes as they inched closer to their ride.

The attendant at the entrance to the transport vehicle held his hand up for Albert to halt while he assessed available seats inside. In contrast with his black spiked hair and red robes, the attendant looked about as thrilled with his job as the dozing guard in the foyer of Cassandra's apartment complex back home. Eyes glazing over, he waited for everyone in the compartment to find a seat before stepping back outside and covering a yawn with the back of his hand.

Oblivious to any tension in his audience of two, Albert prattled on about the various farms located all over the island chain and the many delicious meals one could prepare from the variety of produce and spices. Cassandra watched with increasing dread as the lanky, far future robots slowly worked their way towards the tube line.

The robots hadn't taken an interest in the line yet, but they reminded Cassandra too much of the grumpy Artemis back at her uncle's research facility. Their face plates had an uncanny knack for mimicking human expressions—curiosity and patient listening, a frown now and then, and a glower when they didn't think people were watching them.

Cassandra didn't want to be here when the robots reached the line.

When they'd finished interviewing a couple and their teenage children, the group of five robots panned out to check a wider range of people. Cassandra noticed that the robots seemed to be doing most of their scanning before they even spoke to anyone and she suspected that conversation was merely a polite afterthought, or perhaps a gimmick to hide their real intentions.

Brice took Cassandra's arm and tugged her along with him into the gondola.

She'd been so busy watching the robots that she hadn't noticed the attendant wave them forward.

Cassandra plopped down into a hard seat of molded plastic between Albert and Brice and released a sigh of relief as the doors whisked shut.

The air inside the compartment was cool, though many of the people wore perfume or a lot of smelly hair product. Cassandra wrinkled her nose.

She looked down, alarmed to see that the floor was tinted blue glass, that the entire compartment was mostly glass, with steel bars providing limited structure.

The gondola rocked and then the exterior door sealed and they shot up like a cannon.

Cassandra grimaced as her stomach dropped. Eyes riveted to the floor, she watched a rapidly receding island and an expanse of glittering sea far below as they soared upwards.

Cassandra decided she didn't much care for the ride.

Thankfully, it only lasted a few minutes. They soon hissed to a standstill and the doors whisked opened.

Just one more level to go and then they'd be back to the spot where Octavus had first taken them—the Third Tier and the medical facility.

Cassandra couldn't wait to get out of the gondola, wishing the few dozen people ahead of them would funnel out faster.

They exited the tube in a babbling crowd like an uncorked bottle, but Cassandra stopped short as soon as she saw the robots combing the marketplace. Dozens of gleaming bots that prowled like giant soldiers. Taller than the average person, their presence among the crowd made markedly clear by their bobbing silver heads.

Follow me, Albert said into their earpieces.

Heart pounding, Cassandra stayed close to the hologram as he led them up a broad set of stairs.

She tried to act casual, but it was difficult, especially with all the UFOs in the sky like a cloud of deadly wasps the size of dogs, and the mini Artemis-army questioning everyone in sight.

They had to get on the next gondola before the UFOs scanned them or a robot stopped them for questioning.

Though the city's people were a little alarmed, they were highly cooperative. Most of the new arrivals exiting the gondola with Cassandra actively sought out the robots, no doubt seeking information. At least it kept the robots busy for now.

Most of this second tier seemed to be gardens, and perched as it was on the edge of the floating island, it provided a fantastic view of the lower levels. Cassandra could see the stretch of meadow and ponds far below and hoped the Octagon Room was still safely hidden in the grass somewhere.

Under different circumstances, she would gladly have stopped to admire the view—the gorgeous ocean, the palace-like gardens full of fragrant flowers, buzzing bees and exotic plants, even the Kina-like robot pets that accompanied many of the people—but as it was she could barely keep her feet moving at a respectable pace, could barely prevent her legs from running in a mad dash for the transport platform visible on the upper tier of gardens.

A low wall of polished stone with squat pillars for support skirted the edge of the upper tier and also served as a bench. A party seemed to be going on, now interrupted by the flood of robots.

Albert skirted the party on their way up to a platform with a shorter line than the lower level. Cassandra recognized some of the people from their previous ride now joining the party.

Thankfully the gondola was mostly empty and the line moving quickly.

Brice's typewriter arm, however, seemed to be bothering him. He rubbed absently at it, eyes locked on the nearby party-goers and the few dozen robots roaming the grounds. Huge urns overflowing with flowers marked off the lush lawn, the fragrance drifting to the line on a salty breeze.

Brice rubbed his arm again, trying to be discreet, but Cassandra's heart started thumping harder when she noticed a handful of nearby robots all suddenly look up, directly at Brice like he had a big flashing neon sign over his head.

The robots didn't look worried or angry, but definitely curious. They politely broke away from the party, attention fixed on the transport line.

The attendant waved Albert and Brice inside and Cassandra hurried in right behind them. Two sets of glass walls somewhat blurred the view of the garden, though the silver robots stood out like white paint in a black room. Thankfully only a few more people got on and the doors hissed shut just as the robots approached the attendant. Cassandra could see their shiny faces peering through the glass.

Then the outer doors closed and the gondola shot up.

Cassandra didn't look down through the floor this time, or even out the window walls. Her eyes landed on Brice and stayed there. She wanted to say something, to demand what was happening with him, whether he was feeling the influence of the grid, but there were too many people around them.

Brice must have seen how the robots had taken an interest in him the very moment he'd rubbed his arm. Cassandra didn't know if the grid lines had reappeared. She was tempted to lift his sleeve to see for herself, to determine if her assumption was correct—that the robots had sniffed the grid in Brice.

She didn't know what that meant, if this place was falling under grid influence and the robots had detected Brice as one of their own, or if the robots had detected an anomaly and were merely curious, or if their sudden interest had just been coincidence.

Brice made a point of keeping his gaze forward.

As for Albert, he carried on with his guided tour, oblivious to any of the intrigue around him.

Cassandra sighed and leaned back in her seat.

The ride was a little longer this time, maybe five minutes, but when she glanced through the floor, she wished she hadn't.

They had to be at least a few miles above sea level.

Feeling a little woozy, she looked up at the ceiling again and focused instead on the rapidly approaching upper island.

They whooshed past brown soil, then slowed past green grass and rose up over a high stone wall before coming to a stop at a platform with the number three on it.

Albert deboarded first, behind a family of three and a handful of people that looked like they'd been up all night, ruffled hair and circles under their bleary eyes.

Cassandra stayed close to Albert, tensing in anticipation of a confrontation with Smart Robots, but the Third Tier was relatively quiet compared to the lower level, if extremely wet.

They had Octavus to thank for that, who had decided to land the time machine in a fountain, though nowhere to be seen from their current position. Perhaps it was at the top of the long staircase ahead?

That seemed to be the case, since Albert had stepped off the platform and was heading for the soggy stairs. Not a person in sight. Maybe they'd all gone home to change. Cassandra just hoped no one had been hurt during the sudden tsunami.

Dead fish littered the staircase, bringing the pristine island a little closer to a messy dock replete with rotting fish baking in the sun and soppy steps underfoot. All that was missing were the call of gulls, the curse of sailors, and the salty bite of sea. The cleaning bots descending the stairs gave her the creeps, especially after the interrogations going on in the lower islands.

Why no Smart Robots or mini UFOs up here? Maybe they'd already questioned this whole level and found nothing out of the ordinary? After all, Octavus had quickly taken them away to the spot out on the lowermost island, the spot where Niles had said they should initially land.

The rogue AI had really caused a stir. Hopefully it didn't result in further complications for them.

Brice was doing his best to leave his arm alone as they climbed the stairs.

Cassandra wanted to catch up, but he seemed intent on keeping the distance between them, perhaps well aware of her intentions to question him now that they enjoyed an absence of potential eavesdroppers. The earlier fountain emptying had certainly cleared the area, except for the rotting fish.

She wrinkled her nose and stepped around a plump koi swelling in the sun.

A cleaning bot the size of a small child, rotund trash-can middle and spindly arms shooting in all directions in creepy spider fashion, picked its way down the stairs on six legs, demonstrating agile climbing ability and noteworthy multi-tasking as it simultaneously mopped water, clipped overhanging bushes from the border, and sucked up dead fish from the steps.

Cassandra gave the bot a wide berth.

She glanced over her shoulder to see that the emptied gondola had zoomed on to the next station, seeming to lead back to the lower level in a huge loop.

Cassandra knew they were close to the medical facility when Albert's tour guide mode switched to the topic of Hesperides advanced medical care and their target: *Smart Labs.*

A little out of breath by the time they reached the top, Cassandra scaled the last step, which felt like the thousandth, before Albert headed off for a large green L-shaped glass building at least ten stories high dominating the area to the left and directly ahead.

A courtyard was on the right, with the mostly emptied fountain of bright blue tiles. The fountain had perhaps a foot or two of remaining water and very few fish. Cleaning bots littered the courtyard, mopping up water and dead fish, righting overturned flower pots and scooping up mud.

One human was among the clean-up crew, a man with his hands on his hips. Soaking wet and seemingly in charge of the clean-up process, he yelled and waved his hands, though Cassandra couldn't understand a word. Maybe that was a good thing.

This way please, Miss Bennet, Albert said through Cassandra's earpiece.

The hologram and Brice were already half-way up another staircase, this one leading to the main entrance of the hospital. She didn't see the name of the hospital anywhere, but Niles had been right about the symbols all over the building. What had he called them?

As if reading her mind, Albert told her and Brice all about the *Asklepion* symbol and the Greek deity, Asclepius, who had inspired its design, fashioned after the serpent-entwined rod the deity had wielded. It didn't matter that Niles had already told them. Albert went into even greater length than Niles ever had.

As much as Cassandra appreciated Niles's research into this world, she was going to have to make some changes to Albert's programming as soon as she had a moment alone with him. No more droning lectures, to start.

Albert interrupted his own spiel on Greek deities to inform them that they were about to enter the *Smart Labs* and should be on high-alert.

Cassandra gave Brice a nervous smile as he opened the door for her and Albert.

The detective and Niles had devised this next part of the plan. Her uncle had been optimistic about their success, but Cassandra was with Brice in thinking they had little chance of getting out of here with the intended stolen goods.

If they actually succeeded in gaining entry in the first place.

CHAPTER 26

Albert entered the Hesperides top-notch medical facility first, followed by Brice and Cassandra. Being that the building was almost entirely glass, Cassandra expected it to be lighter inside, but the tinted glass filtered out much of the sunlight and every ounce of heat. It was as frigid as Cassandra's office of employment back home that cranked the air-conditioning way too high and forced employees to don coats in the middle of summer.

It smelled and tasted lemony fresh, with an undertone of antiseptic. Not entirely pleasant.

Keeping in line with the green-tinted exterior, most of the glass in the foyer was green as well, though no wall or panel was exactly the same hue. The exterior walls, which revealed more of the outside than they'd revealed of the buildings' interior, were sea-green. The glass wall separating the foyer from the building proper was moss colored, deep jade, and lime green in three angled segments spanning the entire length of the foyer, fifty feet across.

The ceiling was two stories up and sharply angled. The cloth-covered chairs in the waiting area all emerald green and mostly filled with patients waiting to be called.

A man against the far left wall had fallen asleep, his head lolling back against the transparent wall and mouth ajar. One hand rested on a briefcase on his lap, the other hung down at his side. He was leaning like the tower of Pisa for a lady who had scooted as far away as possible without sitting in the next seat over. A device in her hands cast a soft blue glow on her tight face.

Everyone in the waiting room wore typical Hesperides toga-like fashion, but in varying hues of pastel colors, so that they looked like a row of flowers in a lush field, surrounded as they were in all that green. Even the glass floor was a rich forest green.

All but the sleeping man looked up when Albert, Brice, and Cassandra walked in.

If anyone had been talking before, they'd all fallen so quiet that Cassandra could hear the man on the far end of the room snoring.

At least part of the plan involved neither Brice nor Cassandra being able to speak, so no one would hear a long dead language.

Cassandra forced her hands to relax at her sides as she followed Albert to the sparkly glass counter like a slice of the Emerald City. Her heart pounding so hard now she could have sworn someone would have heard it in the room.

As planned, Albert would alert the lady behind the counter that he served as their translator and had brought them in for replacement voice boxes.

Niles had supplied them with a card, hacked of course, but it would show they possessed more than enough money for the procedure. They would have used it to get a taxi here, but Niles didn't expect the card to work more than once. He had said something about the card exhibiting a fixed account and number tag. The far future networks here in 4327 would read the card, see the amount of credits on it, and accept the amount (they hoped). But if the card were to be read again, the computer system would read the same number tag (which was a time stamp of sorts), and thereby reveal a frozen, and thus obsolete, account.

Cassandra resisted the urge to chew her nail.

Her stomach rumbled embarrassingly. She gave Brice a faint smile when he glanced her way with one brow raised.

She had no idea why her stomach had just growled. Even if Albert offered her a delicious apricot Danish, she'd have turned it away.

Neither of them could follow Albert's conversation with the hospital staff, but the butler was very polite and professional.

The lady, her blonde hair resembling a modern art project dragged through a hedge backwards, extended her hand for Albert's card.

While the lady ran the card through a machine, Cassandra busied herself with peering through the viridian doors currently barring access to the rest of the facility. She could make out movement on the other side, but not much detail.

The lady handed the card back to Albert who said something in response, and the viridian doors opened with a gust of antiseptic-laden air colder even than the waiting room.

Cassandra was confused. Didn't they have to wait their turn?

She glanced over her shoulder. No one really looked surprised at their speedy service, but the lady with the device on her lap, the one with the snoring man beside her, could have popped balloons with the glare she leveled on Cassandra and Brice.

As soon as they were on the other side of the doors, Cassandra released her breath.

They'd made it through the first part.

Now to find three hospital gowns and the operating rooms.

Cassandra gestured for Brice to come closer. He bent over so she could whisper in his ear. "What was that all about? Did we just get

VIP service?" The first words she'd spoken since they'd entered the garden courtyard a few thousand feet below.

The corners of Brice's mouth pressed down and he shrugged.

We received VIP service, Albert said through the earpiece. *Mr. Bennet may have added an extra zero or two to his bank account. And Miss Bennet, might I suggest you refrain from speaking while we are here? "Our cover could be blown", as is the vernacular, I believe.*

Cassandra sighed and gestured for the butler to lead the way.

Albert smoothed the front of his purple and green robes before starting down the long hallway, which came to a crossroads after a short distance and a fair amount of foot traffic and floating tables like haunted beds.

Cassandra shivered and hugged herself, planting her hands in her armpits in an attempt to warm them as her eyes tracked the floating patients. It was so cold, just like a haunted house with cold spots, though everywhere was cold as death.

The hospital staff barely spared a glance for Albert, Cassandra and Brice as they passed.

Albert turned right.

The glass walls displayed various news reels and product placements from cheery faces. Cassandra watched out of sheer curiosity, since she didn't understand a word.

The walls also lit up with directions, or so Albert explained in typical tour guide fashion through the earpieces.

As they wove through the labyrinthine corridors, Cassandra tried to keep track of their route and eventually gave up. If Albert abandoned them now she'd be hopelessly lost. She had no idea how well Brice had remembered their route.

It didn't really matter since they wouldn't be going back the way they'd come. Niles had programmed Albert with an escape route, to be taken after they found the appropriate operating room and stole the medical equipment.

They walked down yet another long deep green glass corridor, the walls becoming increasingly opaque, and made yet another turn, this time into a solid steel corridor.

Albert alerted them that they were nearing the operating rooms.

The hospital reception staff expected them to continue on to another waiting room to await surgery preparation. Albert said they wouldn't be going there, of course. The butler was on the lookout for a closet of supplies, per Niles's instructions, to garner their medical scrub disguises.

In here, Albert said.

A wall panel opened, revealing a closet full of medical supplies—mostly blankets and hospital gowns. They stepped inside and Albert shut the door.

The butler snatched three gowns and handed one each to Brice and Cassandra. They pulled the starchy whiteness over their heads and cinched it around their waists. The gowns smelled laundry fresh but left a talcum-like residue in the air.

Cassandra smacked her tongue as she slipped white booties over her scuffed sneakers and a pair of silky-soft white gloves over her hands.

While Brice adjusted his disguise, Cassandra caught a grid glimmer on his typewriter arm again.

"Brice," she whispered. "Your arm."

"It's nothing."

"Bullshit."

He looked startled. She wasn't one to swear. "I can handle it."

"How long has it been going on?" She thought she already knew the answer, but she wanted to hear it from him.

"Since before we entered the city."

Cassandra's head jerked with surprise. She hadn't expected that. She'd only seen the first glimmer when they'd entered Hesperides and were standing in the alcove.

She didn't even know what to say, except that he was jeopardizing their mission.

"I can handle it," he repeated, his square jaw set and gray eyes narrowed. If ever there was a face of bull-headedness, it was Brice's right then.

Now Cassandra's anger flared. "Did you see those robots? Down at the garden party? They *saw* you, Brice. When your frickin' typewriter arm flared up with the grid." She was still whispering, but only barely. "Who knows how many frickin' alarms you could set off here."

Brice crossed his arms, his expression hard. "I detected a glimmer when we first landed. Nothing more."

"And since then?" She returned an equally hard glare. "I've seen your arm light up. It's been bothering you."

He released an exasperated sigh. "Want me to go back to the Octagon Room?"

Cassandra wasn't really sure what she wanted. But she wasn't so sure Brice could be trusted if the grid continued to creep into him.

"Most of the glimmers are just static," he said, some of his anger fizzling. "A network that's not here. Buildings out in the ocean. Absent control hubs. Must be the grid creepage your uncle mentioned."

"Must be." Cassandra stared at him.

"I didn't think it was anything to worry about. I'm still fine. Still me." He gave her a faint smile.

He might be fine now but she'd seen how the grid had affected him back at the mansion in 2145, when he'd messed up their time jump. And she'd seen how the grid had possessed his friend, Detective Jankovic. A good man, as Brice had described him, and certainly the farthest thought from Cassandra's mind when Jankovic had come after her with those intensely glowing grid-eyes of his.

"Want me to leave?"

"You're already here. Might as well stay."

So why then did she feel like she was making a mistake?

It was a long trek back to the Octagon Room. At least an hour, and with all those robots patrolling the islands Brice would surely be caught. She didn't want that. "You're safer with us."

"The operating rooms are not far from here," Albert said.

The butler made sure Cassandra and Brice were finished dressing before he opened the door, looked both ways, and stepped out into the cold hallway.

Cassandra couldn't shake the feeling that they were being watched.

Heart thumping madly, she followed Brice down the long hall. Eventually they turned left, into yet another silver corridor.

A metallic voice spoke from behind.

Albert, Brice and Cassandra spun around to find a Smart Robot standing in the hall, face plates forming a deep frown of suspicion.

Albert walked around Brice and Cassandra, putting himself between them and the robot, and spoke unintelligible English.

As always, Albert remained perfectly calm, his tone sounding authoritative, though he failed to sway the robot.

It started to lift its arm and Albert acted with lightning reflexes.

One moment the robot was standing there, nearly six inches taller than Albert, and the next its head was flying through the air and its rail-thin silver body crumpling to the floor.

Albert caught the body before it crashed, but the head clanked down the hall and rolled to a stop against a wall.

Brice ran down the hall and retrieved the head.

Cassandra was still staring at Albert as though he'd just sprouted wings.

Brice returned with the head. Though he'd acted quicker than Cassandra, he looked no less shocked than her, and she'd seen Albert take Detective Jankovic down with a chair and battle an entire police force in their headquarters, providing ample distraction for Cassandra to retrieve the orb and get the hell out of there.

Operation Hesperides, Albert said in their earpieces, as if in response to the questions on Cassandra and Brice's faces.

Guess that made Albert their tour guide slash commando?

The butler in hospital scrub disguise dragged the headless silver body down the hall to a set of doors and lifted the robot's hand to a security wall panel.

The doors whisked open.

Thankfully the room on the other side of the doors was empty of people or robots, but it reeked of antiseptic and a faint taste of copper, like stale blood.

Albert dragged the body into the room, with Cassandra and Brice right on his tail.

"This was to be your operating room," Albert told them. "This Smart Robot was kind enough to tell me where I would be operating on Miss Bennet and Mr. Brice." He dumped the body on the floor and shoved a cabinet in front of the door, which grated along the floor, leaving deep grooves. Albert was a lot stronger and faster than he looked.

Hell, he could do the mission all by himself. All Cassandra had to do was tuck his mobile device in his pocket and let him go at it.

"So that's it, then?" Brice asked, indicating the substantial operating table in the middle of the room.

The table was a lot bigger than the one in Niles's current possession. It would fit in the Octagon Room. Barely. It was taller than Brice and wider than the three of them put together, though the table would only hold two in a pinch. It had mechanical arms folded at its sides and a clunky arm that arched over the table. And all white, just like Niles's old table.

"This is the one Mr. Bennet requested." Albert grabbed one of the robot's wrists, took the head from Brice, and dragged the body to a wall, where he opened a panel and shoved the robot in with him.

He left the broken robot inside and came out with an armload of white sheets. The door clicked shut behind him.

"If Miss Bennet and Mr. Brice recall, Mr. Bennet chose particular maladies—broken voice boxes—that would require Smart Organs to remedy. This operating table will perform as Mr. Bennet hopes." Albert went to another wall, typed a code into the panel, and waited for it to slide open, revealing a huge well-lit space with an array of Smart Limbs and other organs. Far more macabre than her uncle's mechanical graveyard in his cordoned off lab back on the Fifth Branch world.

Albert selected the appropriate limbs and organs and placed them carefully on the operating table. He broke a panel off the cabinet, to use as a plank he said, and added it to the other supplies before unfolding the sheets and tossing them over the operating table.

Cassandra decided to help the butler, rather than fret and chew her nails.

They were covering the operating table with the last of the bleach-white sheets when the doors started opening, slowly heaving the cabinet deeper into the room with a terrible screech.

The doors shoved the last of the way open, toppling the cabinet onto its side. Two Smart Robots burst in.

Albert tried to speak to them, but they were already drawing weapons.

The butler-turned-commando disarmed the robot on the right. He tried to swipe its head off, but the robot ducked before Albert's fist could make contact.

Brice fired on the robot to their left and it burst into pieces with a loud pop and tinkling debris and robot innards. The head clanked off into the corner and the bottom half, mostly intact, crumpled with a rattling clatter.

The detective would have fired on the second robot, but he couldn't get a clear shot with Albert popping in and out all over the place. Eventually Albert succeeded in beheading the robot.

Cassandra was happy they were safe, though after what Niles had shared about artificial intelligence, the destruction of Smart Robots felt a little like murder. Maybe these robots hadn't obtained sentience yet, which seemed highly likely since Niles had said the far future had learned from its mistakes and did everything in its power to prevent AI sentience.

"Is that the new weapon Artemis gave you?" she asked Brice.

The detective pursed his lips and nodded, giving the small weapon in his hands a look of appraisal. He tucked the weapon back in its holster beneath the layers of his disguise.

"How did you trick the first robot?" Cassandra asked Albert. "The advertising panels out in the garden knew you weren't human. Do holograms operate on people here?"

"Not at all, Miss Bennet. The advertisements actively scan for appropriate customers and match appropriate material of interest. The robot we encountered in the hallway did not immediately scan me. I was able to obtain the answer I required before it became suspicious. Clearly, it has alerted hospital security. We have very little time to escape the premises."

Albert finished concealing the operating table and asked for Brice and Cassandra to help him wheel it through the doors. The two robots had already cleared the cabinet out of the way, which would have been no easy feat for a human, as it looked like it weighed a ton.

Cassandra thought Smart Metal was nearly indestructible, so she didn't understand how Albert had managed to behead the robots or how Brice's weapon had blown one to bits. As they wheeled the operating table down the hall, she asked Albert. He answered via the earpiece.

Apparently, Smart Metal didn't mean indestructible and the seams of the robots could be severed. The robots they'd encountered were designed as hospital staff, not military personnel. Furthermore, Niles had designed a unique weapon that would prove most effective against the far future tech of 4327, able to penetrate non-military grade Smart Metal.

Still, Cassandra doubted she or Brice would be able to behead a Smart Robot like that. Albert seemed as strong as any robot here.

As they wheeled the huge operating table down a hall barely wide enough for it to fit, Albert assured them they were nearly to the doors that would lead them down a ramp to the exterior fountain where Octavus had first brought them.

The wheels clicked along like a wobbly shopping cart, careening off to one side now and again, with Brice and Cassandra there to buffer it with their bodies. Albert pushed from behind and apologized profusely whenever this happened.

Brice grunted as the table veered off to the left again and a wheel nearly went over his foot. He hopped out of the way just in time.

The detective seemed distracted. Cassandra thought she had caught a grid glimmer on the hand of his typewriter arm.

Dread pooled in her stomach. The grid seemed to be bothering him with increasing frequency.

As they rounded a corner, the operating table's forward momentum slowed.

Cassandra looked to see what had happened. She sucked in a sharp breath of air.

Albert was gone.

"Shit," Brice said. He squeezed between the table and wall and started pushing at the back of the table, where Albert had just been.

He grunted with effort, and the table slowly built momentum again like an enormous snowball.

"They must be jamming Albert's signal," Brice said through gritted teeth, the veins bulging on his temples and his face turning a little purple with effort.

Cassandra went to the front of the table and grabbed hold, to help pull it along and guide it down the hall. "We'll never get out of here now."

"Turn right."

"What?"

"Right!"

Cassandra ran to the left side and started shoving the end of the table, so that it slowly turned into another hall. "How did you know?"

"Grid," Brice puffed, struggling to build speed again. "Get the doors."

Cassandra ran on ahead but before she could open the doors, a group of robots came up behind Brice.

He ducked down to the side of the table, weapon drawn, and fired. The robots weren't prepared. Only one of the five escaped. When it ducked its head back into view, Brice shot it square in the forehead.

Cassandra felt a flutter of guilt for the destroyed robots. "How are we supposed to get Octavus to bring us the Octagon Room without Albert?" She tried to keep the panic out of her voice, but it edged in, her stomach doing so many flip-flops she felt sick.

"Might just be the building that's doing the jamming. Get the doors."

Cassandra ran to the doors and threw them open.

Bright sunlight flooded the hall, just as Brice was getting the table going again.

But Cassandra stopped dead in the doorway, the world seeming to slow to a standstill.

While they'd been busy stealing an operating table, an army had descended on the courtyard.

No way were she and Brice getting out alive.

CHAPTER 27

Cassandra's breath came fast and loud, a rushing roar. Her heart slowed to a painful thump like a propeller blade in slow motion.

A voice called her name. Distant, muted.

Cassandra couldn't make her body work, couldn't turn her head.

All she could do was stare at the fleet of mini UFO's in the sky, a silver cloud that cast dappled shade over the courtyard. There must have been at least a hundred, all with weapons trained on the open doors in the side of the medical facility.

All those weapons trained on *her*.

The first red beam missed her chest, only because Brice collided into her, shoving her out of the way.

They slid across the shiny floor and thumped into the wall together, Cassandra first and Brice smashed up against her.

He was heavy and warm, but he didn't stay long.

He grabbed Cassandra's wrist and dragged her from the sunlight.

They huddled at the side of the operating table, out of the line of fire, though the security bots in the sky didn't give up. Red lights flew around the medical facility's corridor, searching for them, yet damaging nothing—not the walls, the floor, or the operating table and its sheets.

As for Cassandra, her right arm throbbed. She glanced down to see a tear in her robes. It could have been worse. A lot worse.

"Thanks, Brice." The world was coming back into focus again.

"Thank me later. We have to get out of here first." He ducked out into the sunlight, weapon in hand, and shot a UFO.

The security bot faltered and collided with its neighbors.

No explosions came, however. No bots fell from the sky.

"Must be military-grade Smart Steel," Brice muttered.

He checked behind them, into the hospital.

"We need to get out of here, see if we can get Albert back as soon as we clear this facility." He crawled to his position at the back of the operating table and readied to shove it.

She couldn't believe what she was hearing. "You want to go out there? You're insane!"

"No other choice. They've got us surrounded. Best bet is to get out there and see if we can summon Albert. That hologram's our only chance of getting the Octagon Room."

Crazy or not, Brice was right.

She got to her feet. Best to act before she could second-guess it. "What do you want me to do?"

"We need to keep moving. I'll get this table going down the ramp. It's not too steep, but it'll get moving pretty fast before long. Try to stay down, call for Albert."

"Okay."

"Ready?"

She gritted her teeth and nodded.

Brice grunted and started pushing.

The operating table squeaked along, slowly at first. It crossed the threshold and began its descent down the concrete ramp through lush gardens.

Red beams roamed everywhere, harmless to everything but Cassandra and Brice.

They both suffered burning streaks on their arms and backs, wounds like cat-o-nine thrashings or laser-fire, but they were moving too fast and fairly well covered by the operating table and the ramp's five-foot-high walls to be severely injured.

Cassandra did her best to stay low, to hide behind the white sheets as the heavy operating table continued to build momentum. Overhanging vines and waxy leaves from spicy-smelling plants in the ramp's high borders smacked her in the face. "Albert!"

She struggled to keep up in her crouched position, but the ramp had the operating table moving too fast, headed for an eventual collision with the side of the fountain below.

"Albert!"

Brice was behind her, weapon in hand and doing his best to pelt the UFOs overhead.

Cassandra cried out as a beam grazed her cheek.

She ducked down again, straight into a clump of big waxy leaves covered with faint white lines.

Heart thumping madly, she almost stopped for a closer look, but the table was moving too fast.

She worried it would get away from them, and then the table suddenly slowed. Cassandra looked up to see the butler, hands braced on the front of the table.

She'd never been happier to see the hologram. "You're back!"

Runaway table now under control, Albert fished under the sheets and withdrew the make-shift plank he'd taken from the side of the operating room's steel cabinet. He ran down the remaining span to the fountain and threw the plank down, making an easy path for the operating table to launch into the middle of the fountain.

I will return with the Octagon Room, Albert said in the earpiece and vanished from the courtyard.

The operating table was picking up speed again.

Brice was still at the back of the table, firing away.

They were nearly to the end of the ramp, where they'd have to cross open courtyard with very little cover.

As she passed another group of plants, she couldn't help but notice the white lines. Brighter and more numerous now, there was no mistaking the grid.

Her skin went cold.

She'd never seen the grid in anything but a person before.

She glanced back over her shoulder at Brice and sorely wished she hadn't.

His face was strained, the veins bulging in his temples. He was struggling with something and it wasn't just the table, picking up speed again.

If Albert didn't return with the time machine right that instant, all was lost. She could just feel it.

"Help me," Brice said through gritted teeth.

He meant the table. They had to keep it on course, aimed for the plank.

He'd pocketed his weapon (he had to if he was to steer the table), and the UFOs descended upon them without fear of retaliation.

They started jogging, red lights grazing them, the taste of blood in the air and the table squeaking for the ramp, when a sudden horrendous splash emptied the rest of the water from the fountain.

Water gushed over the sides, soaking Cassandra and Brice up to their knees.

Cassandra slipped but managed to stay upright to help guide the table onto the ramp.

The operating table soared up the narrow ramp, wobbled, and then the plank tipped and the table slid down into the fountain where it rolled into the side of the invisible Octagon Room with a clank.

Cassandra breathed a giddy sigh of relief.

She turned to Brice . . . and froze.

The detective was standing in the spot where he'd last been helping guide the table, still as a statue, his eyes fixed on Cassandra. But that wasn't what terrified her.

It was the hundreds of Smart Robots pouring into the courtyard. Climbing down the sides of the medical facility from the hill up ahead, pounding up the stairs from the lower level of the Tier Three island, and descending from the sky in hovercars as shiny as their bodies.

Hundreds, perhaps thousands.

And in the ocean all around them materialized enormous neon blue and green towers, just like the ones Cassandra had seen in San Francisco in 2145. The towers that Niles had said had not been present in 2143.

It could only mean one thing.

The grid had arrived and rewritten history.

Cassandra backed up into the side of the fountain, her sneakers slipping in the water, the tiles hard against the back of her legs. "Brice?"

He clutched his head, white grid lines visible all over his arms where the sleeves of his layered disguises fell away. Grid lines glowed brightly from his hands and forearms, from his neck and forehead. And when he finally looked up, his eyes glowed with the same intense grid-white that Detective Jankovic's had.

Whatever struggle Brice had been carrying on with the grid, he'd just lost.

Cassandra didn't want to turn her back on him, but she had to get away and into the time machine. The island was overrun with Smart Robots and the grid had taken over. This world had just gone to hell.

Octavus had to open the doors. It just had to.

Cassandra scrambled over the lip of the fountain and tripped, landing on her knees with a painful thump into an inch layer of frigid water and flapping fish.

She crawled on her hands and knees until she could stand up, using the operating table as leverage. . .

. . .and landed on her back with a smack, the wind knocked out of her.

Brice fell over her, those cold grid-eyes boring into her and a smile on his face that sent icy prickles through her whole body.

He pinned her arms to the fountain floor with his knees and pinned her body with his weight as he sat and laced his fingers around her neck.

Cassandra bucked under him, but he was too heavy and had too good of a lock on her. She desperately wished she'd taken some form of self-defense classes in her life. Shirley had always tried to get her to go.

"Please, Brice. Let me go. We can still get out of here."

"Open the door," Brice said, his voice devoid of mercy or humanity.

"I can't. Let me up and I'll open it for you."

Screams erupted from the courtyard.

Robots didn't scream.

Cassandra's body went rigid as Brice started squeezing her neck.

She didn't understand. She'd offered to help!

"Open the door, Octavus," Brice said darkly.

Cassandra's heart pounded in her ears.

Brice didn't care about her. He was using threat of her death to blackmail the rogue AI.

Cassandra's throat burned as Brice squeezed harder.

She struggled, her eyes feeling like they were going to pop.

The world started blacking out.

Brice lifted her from the fountain floor and slammed her into the side of the invisible Octagon Room.

She couldn't breathe, her vision going, her head throbbing. She only had one chance. "Al—!"

Brice kneed her in the stomach. While she coughed and gasped for air, he fished the mobile device from the satchel at her waist.

Cassandra realized too late what he was doing. She reached for the mobile device in his hand, fumbling at his arm as he launched the device into the air.

Fury coursed through her, replacing her fear.

She kneed Brice's crotch, and as soon as he released her throat she screamed Albert's name at the top of her lungs.

Brice reeled and stumbled back, clutching himself.

Cassandra scooted away along the invisible wall. "Octavus! Open up!"

Brice recovered and lunged after Cassandra.

She tried to dodge, but he was a trained fighter, a trained killer. He anticipated her moves like a professional chess player planning eight or more moves ahead.

She landed on her bottom as he swept her legs out. He grabbed a fistful of her short hair and yanked her up.

She kicked at him, but he pinned her to the side of the time machine. The fight abruptly left her as she felt his weapon press to her temple, his face uncomfortably close to hers.

His grid-crazed eyes seemed to spark. "*Door*, Octavus, or you both die here."

Cassandra's breathing had become erratic, her heart beating fast enough to leap from her chest. "Please, Brice. Don't you remember me?"

He slammed her into the wall. "Last chance."

Bodies fell from the hospital roof behind Brice. People running for their lives and robots chasing them down, hunting them, ripping them to shreds.

Cassandra squeezed her eyes shut and bit her lip hard enough to draw blood. It mingled with the tears in her mouth. "Please, Octavus. Open the door for him."

The door remained shut.

Dread replaced any hope Cassandra had harbored that the rogue AI could ever be trusted. How could it ever be good without a moral compass?

She wished she'd never agreed to take it from the mansion, wished she could blow it up right then. But as it was, she was going to die by Brice's hands and the robots would surely shred the Octagon Room to pieces once they'd finished with the city's human inhabitants.

"Time's up." Brice leaned in close, his metal weapon digging into Cassandra's temple.

A shape seemed to come out of nowhere, colliding into Brice and knocking him off her.

"Albert!" Cassandra almost fainted with relief.

The butler had knocked Brice over, but the detective was scrambling to his feet, those crazed eyes locked on Cassandra.

She kicked him in the head. Hard.

The detective landed face first in the water.

Cassandra breathed heavily, her hands clenched into fists, salty tears streaming down her face.

Screams pierced the air. Hundreds . . . *thousands* dying throughout Hesperides.

Albert picked the detective up by the back of his clothes and cradled him under one arm.

The door to the Octagon Room finally opened.

Cassandra was too relieved to yell at Octavus or threaten annihilation.

Albert ran inside with Brice and dumped him on the couch, then rushed back out to get the operating table.

The butler shoved the table from behind as shiny robots rushed towards them, metal feet clanking and long fingers dripping with blood.

Cassandra helped as much as she could to drag the table in. It filled the room like a white elephant.

Albert squeezed in and the door sealed behind him.

Pounding erupted all around as the robots tried to break in.

Albert flickered like static, then solidified.

Cassandra frowned at him, about to ask if he was okay, when Octavus spoke.

"They will break through in five minutes. Incoming reinforcements from the oceanic control hubs."

Cassandra resisted an urge to take a crowbar to the AI's innards. First things first. They had to get the hell out of 4327.

She rushed to the control station and turned the key in the top of the octagon.

While the petals were unfurling, she noticed Albert flicker again.

Then she remembered that Brice had thrown the mobile device.

She glanced down at Albert's hands. He didn't have it. "Albert, where's the device?"

He gave her a thin smile. "Far from here and damaged, Miss Bennet."

She came around the enormous operating table and tried to shove past the butler. "We have to get it!"

The banging grew louder as more robots piled onto the time machine. The noise was horrendous.

"When you called I came as soon as I could, Miss Bennet. There are too many. We cannot allow you to leave this room."

Cassandra stopped trying to push past the butler and looked up into his brown eyes, no longer glassy as she remembered them, but warm. Caring.

"Take Miss Bennet home," Albert said. He flickered again.

Cassandra's lower lip trembled. She grasped the butler in a fierce hug.

They had Albert to thank for everything. She couldn't leave him behind.

Wind stirred through the room, barely rustling her wet hair and bringing a faint trace of their morning's breakfast. "Thank you," she whispered.

Albert hugged her back, just as tight and heartfelt as any she'd received from her friends back home, and then her arms collapsed on thin air.

Chapter 28

Albert wasn't really gone.

At least that's what Cassandra kept telling herself in the moments after he vanished.

They'd abandoned him in a world gone mad, in a 4327 fallen to robot domination and grid influence. Would Albert keep fighting? Would the robots destroy his mobile device? Would the grid make him one of them?

She felt depressed despite having gotten what they went into the far future to obtain. They had the operating table and Niles's replacement limbs. They'd even made it out in one piece, well, except for Albert.

But the hologram wasn't really dead. He was here, in the research facility. Or at least that's where she thought they'd arrived. She trusted Octavus about as much as the plague.

And as for Brice. . .

Cassandra cast a wary glance at the comatose detective sprawled on the velvet couch.

He'd just tried to kill her.

She was so beyond overwhelmed.

Wet, cold, covered in wounds, and her throat hurt like hell.

The door opened, revealing her uncle's research facility in the Fifth Branch.

Familiar smells greeted her—faint citrus with a bite of smoke.

The hubbub of a busy workshop, the familiar sounds of robot employees busily creating, cleaning, and experimenting for Niles.

Her uncle had surrounded himself in ticking time bombs.

Cassandra had seen it firsthand in the far future. Robots couldn't be trusted, and neither could Octavus, a rogue AI.

Niles had what he wanted, though. His operating table and new limbs.

She would deliver them, as promised, and then she'd be on her way. Her uncle didn't need her anymore. He could travel, explore, and fight his own battles.

Albert had been wrong about one thing during his parting words, though. Octavus had *not* brought her home.

Home was back in San Francisco, in 2017, with her cactus Gus and her secretarial job. Home was safe, where friends didn't abandon you to die or strangle you.

"Cassandra?" Niles called from outside the Octagon Room.

His far future robot pet, Kina, came slinking in, big ears twitching and lambent blue eyes roaming all over the Octagon Room's interior.

Cassandra recoiled a little from the robot's presence.

It seemed not to notice her as it sniffed the operating table and white sheets drenched in fountain water and blood. The once bleach-white sheets seemed more suitable for a butcher shop than a hospital.

"There you are!" Niles said as he limped into the cramped room, maneuvering awkwardly around the massive operating table. His eyes gleamed madly as he pulled the filthy sheets free of the construct.

He turned on Cassandra. "You did it!"

She flashed him a humorless smile.

Niles frowned as he noticed the sprawled detective on the couch.

"Long story," she said, her voice hoarse.

"And you're hurt!"

She waved away his concern. It hurt too much to talk.

A tall glass of cold water sounded good, and maybe a bite to eat. Her stomach was growling. Again.

She wanted to plonk down in a chair and sleep for a thousand years.

But her uncle was eager to get his limbs replaced. She couldn't blame him. If she had the grid infecting her body she'd want it out, too. Though she couldn't decide which was worse: grid infection or being rebuilt with robot parts.

Niles hurried from the Octagon Room and returned a few moments later with an entourage of robots that all squeezed into the hampered space, Artemis unfortunately among the helper crew.

Cassandra gave that robot a wide birth, backing all the way up against the bookshelves.

Artemis directed the other robots until the operating table was soon squeaking away, more than one wheel loose after its mad escape from the hospital and flight into a fountain.

As soon as the robots were gone, Cassandra breathed a little easier. She moved away from Brice to stand in the center of the Octagon Room.

"This shouldn't take too long," Niles said, ducking his head back inside. "We'll have the new table set up in no time. Shall I send Albert? Yes, yes. He'll take care of everything while I'm preoccupied." He waved his warped left arm. "Infection's gone nasty since you left. Best to deal with it as soon as possible." He gave her a wild look of intense excitement and nervous energy. "Thank you, Cassandra. This should work. But if it doesn't, Artemis knows what to do."

Cassandra blanched.

Niles waved his good hand at her, dismissing her concerns. "If I survive the operation but it doesn't fix me, only Artemis and the others will be able to take me down after what I become."

Cassandra didn't want to think about what her uncle could become—in either circumstance he'd be a monster of sorts. "Albert could handle it, too," she whispered through her sore throat.

Niles smiled sadly. "And Albert."

Cassandra went to her great uncle and gave him a tight hug. She never knew she'd had an uncle until a few days ago, and now she stood a good chance of losing him. "You better survive after everything we went through to help."

"I'll do my best." He limped away after the squeaking operating table.

Cassandra didn't know what to do with herself, but her legs had started shaking and her mouth was dry as chalk.

Brice groaned from the sofa.

Cassandra spun around.

Brice had sat up, both feet planted on the hardwood floor and the heel of his hand pressed to the side of his head. "You kicked me."

She crossed her arms and glared at him.

The detective hunched over. His white hospital gown was ripped and bloody, crisscrossed with enough scorch marks to rival a full-on grid infection. Thankfully his skin had returned to a normal hue, if a little beat up and bloody.

He groaned again and rubbed his head, then fell so still Cassandra wondered if he'd fallen asleep.

His gray eyes slowly found Cassandra's. A shadow seemed to pass through them. His hair was a disheveled mess, seeping gashes marred his face and arms, and dark circles hung under his eyes. Haunted was the look he gave her.

"Oh, God," he whispered.

Cassandra's lip trembled.

He pushed up from the couch and took a step towards her.

Cassandra stumbled away from him, palms facing out.

Brice halted. His gaze fell to her neck. "Did I . . . Did I do that?"

Her hand went to her neck, as if to hide it from him. "How much do you remember?" The words were strained and hoarse, like a croaking frog with laryngitis.

He sucked in a deep breath and released it with a shudder. "Not much." His face crumpled and he dropped his head. "But enough to know I deserved that kick." He looked back up, anger flaring in his eyes. "You should have left me."

Cassandra backed away.

"Too fucking cocky." He clenched his fists and ground his teeth. "Almost got us all killed. Almost killed . . ." His voice broke off. "Fuck it all to hell." He started pacing, muttering and swearing.

Cassandra was too tired to forgive him, too tired to say anything. She turned and walked out the door.

CHAPTER 29

Cassandra stood on the veranda, hands braced on the cold steel railing. Her legs still trembled, most likely due to shock, not hunger.

She desperately missed the cry of gulls, the drone of traffic and idle chatter of strangers. She needed something grounding, like a tuna sandwich (though it'd be a pain to swallow). Or a bath or a walk. Any hint of normalcy, really.

Anything to stop the images from playing in her head, over and over.

The screams. The people being torn apart by robots. Brice's grid-lined face and glowing eyes as his fingers wrapped around her neck.

She squeezed her eyes shut and chewed the inside of her lip.

A tear trickled down her cheek, cold and salty. She angrily wiped it away and winced as she rubbed salt into the gashes on her face. She had no idea what she looked like, but if it was anything like Brice, it wasn't pretty.

She cleaned her bloodied hand on the front of her hospital gown.

A shower and clean clothes, that's what she needed. *Her* clothes, the ones Albert had mended for her before she'd gone into the far future.

She bit back another wave of sadness.

She still hadn't seen Albert since returning to the research facility, though to be fair she'd left the Octagon Room pretty quickly. She'd had every intention of escaping to the beach, but her legs had been shaking too badly. As it was, she had barely managed to climb up here to the veranda. At least she was alone.

However alien, the crashing surf was soothing, the ozone-laden air refreshing.

And that serene and eerily empty landscape of timeless sunset and heavenly body hanging like a sister planet on the horizon could give her eyes something else to process instead of maimed bodies.

She'd had enough adventure for a lifetime.

As soon as Niles was well enough, she'd have him take her home.

"Thought I might find you out here." It was Brice.

Cassandra didn't turn around. She heard him slide the glass door shut.

"Words can't express how sorry I am," he said. "I don't expect you to forgive me."

"You weren't yourself," she croaked. "Believe me now about the grid?"

Brice was quiet.

What could he say? He'd denied that he'd ever lost control under grid influence before, back in the mansion in 2145, and he'd denied that he could possibly lose control when he felt its impending influence in 4327.

It didn't feel good to be right, to shove it in his face that he had a new reality to accept—that his whole life, the one he remembered at any rate, was a grid lie. Just like 4327, Brice had been rewritten.

Cassandra forced herself to turn and face him.

The grid was gone, leaving only pain in his gray eyes.

He had a welt where she'd kicked him in the side of his head, a big goose egg. Though it had felt necessary at the time, she cringed now. The welt was nothing, however, to the gashes all over his face and the particularly deep one along his jawline.

His shredded hospital gown revealed glimmers of his toga disguise beneath, and where both disguises failed him, blood-crusted skin showed.

"I don't have anywhere else to go." The way he said it sounded so pathetic, so final.

He rubbed the back of his neck and winced.

"You can stay here." She didn't care if Brice wanted to stay with her uncle and all his crazy robots.

He looked surprised. "You don't mind if I stay?"

"Why should I care? I'm going home."

"Oh." He looked down.

"I've had it, Brice. I really have. I'm done. Once my uncle's all fixed up, you two can go gallivanting about the universe."

Brice looked up, a slight frown on his face, or perhaps a pained look. Hard to tell with his face such a wreck. "I'm sorry," he whispered, his frown collapsing, his voice cracking. "Oh, God, Cassandra. If I'd known I'd be capable of . . ." He trailed off, his gaze falling to her throat like people did when passing a car accident. They didn't want to look but couldn't help themselves. He turned away, bracing his hands on the railing and ducking his head. "If I'd known, I'd never have gone."

She almost said it was okay, but it wasn't really. He'd tried to kill her. But she could say the truth. "It wasn't your fault. The change that happened, it was the grid. I saw it, how it took over." How it had transformed him into a monster, just like it had done with Detective

Jankovic in 2145. "You tried to fight it. And if you hadn't been there, who knows if I'd have even gotten out. I couldn't have pushed that table out the door all by myself."

Nor could she have hit all those robots with the gun. She'd never fired a gun in her life and certainly didn't know how to use the weapon Artemis had given Brice. That was really why she'd wanted him along, and they'd known the risks. Well, maybe Brice hadn't, but she had. In the end, she'd decided to risk it in the hope the grid creepage wasn't bad. "I might have escaped, but not with the table, not once the hospital took Albert offline."

Brice kept his head ducked, arms braced and knuckles white.

"No use beating yourself up over this. What's done is done." A corner of her mouth turned up. "You strangle me and I kick you unconscious. I say we're even." Concussions could kill just as readily as strangulation, or so she'd heard.

He shook his head, still not looking up.

Despite her efforts to clear the air between them, she couldn't stop seeing grid-Brice looming over her, hands around her neck.

"Here you are, Miss Bennet."

Cassandra and Brice both turned to see Albert standing on the veranda, hands clasped in front of him and butler suit neatly pressed.

"Mr. Bennet is through his surgery."

Cassandra stood up straighter. "How is he?"

"As well as is to be expected, given the circumstances." Albert paused. "There may be an adjustment period."

No kidding.

"I am to bring you to him now."

The medical facility had been curtained off for a few hours now, or at least what seemed like a few hours. Cassandra had no way of really knowing.

"You saved him just in the nick of time," Albert said, a faint smile touching his mouth. More sincere than the smiles he'd given, back at the mansion. "I have arranged refreshments in the Octagon Room, to be enjoyed once you've spoken with Mr. Bennet."

"Thank you, Albert." Cassandra studied the hologram. She missed the Albert who'd acted as tour guide and commando in 4327. But they were the same hologram, weren't they? Did it really make a difference that this Albert didn't share those memories of 4327?

Albert didn't make a move for the door. He seemed to be waiting for something, or perhaps trying to get up the nerve to ask something.

"What is it?" she asked him.

"Miss Bennet did not return with the mobile device."

"No," Cassandra said, her voice hoarser than it should have been.

"I did not receive an update from your travels in the far future. Am I to understand that the mobile device is no more?" Despite Albert's relatively impassive face, there was a hint of sadness in his eyes.

"The mobile device didn't make it." Cassandra avoided looking at Brice. Though it wasn't really his fault. It was the grid's fault, but Brice had been the tool used to toss the mobile device out of reach and effectively kill that copy of Albert.

Albert was quiet, seeming to take this in, breathing a little deeper and leaning back a fraction, as if leaning away from a precipice.

There was only one conclusion to be drawn from this: Albert had perished in the future.

"Was I brave, Miss Bennet?" Albert finally asked, his brown eyes fixed on her, a hesitation in his voice. "In the end?"

Cassandra swallowed a painful lump in her throat. "Yes, Albert. You were brave. If not for you, we would have died." Her throat constricted too much, making it feel like she was being strangled all over again. She didn't mention how she had hugged Albert in the end and thanked him, how in the end Albert had been one of them, a friend.

And as much as Cassandra realized Albert was still with them, in effect, there had been two separate versions of Albert and the other had perished.

She rubbed the corner of her eye with the heel of her hand.

Brice was watching her, she could feel his eyes on her, studying her. He'd been unconscious for the final goodbye.

It must be odd, to have fractured memories like the hologram did, almost like having a fractured personality. Albert would never know what had happened. Maybe Cassandra would tell him, someday.

And with his mobile device destroyed, he was trapped here, just like Niles.

Unless Niles copied Albert into the new Octagon Room, but the hologram wouldn't want to share space with that psycho rogue AI, Octavus.

Why Cassandra had never feared Albert, and still didn't, was a little baffling. But he was different from the robots. He was family. And not once had he ever let her down. That was more than could be said for Brice or her own family.

She gave Albert a hug.

He stiffened, a little surprised, which was hard to do to a hologram.

Cassandra pulled away and smiled up at him. "I'm ready to see my uncle now."

"Yes, Miss Bennet." The hologram studied her a moment before turning on his heel and opening the sliding glass doors for them.

* * *

The workshop slash factory was surprisingly quiet, the odors and acrid smoke at a minimum. No clanking of robot feet, no hammering or hissing.

It was like they'd all taken the day off.

But as it turned out, the robots had all just come to witness the unveiling of her uncle's new body.

Cassandra nearly froze as she and Brice followed Albert towards the circle of white curtains cordoning off the operating table. Apparently, according to Albert, Artemis had led the operation, being a medical robot from the far future. A nurse of sorts, then, turned generator mechanic and weapons specialist.

And future killer.

Cassandra couldn't make herself walk into all those robots, into a forest of shiny silver bodies with inhuman faces watching her in a disturbing mimicry of wonder and curiosity and concern.

She'd seen what they were capable of.

And now her uncle was becoming one of them.

There had been no screams during the procedure. The advanced operating table possessed an adequate supply of far future anesthesia. Her uncle would have slept through the whole thing.

Artemis pushed through the curtains, its long face serious, eyes searching the crowd of robots until they landed on Cassandra. The robot hooked a finger and performed a come-hither gesture.

Cassandra stiffened, but she went, with Brice and Albert right behind her.

She avoided looking at a single robot on the way into the medical facility.

Inside the ring of curtains, her uncle sat on the substantial operating table, perched on the edge, legs hanging down and hunched over, flexing his hands in front of him.

He wore a white hospital gown, so his torso was hidden, but his Smart Limbs on his left side were bare to the world. Half man, half robot. Cassandra had no idea how much of his torso and insides had been carved out.

"How do you feel?" Cassandra tentatively asked.

"Cassandra!" Niles looked up, a mad gleam in his eyes. He slid off the table and landed a little shakily, one foot clanking. "Not bad, not bad. Artemis, my dear, you've done a fine job. Nice and even, almost can't tell the difference."

"Thank you, Sir," Artemis said, a hint of pride in its voice.

Niles did a little jig, hips wagging, one bare foot landing quietly and the other with a clank, so that it sounded like he still had a limp. "I'll be back on the dance floor in no time!"

Cassandra pulled a face. "You dance?"

"Of course!"

"Not that he's any good," Artemis said, flashing Niles a smirk.

"She doesn't know what she's talking about," Niles said, continuing to hop while he waved his hand at the robot.

"Explains the disco globe," Cassandra muttered.

"Yeah," Brice agreed.

Niles came to a sudden stop, breathing heavily. "Out of practice, but the limbs are fantastic!" He rubbed static into his white hair with both hands, though the Smart Limb on his left side seemed to do a better job of making his hair stand on end, the white locks reaching for the metal like eels waving in their burrows on the seafloor.

"Artemis, please see to Miss Bennet and Mr. Brice."

"My pleasure, Sir." Artemis turned on Cassandra. "Your turn."

Cassandra cringed, unable to tell if the robot looked happy or smug to be working on her. She gave Brice a look that said "help", but he gestured to the table with a chivalrous flair and said, "Ladies first."

Cassandra hopped onto the table and laid down as Artemis went to work.

"This will only take a moment," the robot said. "Your wounds are superficial."

The arm made a whirring sound as it lowered and then widened, plunging Cassandra in near total darkness. She hadn't known the table could do that.

She started to panic, feeling claustrophobic, when the darkness lit up with a light show like Fourth of July and her body prickled with static electricity. Just when it was starting to pinch and she was about to cry out in alarm, the arm whirred up and Cassandra squinted into the bright overhead lights.

Artemis gave Cassandra a hand, gripping her forearm in its hard fingers and helping her to sit up.

"Thank you." Cassandra pulled up her battered sleeves to admire the smooth skin. The terrible scars from her earlier injury in the mansion explosion had been reduced to the faintest of white lines. She touched her face and felt no gashes. Good as new.

Except for the terrible memories. The screams. The bodies.

Cassandra hopped off the table and went to stand by her uncle. At least he was only half robot, though his sanity remained questionable.

Brice climbed onto the table, closing his eyes as the apparatus enclosed him like the MRI tables from Cassandra's time. A few minutes later the detective was as good as new, sitting up and flashing an almost normal smile, a glimmer of a twinkle in his gray eyes, black hair tousled, and handsome mug screwed up as he rubbed his nose with the back of a finger.

Niles was eager to discuss their adventures. Cassandra only went along for the ride so she could finally have a glass of water and a bite to eat.

As soon as she satisfied her uncle's curiosity and made sure he was fine, she'd leave. She didn't want to spend one more night away from home.

A shower and a long, deep sleep in her own bed sounded divine.

CHAPTER 30

"Sit, sit," Niles said, gesturing to the Victorian velvet couch in the Octagon Room.

The lights were dimmed, a nice break on the eyes from the bright research facility.

The door closed, shutting out the clamor of robots returning to work. Her uncle's metal army had been thrilled to see the new Niles unveiled, many clapping, just like real people.

Cassandra plopped down on the sofa, on the opposite end from Brice, and promptly poured herself a glass of water. Her throat had finally stopped hurting. She could swallow properly and didn't feel like she had the worst case of strep or that it was going to seize on her at any moment and cut off her air supply.

Albert had put lemon slices in the water, which made for a nice refreshing thirst-quencher. Cassandra had three glasses before she successfully banished the whole "swallowed a desert" feeling.

Brice downed a few glasses, too, though Niles seemed not to notice as he prattled on about his new limbs.

Albert had included some of Niles's infamous chocolate biscuits and Cassandra helped herself to one now. She finally understood why her uncle had wanted them so badly. They were the best thing she had ever tasted. Just the right amount of bitter-sweet chocolate and crunchiness. She spilled crumbs all over her lap, which she brushed on the floor.

After the chocolate biscuit, everything else sort of paled in comparison, though the subsequent banana went quite well with the chocolate.

Brice didn't seem to have much of an appetite. He kept giving her tight smiles that never touched his eyes every time she looked at him.

Now that Cassandra could think again, she thought it was time her uncle knew a few things. She leaned back on the sofa. "You can't trust Octavus."

Niles stopped what he was saying. "Whatever do you mean?"

Cassandra started with the rogue AI's landing in the fountain and alerting Hesperides security from the moment of their arrival and how it had triggered all the robots searching for them, and she saved the best for last—grid-Brice strangling her and Octavus refusing to open the doors for her, even to save her life. "Your AI lacks any moral compunction. I'd be dead if not for Albert."

Her eyes were on her uncle, but she thought she could feel the detective stiffen on the other end of the couch. "Octavus can't be trusted, especially with the Octagon Room."

"You are incorrect," Octavus said. "As I mentioned after the initial jump, Niles miscalculated. There was ample room to jump closer to your destination."

"But look what happened!" Cassandra exclaimed. "We picked that spot out in the middle of nowhere for a reason."

"Is this true?" Niles asked, turning to face the control panels.

Octavus didn't answer right away. "Your calculations proved false. My correction allowed your operating table to be obtained. Had I not traveled to that spot, Cassandra and Brice would not have made it back down."

"Fine, but what about refusing to open the door for me?"

"You are alive, Miss Bennet," Octavus said. "Detective Brice was bluffing in an attempt to obtain the Octagon Room. Once he was dealt with, I opened the door, as requested."

Cassandra clenched her hands.

"There is logic to what you say," Niles said thoughtfully, "but do you fail to understand why you should have opened the door? Did you see the distress Cassandra was under? The pain? The fear?"

Octavus said nothing.

Niles turned back to Cassandra. "Understanding why these things matter will not come easy for the AI. I am pleased it acted autonomously and attempted to make decisions to best aid the mission and your success."

Cassandra crossed her arms. Leave it to her uncle to side with the rogue AI. At best, the AI was like a rebellious teenager who thought it knew best. A cocky teenager brimming with apathy for human suffering. A dangerous combination in any book.

But then, what comparison did the AI have? It had never felt pain or fear.

Still, when people lacked empathy, you called them psychopaths. Cassandra didn't like the idea of allowing a psychopath to remain in control of the Octagon Room.

Niles whirled on Brice. "You strangled her?"

Brice looked a little shocked. The question had seemed to come out of nowhere, as though her uncle had only just realized what Cassandra had mentioned earlier.

"He was under grid influence," Cassandra said.

Niles's eyes widened. "The creepage worsened?"

"If you prefer, I have recorded the collapse of 4327," Octavus said.

Niles hurried to the control panel, his metal foot no longer clanking now that he wore shoes again, and sank into the chair. Cassandra and Brice came up to either side of him. They all watched the Smart Metal wall as it came alive with the chaos in the final moments of the courtyard before their escape.

The Octagon Room must have had cameras embedded in its walls, because there were images from all around it, each and every one distressing.

Cassandra found her eyes riveted to the images as the chaos unfurled. The operating table flying through the air and crashing into the side of the Octagon Room, the descending robots, the people, the death . . . Brice attacking Cassandra and strangling her.

Cassandra couldn't watch. She moved away, hugging her middle and forcing her breathing to slow.

Brice, on the other hand, watched the whole thing.

Whether morbid fascination or guilt or just a need to fill in the blanks of his hijacked memories kept him there, Cassandra didn't know.

"Fascinating," Niles said when the video feed finally ended. He spun around in the chair. "Thank you, Octavus. I will study these videos."

"I also captured the grid transition."

Niles insisted on watching those videos, too, but Cassandra didn't want to relive it. She sat on the couch and waited until they had finished.

"So the mobile device is gone, then," Niles said. "A shame. I know Albert will be disappointed."

"Can't you just make a new one?" Cassandra asked hollowly.

"Not easily, no," Niles said. "Albert is far future tech with alien influence. I copied the device from the mansion and used parts from the Smart Walls as well as far future tech. Now that 4327 is off-limits, building a new one would be near impossible."

"Why not just go to 4326 or 4325?" Cassandra rubbed her temple.

"Grid creepage," Niles said. "The tech I need wasn't invented until that year. Perhaps it could be found in the year prior?" He shrugged.

"I want it out of me," Brice said quietly. He'd backed away from the screens, that haunted look back in his eyes. "Put me on the operating table and cut it out."

Niles shook his head. "Doesn't work that way, I'm afraid. I'm still tagged."

Brice frowned.

"I still have the grid in my body. What Artemis removed is that advanced infection I received from the Sixth Branch." Niles rubbed absently at his high collar. He'd dressed before coming here. Only his left hand revealed his robotic side. "This leads me to believe it was not just an advanced infection, but something else entirely." He rubbed his head like he was trying to rub the hairs right off his head. "It will need more thought, further study." His piercing gaze landed on Brice. "I saw the level of infection in 4327, and yet here is Brice, barely a glimmer in his arm. Dormant, as is mine again, now that the other variety has been excised."

Brice looked crestfallen. He took a seat in one of the leather swivel chairs. Cassandra felt a little bad that he didn't join her on the couch again.

"You witnessed something significant," Niles said. "The start of humanity's ultimate collapse and extinction."

"What?" Cassandra bolted upright. "That was the end of humanity we just witnessed?"

"The beginning of it, yes," Niles said.

Goosebumps prickled her arms. She'd been right—robots led to the downfall of humanity.

Before she could say anything, however, Niles said, "I know what you are going to say, Cassandra, and though it appears robots are responsible, they are not. The grid and its rewriting of history is to blame." He rubbed his head. "Wish I knew how and why. Wish I knew what those control towers were doing and why they only appear in grid-controlled times."

Niles rose from his chair and started pacing and muttering.

He eventually came to a stop, his eyes riveted on Brice. "I wonder if it had something to do with your presence. A tagged individual that attracted creepage from a neighboring infection?"

Brice looked like he'd just been told he had killed millions of people, which is precisely what Niles had just implied.

"No worries, Brice," Niles added hastily. "The infection would have happened anyway. I merely suggest it occurred at a faster rate. Perhaps it detected the orb? The grid seems capable of possessing individuals. Can't say whether it controlled the robots or not."

"Niles, why have I never met you until now?" It still felt a little odd not to call him uncle. Though calling him "Uncle Niles" would feel equally strange. Until meeting Niles, her estranged parents were the only family Cassandra had ever known.

Niles slowly spun around to face her, bushy white brows furrowed. He didn't make immediate eye contact. "I saw you once, when you were little. At your grandfather's funeral, my elder brother's, Frank Bennet."

Cassandra stared at him. She knew next to nothing about her family, but Niles looked uncomfortable and insisted it was a topic best left for another time.

"Once I've studied this footage, I will devise a potential jump to further study the grid. We need to gather as much information as possible if we are to understand it and potentially stop it."

"I'm going home," Cassandra said.

Niles blinked.

"You and Brice can go."

Niles lifted his arm. "I'll be limited in my travels. Look what happened to Brice. Not a risk I'm willing to take. And I'm not entirely sure every ounce of Sixth Branch infection was eradicated."

Cassandra stood before he could make the next logical statement: Niles and Brice were both ticking time bombs when it came to study of the grid. Only Cassandra was untagged and safe to approach grid-controlled time blocks.

"I'm exhausted, but I'll think about it." Not true. She just wanted to go home and never hear about the grid again. She wanted her life back.

"Can I convince you to take the night to sleep on it?" Niles asked.

Cassandra sighed. "So long as I can shower and have my old clothes back."

What harm could come of staying one more night?

* * *

"Cassandra." It was Brice, coming down the underground tunnel within her uncle's research facility.

She'd showered and put her mended clothes back on. It felt so good to be wearing her comfortable jeans and top again. Albert had done a fine job stitching the tears. Her clothes would never be the same, but they were hers. Same with her scuffed sneakers.

She smelled Irish Spring fresh, thanks to the bar of soap in the shower. A strong enough scent to taste, but it sure beat reeking of blood, sweat, and far future fountain scum.

Brice hadn't had a chance to shower yet, or change. His disheveled disguise had sort of grown on him, though, especially now that he'd ditched the bloody hospital gown. He just looked like a battle-worn Greek god.

"Don't suppose there's anything I can say to convince you to stay?"

"Nope."

"But you told your uncle you'd—"

"I lied." Cassandra opened the door to her little room and tossed the damp towel on the bed. She'd dumped her ruined disguises in a pail outside the bathroom.

"Then this is goodbye?"

"Not just yet. I'm leaving tomorrow morning. Promised him one night to think on it."

"What's the point if you've already made up your mind?"

She shrugged. Because she said she would give her uncle the time. And he was family. She'd miss him. Maybe he could visit, though he'd have to disguise his metal limbs. Probably not the easiest thing to accomplish in 2017.

"I'm . . . I'm sorry. Hurting you is the farthest thing from my mind." He rubbed the back of his neck. "It's been a pleasure, Cassandra."

She felt a quiver of sadness. Despite everything they'd been through, she was really going to miss him.

She surprised them both by hugging him.

He smelled of chocolate biscuits, blood, and sweat. Not a hint of aftershave.

His five o'clock shadow had thickened, she turned her face during the hug to avoid getting scratched with the bristle.

She held him and he hugged back, gingerly at first, and then his embrace tightened.

"I'll miss you," she said. "You take care, okay?"

It seemed like such a lame goodbye after all they'd been through, but she wished him goodnight and he was still standing there, watching her, as she shut the door.

She tossed and turned for some time, thoughts of humanity's collapse, the grid, her altered uncle, and Brice swimming through her head.

As she drifted into dreamland, she found herself sitting at the table in her uncle's mansion in 2145 with an array of tasty rolls and pastries spread across the shiny tabletop. The scent of aftershave filled the air as Brice's warm hand slid over hers and guided her finger onto the fifth petal. The dining room started spinning, and the walls ripped apart as they crash-landed in the Fifth Branch. Cassandra hurried to catch up to Brice, but plants burst from the cliff and stabbed her palms with needles. Brice watched her writhe in pain on the ground at his feet, full-on inspection mode devoid of sympathy. He bent over and helped her to her feet, a burgeoning smile and twinkle in his gray eyes turning her legs to jelly.

But the warm and tingly feeling didn't stay.

Grid-lines erupted in his eyes.

Cassandra backed up into the Octagon Room, the look of longing and regret on Brice's face a painful throb in her neck as she closed the door on him.

CHAPTER 31

Gravel crunched beneath Cassandra's sneakers as she walked to her black Civic parked in the circular driveway at the front of her uncle's mansion.

It was like she'd never been away. The warm sun overhead. The wind rustling through the forest. Birds perched on the edge of the mermaid fountain, chirping excitedly.

The keys were still in the ignition, right where she'd left them. It was warm and stuffy inside, filled with that familiar car smell. *Her* car and link to home.

She settled into the driver's seat, hands on the steering wheel. She was going home!

Ducking her head forward, she peered through the windshield back up at her uncle's dilapidated mansion. Niles stood in the doorway. He waved to her.

He'd be going back to the Fifth Branch as soon as she drove off. She had given him a huge hug and was a little sad to be driving off.

But only a little.

It felt like years since she'd been home, though it had really only been about an hour since she'd driven her car up this driveway.

She gave her uncle one last wave and started the car.

Gravel churned under the wheels as Cassandra pulled away from the mansion with its peeling paint and dead gardens overgrown with weeds.

She'd come here expecting to assess whether she'd be keeping the mansion as a home or selling it off to buy something better, and instead she'd discovered a long-lost (supposedly dead) uncle and a dimensional- and time-jumping machine. She'd made new friends in the hologram, Albert, and Brice. Had more adventures than she'd ever thought possible. In her previous life she'd had a boring job and life, always shied away from risks.

No more. Cassandra was a new woman.

Soon as she got home, she'd be taking those self-defense classes with Shirley, and she was looking forward to dinner and a night out on the town. Eager to enjoy herself, rather than rush back to her quiet apartment and pet cactus.

She'd lost her apartment, of course, but Cassandra was fine with that now.

Shirley would be more than happy to help her find a new place.

She'd be keeping the mansion, too. Though no one would learn that its previous owner was still alive and well, living his life in another dimension with a detective from the future and a small army of robots.

Cassandra's friends would never believe her. And for now, she was fine with that secret.

No need to tell Shirley that she'd only be staying a short while. Just long enough to get the rest she so desperately needed, to find some normalcy and grounding. And plenty of time to buy her uncle's biscuits and stockpile them in her apartment for his return.

Turned out one more night really could make a world of difference.

Nothing like a good night's sleep and a little perspective.

The grid had to be stopped, and Cassandra wasn't about to let anyone, including herself, stop her from doing just that.